Praise for T. R. Mousner's

Being

I highly recommend "Being." I felt it offered a view of humanity that while acknowledging our worst flaws held out hope for the future and I also felt it offered an `alien' who was enough like us to be someone I could relate too but at the same time was different enough, and who came from a different enough culture to make the story believable.
--Tracy Riva, Midwest Book Review

I absolutely loved this book!! I do not think I have ever read a Young Adult book about extraterrestrials, and I have to say that it amazed me. The plot of the book was so engaging I was hardly aware of the book going by so fast!! It has some really good attention grabbing, exciting scenes as well as very good character development. You can hardly tell it is planned development-- it flows very naturally, as does the whole book. It really leaves one wanting for more. I cannot wait for more from this author and to find out what happens with EBN, Aix and Shale next!! I HIGHLY recommend this book to anyone who is looking for an excellent one-day read and loves Young Adult novels.
--Holly Polk, Full Moon Bites Reviews

This book will suck you in with all the great characters and flowing plot. I did not want to put this book down and hate that it took me so long to pick it up. You will not be disappointed whatsoever. The author does a tremendous job and will be looking for more books from her.
–Babs Hightower, Babs Book Bistro

T.R. Mousner's debut YA novel is a must read. The story is filled with adventures and characters that should not be missed! Whether you like the science fiction angle or sense of family and connections made in life, there is something for everyone in this book. I will definitely be on the look out for the sequel from Ms. Mousner!
--Talina Perkins, Night Owl Reviews

EBN is a fantastic character. She's super courageous and brave like you wouldn't believe... Honestly, I'd like to see more characters with her qualities in YA. Overall, Mousner's writing style is amazing making for a fast paced enjoyable read. She creates a vivid image for the reader as if you were a character yourself. This is the perfect book for readers who haven't taken the sci-fi plunge. Readers that enjoyed Gini Koch's Touch By An Alien or Stephenie Meyer's The Host will really enjoy were Being takes you. I only want one thing, more of EBN.

--Jennifer Shaw, Book Noise Reviews/Fictitious
Musings

I loved the unpredictability of the book and the originality of the plotline... The ending provided a good bit of resolution while also managing to leave me anxious and excited to see what happens next. I can't wait to read the sequel!
--Zareen, Reach for the Books Reviews

I love everything about this book - the writing, the plot, the world building and the characters. Author T.R. Mousner sure knows how to grab her readers and take them along with her on an unforgettable ride from Earth to the stars and beyond.
--AO Bibliophile, AOBibliosphere

Being is an exciting new novel from TR Mousner. Being, for me, sometimes read as a statement on the human condition. But it also had engaging characters and action. And wow, hold on to your seats because the cliffhanger ending is quite a doozy! Also, when you read the book, you will appreciate the genius of the gorgeous cover.
--Andrea Thompson, The Bookish Babes

Being

by

T. R. Mousner

For my beloved husband, Jim, without whom there
would be no Being.

Chapter One: First Contact

In the tranquil moments following my mission, no warnings betrayed the perfect silence inside my spaceship, the Protectorate's *Surety*. Blissful thoughts entered my mind as my cloaked craft zipped toward vacuous space. Soon I would return to my home world and family.

The reconnaissance mission had been simple. I had flown over two alien military installations on the planet Erox — Wright-Patterson Air Force Base and Area 51 — where my ship lingered undetected. The *Surety's* computers copied every bit of data from both facilities. The files numbered in the billions.

Within a blink, the *Surety* reached Erox's exosphere. Traveling near Erox made me nervous because the planet's gravity often interfered with my ship's force field. Because this inconvenient truth matters most just beyond the demarcation line where blue meets black, I slowed the craft. I took a deep breath, loosened my tightening muscles and focused on navigating the gauntlet of space trash orbiting Erox.

Countless massive objects — many dwarfing my ship — threatened from every distance and direction. While the cosmic junkyard streaked across the void, my eyes darted this way and that, searching for patterns.

Suddenly and without warning, an unseen force slammed the *Surety*. A deafening crunch roared, destroying the bucolic quiet. Alerts followed, blaring throughout the control deck.

Engine three failed. The systems screen indicated debris had penetrated the ring-shaped cabin rotating around the craft's rear. I gasped against the lost air pressure as I redirected power to engines one and two. The ship spiraled, falling. Not even Erox's thick, polluted atmosphere slowed the plummet.

I fought for control, engaging the repair systems and visualizing the *Surety* whole and intact. The craft failed to respond to my vibrating thoughts, confirming my worst fears.

As I wrestled the plunging, spinning ship, I gulped for air. Time slowed to a crawl and a surreal sense of loss gripped my stomachs. This could be it for me. But I was only six hundred Scyros cycles old. My life had just begun.

Disoriented and suffocating, I lifted my hand off the command module embedded in the armrest. At once the ship stabilized and held steady, however our velocity continued unchecked. With Erox's rocky surface nearing faster than I could measure, I aimed for an uninhabited patch of land, activated the crash shields, fired the thrusters and braced for impact.

Then everything went black.

When I bolted awake, I sat strapped in the pilot's seat. My head pounded; ringing buzzed in my ears. My vision wavered in and out of focus.

Gray smoke fogged the air. The laser screens and console lights flickered. Tremendous pressure squeezed my body from every direction. I felt groggy and ached all over—even my skin hurt.

The symbol for *Erox* glowed red from the flashing navigation screen. Ignoring the sense of dread twisting my stomachs into knots, I touched the symbol. A satellite image of a landmass called California appeared on the screen with a solid black dot marking the city of Los Angeles. A second black dot blinked above it, indicating the ship's location. I touched it. After a map expanded of a place called Lancaster, the screen shorted out.

I groaned. This never should have happened. I was not scheduled to fly this mission. I held enough knowledge to survive on the alien planet, but I also knew enough about the indigenous people, called *Sents*, to be disgusted by my situation.

I removed a slim crystalline disk from my flight suit interior pocket and pressed a tiny button on its side. The disk quadrupled in size, expanding into a small computer screen. With one finger pressed against the console port, I held another finger over my computer's port and copied the Sents' military files onto it. It was critical my superior officer receive the files.

Before I could check for injuries or assess the damage, a second alert wailed through the ship. Two white dots pulsed on the wavering systems screen. Sent airships approached the crash site. I froze. My breathing grew rapid and shallow.

The piercing alarms coupled with the hammering in my head made thinking almost impossible. I touched another port on the console and struggled to focus my concentration. After what felt like a very long time, my vibrating thoughts appeared on the communication screen:

High Chancellor – Surety crashed on Erox. Sents approaching. Rescue requested. Guardian of the Sky EBN-Reyoz-X

As soon as I sent the transmission, a *beep* issued from the console. A transmission arrived from the only Being with knowledge of my whereabouts, my grandfather known as *Gran-Ada:*

EBN – Rescue forthcoming. Enact emergency protocols and retreat to Protectorate outpost. Await further orders. Coordinates, map and briefing attached. Protectorate High Chancellor Eesh-Slic

Disheartened, I reviewed the attached files. Since when did a Protectorate outpost exist on Erox? I tried to imagine the Protectorate officer who would volunteer for such an assignment. I would prefer to live under the methane cloud in the compost city of Swarthmur before choosing Erox.

The smallest movement required colossal effort. Feeling heavy and awkward as though moving through mud, I hoisted myself out of the pilot's seat, pushed to the back of the cabin and heaved two black duffel sacks from the *Surety's* floor and storage compartments. I disrobed and glanced over my life support system — a humanoid skin suit worn over my body — but found no injuries. Uncertain how I had survived the crash unscathed, I removed a bundle of Sent clothes from one of the sacks.

My eyes darted between the clothing articles and my computer where the garment names were displayed. There was a green and blue Hawaiian shirt, faded jeans, tan work boots and a bulky camouflage jacket. I held up the Hawaiian shirt and inspected it. Surely Eesh was not serious. These garments were too big. I dug through the duffel for another but all the shirts were similar.

I could not imagine going unnoticed in such bold, ridiculous costumes. I knew Sents were primitive but I had underestimated their foolishness. As I dressed I thought my younger brother, Aix, would have been better for this assignment.

Aix loved Sents. He spoke their languages and knew the names for things. I spoke Sent as well, but not because I had studied. All Guardians received language implants that translated any known foreign language into the Guardian's native tongue and retranslated the Guardian's vibrating thoughts into the appropriate language before they spoke. However, no implant was perfect and I would rely on my computer to fill in the gaps.

While gathering my uniform to collect my computer and weapon, I felt something else inside the pocket. The black envelope! I had almost forgotten. I fished it out, tore it open and removed something my computer identified as a stack of Sent currency and folded sheets of beige paper. I unfolded and leafed through the pages. They were blank.

Bewildered, I flipped through them again, looking at the front and back of each empty page. When Eesh handed me the envelope he had said, "Supplemental orders and information regarding emergency protocol." At the time, I thought it unusual because I had never received written directives before. Eesh's words made even less sense now.

An unsettled feeling crept over me. Unless this was a test, I did not understand why Gran-Ada would do such a thing. Concerned there were orders and information I did not have, I shoved the items into one of the duffels. As I prepared to exit the ship, I tucked my stone-sized weapon — a Disintegrator — into my pocket before opening the *Surety's* door.

There was a faint hiss as the ship's hatch rose. Rancid air blew against my face, choking me. I gasped, unable to breathe. Chemical and refuse tastes filled my mouth. For reasons unknown, Erox stank like steaming *grek*. I slung the heavy duffels over my shoulders and stepped outside, coughing and spitting to expel the death tastes. The hatch automatically lowered behind me.

With my computer in hand, I scrutinized my surroundings. This part of Erox was a gritty, dusty place. My damaged but intact ship had crashed behind a crescent shaped boulder outcropping jutting from the side of a mountain. A discolored ring marked the impact site. I stepped on it and the melted sand cracked like ice under my weight.

Clumps of dry grass and low shrubs surrounding the airship still smoldered. At least the cloaking mechanisms were not damaged. They regulated the craft's external temperature to avoid detection by thermal imaging and replicated the ship's surroundings, disguising it as a lichen-covered boulder identical to those near it.

I heard the noisy Sent airships approach. I scrambled away from the crash site and followed a rocky trail skirting the outcropping. At the trail's end, I ducked behind a boulder and peered out of the shadows.

It was a clear night. Starlight dotted the indigo sky and a gibbous moon frosted the arid terrain with silver light. Desert foothills rolled from the base of the mountain before stretching into a wide plateau. Beyond the desert, the lights of Lancaster glowed from a basin ringed by remote mountain ranges.

Uniformed Sents scoured the desert and foothills. The Sent airships flew low. One scanned the desert while the other searched the foothills and mountainside with blinding spotlights. Then a third airship swooped out of the sky. Dust clouds whipped and whirled as it landed at the base of the foothills, directly below my vantage point. When the ship touched down, streams of armed, uniformed Sents poured out and ran up the mountain.

They headed straight for me.

I fought my first impulse to turn and run. My pulse raced and my heart galloped in my chest. Before I could slip the computer into my pocket, one of the airships flew close. The drone of the rotor blades drilled into my brain, amplifying the incessant throbbing. The searchlight passed over the boulder shielding me and moved up the mountain. As the light swept over the mountainside, I saw a cave nearby.

When the Sent airship turned away, I slipped out from my hiding place. I moved in the shadows, climbing over rocks and dipping behind boulders until I crossed the distance to the next gorge. Below me, the Sents climbed closer. Their shouts grew steadily louder. Each time I heard their voices, fear gripped me anew.

Only a steep slope separated me from the dark, yawning cave mouth. I had to hurry. The nearest airship turned my direction.

As I dashed for the cave, I stumbled under the weight of the duffels and stepped on a patch of loose rocks. My feet flew out from under me and I slid feet-first down the mountain until I collided with a tubular, spiky plant, which sent sharp waves of pain up my leg.

When the dust cleared I glanced up. I stared up the end of a long-barreled weapon. Though primitive, I knew this weapon to be effective.

"Hold it right there," a uniformed Sent barked.

The musky scent of the indigenous invaded my nostrils and I gagged. I swallowed hard and stared up at my captor. The word 'Johnson' appeared on the nametape over his pectoral pocket. The Sent emitted an emerald energy field that darkened when he spoke into his headset. Our close proximity caused a stream of thoughts and impressions to flow into my mind. The Sent broadcasted his thoughts loud and clear.

Staff Sergeant Johnson was ending his shift at work when an unidentified object flew through restricted airspace. He should've been home by now. He'd planned to go camping in the woods with his girlfriend, Pam, and hadn't called to say he'd be late. Pam was going to be pissed.

Cramps shot up my injured leg, pulling my attention from Johnson's thoughts and I looked down. Countless spikes skewered my boots, bunched pant leg and skin suit beneath the knee. To my horror, part of my skin suit had also scraped away, revealing my lacerated teal flesh underneath. When I reached down to lower the fabric and cover my exposed teal skin, Johnson lunged forward and whacked my head with the butt of his weapon. I sprawled sideways, slamming my head against the rocky ground.

"I said don't move!"

My eyes narrowed. The strike only justified my low opinion of Sents.

Behind Johnson, there was a flurry of movement and strange sounds. Within moments more armed Sents surrounded me. One yanked the duffel sacks from my shoulders and dragged them away. An airship hovered overhead and aimed a spotlight on us. I squinted against the white-hot light. I had no idea how I was going to get out of this situation.

"Put your hands on the back of your head and stand up," Johnson ordered. "Do it slow. No sudden movements."

There was a hushed murmur of Sent voices as I rose to my feet. Because of the slope's incline, I stood almost three heads taller than Johnson.

"Damn, she's a big 'un," one of the Sents whispered.

"Dude, you hit a girl," another said.

"I thought she was reaching for a weapon."

"What's she gonna do, Johnson? Throw cactus barbs at you?"

My captors seemed to be waiting. I glanced over Johnson's shoulder. Two more Sents climbed the mountain. One wore a brown uniform with a gold badge and brimmed hat; the other wore an olive suit and black-framed spectacles with dark tinted lenses.

"Extend your arms out," one of them ordered.

I straightened my arms. One of them grasped my sides and I flinched.

"Take it easy," Johnson said. "Just checking for weapons."

I glanced to my right. One of the Sents squatted, opened the duffels and ransacked the contents. I held my breath as he opened my medical and supply kits, tore open each silver packet and poured the various liquid supplies I desperately needed into the foul soil.

A moment later the touching stopped. Another voice said, "She's clean."

"What's your name," Johnson asked.

"EBN." My name squeaked out of my mouth and sounded jumbled like a recording played back at the wrong speed. I cleared my throat and pronounced it again in a slower cadence so it sounded like the Sent language I had heard while watching their broadcasted programs with my younger brother, Aix.

"What's your last name, Eden?"

"Reyoz."

"Got any identification, Eden Reyes," Johnson asked.

"No."

"Where you from?"

My mind blanked. I looked down then recalled the words from the navigation screen. "Los Angeles," I blurted.

Johnson thought of Pam again and how he wasn't supposed to be here. I knew exactly how he felt.

After what seemed like an eternity, the suited Sent reached our position. Though he was small in stature, he moved with an air of seriousness and authority. Opaque gray energy haloed his body. Although he carried no weapon I could see, this Sent intimidated the others. From the greetings I heard, I deduced the Sent's name was 'Sir.'

Johnson retreated a few steps, turned away and briefed Sir. I stared at them and pricked my sensitive ear holes. In spite of the loud airships, I heard every word.

"Whadda you got?"

"Says her name's Eden Reyes, from Los Angeles," Johnson replied. "But I don't believe her. I doubt she's eighteen yet. Check out the shape of her head."

"Did she see anything?"

"I didn't ask."

Sir gave a stiff nod then stood before me, staring in silence. I watched his lower jaw chew and grind in a steady rhythm. Unlike Johnson, Sir did not broadcast his thoughts.

I caught my reflection in the tinted lenses of Sir's spectacles and relaxed a little. The organic, carbon-based skin suit disguised my true appearance. With its shoulder length blonde hair, blue eyes and fair skin, I looked like one of them. There was no indication of the Being underneath, an Adelian-Nadreen hybrid from the Xionin star system, located four sectors from this alien grek-hole.

"You got some identification, young lady?"

19

"No."

"Why not?"

"I lost it," I lied.

"How old are you?"

"What is age, but a number?"

Sir dragged one thick-soled, black shoe against the rocky ground and placed his hands on his hips. When his jacket gaped, I noticed a weapon strapped to his side.

"Let's try this again. How old are you?"

"Eighteen." Another lie.

"What's a pretty girl like you doing in the middle of nowhere, Eden Reyes?"

"Passing through."

"Where are you going?"

"That remains to be seen," I said. "Does anyone truly know where life's journey will lead them?"

Sir shook his head. "Sounds like you ran away. Did you? Don't lie."

"No, Sir," I replied.

"What brings you out here tonight?"

Although I was uncertain of the word's meaning, I took a chance. "Camping."

"By yourself? This area's not a public campground. Where's your gear?"

I pointed to the black duffel sacks. Piles of rumpled Sent clothing, discarded supply wrappers and the ruined medical kit sat in the dirt next to the bags.

Sir looked around. "Who searched the bags?"

"I did, Sir," said a uniformed Sent with a maroon aura. He turned his head and spit out the side of his mouth.

"Where's your tent? Food? Water?"

"I travel light," I said.

"Where's your campsite?"

I twisted my head and pointed. "The cave."

Sir pointed to two Sents then jerked his thumb over his shoulder. The uniformed captors ran up the mountain to inspect the cave.

"How long have you been camping out here?"

I shrugged. "One night."

"I'd like to believe you, but your clothes are too clean for someone who's been living in a cave." Sir's eyes bore into mine. "How'd you get here from Los Angeles?"

"I walked."

"You walked," he repeated in an incredulous tone. "Lift your feet."

I lifted each foot off the ground and winced when I moved my injured leg. One of the Sents directed a light at the soles of my boots.

"Those boots don't look like they've walked forty-five miles."

"These are new," I said.

"I can see that," Sir snapped, raising his voice. "Come to think of it, nothing about you looks right. Why are you wearing men's clothes? With that Jimmy Buffet shirt and GI Joe jacket, you look like a colorblind parrot trying to blend in jungle foliage in the middle of a damn desert."

———
21

"If that a crime, then arrest me," I lifted my hands in surrender.

Sir made a *tsk* sound, chuckled and shook his head. "I suppose you were you in that cave all night?"

"Until I saw the light."

Sir's jaw stopped moving. "What light?"

"A bright light shot across the sky. It made a loud, high-pitched noise. I left the cave to investigate."

"Where'd it go?"

"Over this mountain."

"Are you sure?"

"Yes."

"You hear anything after that?"

"Yes, something far away."

"What?"

"Boom," I said softly.

Sir ran a hand through his black, close-cropped hair that formed a sharp point in the center of his forehead. "So why were you running? Why not stay in the cave?"

"I feared for my safety, not knowing what it was. Then you came and scared me more," I said, raising my chin toward the airships.

Sir smiled, revealing yellow, crooked teeth. "We are a scary bunch."

My captors laughed. "Did you see anything else? Could you tell what the object was?"

"No. It happened very fast." I heard footsteps behind us and knew the cave inspectors had returned. I held my breath as perspiration bubbled on my brow.

Sir stepped away and spoke to them. When he finished, he pulled Johnson aside.

"Her story checks out. Have someone treat her left leg and let her go."

"But Sir, shouldn't we take her in for further questioning?"

The Sent shook his head. "Waste of time. Our targets are reported to be half her size."

"With all due respect, Sir, what if the reports are wrong?"

As Sir considered this, his lower jaw moved side to side. "If we had unlimited resources at our disposal, we'd take her in. She's strange, maybe on drugs, but we're not out here to capture smart-mouth cross dressers. Now let's find and secure our target."

It was a relief when the Sents released me. I refused to let them touch my injured leg, though. Convinced they would follow me, I sat on a boulder, plucked the cactus needles from my boots and leg and repacked my duffel sacks. While I waited for them to board their airships and land vehicles, I collected the discarded supply wrappers and stuffed them into the duffels.

Within a matter of *mangnas*, Sent trash had wrecked my ship, Sents had assaulted me, destroyed my food and medical supplies. For the first time in my life, I knew what it meant to despise another. At least my canisters of Re-breather formula sat untouched. I figured the Sent who searched the duffels was not smart enough to open them.

Once they vacated the area, life returned. Insects buzzed and chirped in the darkness. Something howled in the distance, startling me. Creatures rustled around my feet and scurried in the underbrush.

When I was certain I was alone, I marched several hundred letrs down the mountain toward the valley. Strong wind gusts pushed against me. The death stench pervaded my senses and made me queasy. Each time I inhaled, I had to consciously fight the urge to sputter after each breath.

I followed a winding trail into a canyon with steep walls. Up ahead where the trail tapered, an orange light burned through a narrow pass. As I moved toward it, I heard muffled laughter. Then a loud crash pierced my ears. Something hissed and let out a shrieking howl. I stopped mid-step and waited, my breath seeming unnaturally loud. When things grew quiet again, I crept forward and peered through the gap.

A small clearing lay on the other side, surrounded by rock walls and clusters of bushes. Two male Sents emitting murky brown energy fields sat before a blazing campfire. Their elongated shadows danced on the boulders behind them. The one with a beak nose and close-set features wore dark, stringy hair that fell to his shoulders. He tipped a brown bottle to his lips, swallowed the contents and pitched it at the gap.

I ducked behind the rocks just as the bottle shattered. Glass shards flew through the crevice and landed on the sand at my feet. The Sents' laughter rang through the clearing, punctuated by another fierce yowl.

I looked up and behind me. The canyon walls were insurmountable, especially with the duffels and my injury. I had to turn back and look for another route. I refused to continue through the clearing; I had encountered enough Sents for one lifetime.

While I considered this choice, a black, furry paw extended past the rock wall and batted at glass shards twinkling in the firelight. I leaned forward for a better look.

An emaciated animal with gold eyes, pointed ears and a dull, black coat with bald patches cowered as the Sents launched another bottle at it. The animal flattened, squeezing its eyes shut as the bottle smashed near its head. When the danger passed, it scurried here and there but could not escape because of a cord tied around its neck. The second Sent, a stocky male with wavy copper hair and a spotted face, held the other end of the cord.

"Where's the gun," he muttered.

The dark-haired Sent grabbed a long-barreled weapon leaning against a boulder.

"Here Chaz. Take this." The copper-haired Sent held out the cord and reached for the weapon.

"I ain't taking that thing," Chaz protested. The animal spit and hissed.

"If you don't hold it, we can't shoot it," the copper haired Sent argued.

Rage boiled in me. What kind of Sent custom was this? On Pharralax, all animals — even those raised for food — held a sacred status. Their protection was required by codified principles known as *The Way*. If only we were on Pharralax, where animal cruelty carried the death penalty.

I reached for my Disintegrator and with some hesitation, adjusted the setting from 'disintegrate' to 'shock.' I stared at the animal and glanced at my computer. The Sent word for it was cat. My hands shook as I pocketed the computer and set the duffels on the ground. I did not want to do this.

The stocky Sent pumped the weapon, raised it to his shoulder and aimed. "Hold it still," he demanded. His finger curled around the trigger.

I rounded the rock wall and stepped into the clearing as the dark haired Sent called Chaz yanked the screaming cat close to the fire.

"What are you doing," I asked, genuinely curious.

The Sents looked up, speechless. Chaz's mouth dropped open.

"Get out of here," the copper-haired one said. He raised his weapon and pointed it at me.

I fired two pulses from my Disintegrator. The Sents hit the ground face first, incapacitated. I scooped up the frightened cat and yanked the cord from the Sent's hand. Unlike my mother, I do not speak animal languages, but I knew how to communicate empathy and directed my energy at it. Immediately soothed, the creature went limp and purred loudly.

I pocketed my weapon and examined the vibrating animal nestled in the crook of my arm. It was uninjured, however, the bald patches resulted from a skin condition my computer identified as mange. I set it down and untied the cord around its neck with shaking hands.

"Go home tiny creature," I whispered, envious the animal was free to do so. Instead of running away, it wound its lithe body around my legs and almost tripped me as I retrieved the duffel sacks. Back in the clearing, one of the Sents moaned. There was not much time; soon they would regain consciousness, although without any memory of me, or what had happened. As I shouldered the duffel sacks, the cat mewed and blinked at me. I bent low, picked it up and stalked through the clearing.

I moved fast in spite of my injury. When I reached the base of the foothills, the ambient noise around me swelled. A faint but annoying electrical hum buzzed in my ears. I trekked down an incline toward the bright, glowing valley and blinked several times to ensure my eyes were not playing tricks.

Contrary to the images I had seen depicted in Sent broadcasts, it was not a war zone. The buildings sat intact. There was no evidence of recent explosions or destruction, but perhaps when their sun rose chaos would ensue.

The supply sacks grew heavier with each step as I trudged along. The buzzing noise steadily grew louder, filling my head. I pricked my hypersensitive ear holes and listened closely. From the vibration it sounded like the transmission of information along metal or fiber optic lines.

A short distance later the thick vegetation abruptly ended. The stretch of desert before me contained low scrub, trees with thorny leaves and Sent trash. Discarded bottles and rusted cans littered the field. The broken glass covering the ground glittered in the moonlight.

A rustling, snapping object blew past me, carried on a burst of wind. The language implant held little use when items in question did not exist on Pharralax. In those cases, my computer filled in the gaps by providing the English word for the visual stimuli.

The computer identified it as a plastic bag. When I advanced, I noticed more bags tangled in bush branches and impaled on the thorny plants. Only low, worthless Beings desecrated their environments. This was yet another reason to abhor Sents.

I continued walking until I came upon a dry riverbed with steep banks. I set the cat down, slid down the embankment and clambered up the other side, where I leaned against the duffels and rested. The cat followed, scampering at my heels. During my rest, the animal rubbed its head against my arm and flopped down against my healthy leg.

For reasons unknown, the purring creature looked fuller and healthier than it had in the clearing. I did not understand how it healed so quickly but figured it was the cat's nature because the bare patches on its fur had filled in and its coat was now sleek and shiny.

Only a barren field dotted with rocks and more Sent trash separated me from the Protectorate outpost. The outpost, or barracks, was located in something called a 'mobile home park.' From what I could tell, there was nothing park-like about the rectangular habitat boxes lying some distance ahead. Light poured from a few square windows, but most gaped darkness.

Tall, branchless trees with horizontal vines strung between them stood outside the boxes. They seemed unnatural and unlike anything I had seen before. It was awhile before I realized they were not trees or vines at all. The poles and lines created the buzzing in my head.

I crossed the fallow field. The outpost would have been difficult to discern had I not been briefed about its appearance and exact location. I approached the white habitat box, only one of three sitting on a dirt road at the edge of the mobile home park.

The barracks had a green awning, manufacturer stickers on the windows and dusty newspapers scattered about the patio. The numbers next to the entrance matched the numbers contained in the briefing — 213 Stellar Way, Space 87.

Tingling with anxiety, I stared at the square entrance and imagined the door rising. I heard a loud clicking noise but when the door failed to elevate, I grasped the handle and pushed it open. The door banged the wall behind it and slammed shut.

If not for my exhaustion, I would have marveled at the Sents' square, disconnected structures with locking doors that kept each other out. Their harsh treatment of me made more sense now. On Pharralax, transparent corridors called *tubes* connect our sphere-shaped homes to foster a sense of connectedness and none of the doors hold locks.

I pushed the barracks door open and ducked under the doorway to avoid bumping my head. As I stepped over the threshold every light and electrically operated mechanism inside the structure clicked on.

I had arrived.

I had never dwelled within square chambers before and found hard angles gave me an uneasy, unsettled feeling. Weary from the weight I carried, I placed the black duffels on the white entryway tiles and removed the computer from my pocket.

The cat slinked inside and sniffed the furniture. Two ceiling fans whirled at top speed dangerously close to my head. Unfamiliar noises resonated from the barrack's unseen depths, including the amplified buzz of electricity.

Grek-stench permeated everything, crinkling my eyes. I lifted my shirt over my nose but the fabric held the nauseating stink as well. My eyes watered and my face puckered in disgust. When I pulled the shirt off my nose, a tear fell onto my dry lips. I licked it off and gagged at the gritty film on them.

The outpost was a tiny command. My head almost grazed the ceiling. My eyes darted between my computer screen and objects in the barracks as I learned their names. In the front chamber the sparse furnishings either had legs or rested directly on the floor—none of the pieces hovered like the diamagnetic furniture back home. I reached out and brushed my fingertips over the entryway wall. It was coated in a permanent white substance that could not be programmed to change color or pattern.

A blue sofa stretched across the wall opposite the entryway. Noise bellowed from two viewing boxes called television sets that sat on a long table, right angled from the sofa. A black and white chronometer hung on the wall above the table. Two brown reclining chairs sat side-by-side, facing the televisions. A set of sliding glass doors covered by white vertical blinds sat a few paces behind the chairs. I shook my head, reminded of how very far from home I was now.

The noise in the chamber interfered with my ability to think, so I imagined the televisions in the 'off' setting and the machines shut down. I then explored the barracks, walking from chamber to chamber, shutting off lights, fans and appliances that had sprung to life.

The common chambers were sparsely furnished. They all had white carpet and bare white walls. The decompression chambers, though, held multiple decompression platforms stacked two high. The Sent term for these objects was bunk beds. As I inspected the outpost, I wondered who else had been here and how many others were expected.

Down a short hallway I found a bath chamber. I stripped then ducked inside to inspect my skin suit for additional damage. I stood before the mirror but saw only my chest reflected. When I bent my knees, painful twinges coursed up my injured leg. Letting out a dissatisfied grunt, I kneeled on the floor.

I stared at the stranger in the mirror, overwhelmed. I had seen myself in the skin suit only twice before. First I stroked the thatch of blonde hair crowning my head. Then I touched the prosthetic lenses covering my cobalt, compound eyeballs. With the skinsuit's white sclera and blue irises, I looked like my Nadreen mother and younger brother, Aix. The skin suit even had prosthetic ears as well as a prosthetic digit on each hand and foot to give me ten fingers and toes.

I turned my head side to side. The skin suit diminished the wrinkles etched into my skin — courtesy of the Adelian aging process, which was the opposite of how Sents aged. Besides the gashes on my leg, the skin suit sustained no other damage but the numerous cuts ran deeper than expected.

I exited the bath chamber and searched the decompression chamber across the hall for supplies. Bunk beds and empty chests of drawers lined the walls.

Finding nothing, I crossed to the only window centered in the wall opposite the door. Dust motes clouded the air as I raised the white plastic blinds and looked outside. A narrow space separated the barrack's back wall from a green gravel-topped driveway. There was a dusty, red Sent vehicle parked mere letrs from the window. Beyond it, cracked wooden slats called stairs led to an elevated patio with faded brown paint.

The dilapidated habitat box was a dingy shade of brown with darker, dingier brown trim. The window and patio door screens hung in tatters on bent and rusted frames. A corroded metal box sat at the end of the driveway atop a splintered wooden post that leaned to one side. I wrinkled my nose in distaste, lowered the blinds and exited the chamber.

This dismal place looked and smelled putrid. I could not wait to send a transmission to Aix and tell him what Erox was really like. The truth would not change my brother's mind, though. Aix revered Sents for their artistic talents and thought Adelians should learn from their example. As his only sister I entertained Aix's follies, but secretly found his ideas laughable.

I rubbed my heavy-lidded eyes before dressing and returning to the front chamber. As I lowered my tired, aching body onto one of the reclining chairs, I expanded my computer to full size and held a finger over the port. My vibrating thoughts appeared on the screen:

> *High Chancellor — Clandestine insertion accomplished. After a close encounter with Sents, barracks located. Awaiting further orders. Envelope contained no orders nor additional information as stated. Guardian of the Sky EBN-Reyoz-X*

I attached the Sent military files to the transmission and sent it.

With thoughts of decompression dancing in my head, I pushed out of the seat, cringing from the pain in my leg. While I limped down the hallway, the computer *beeped.*

> *EBN — New mission objectives: observe Sent activities and report findings. Watch for signs of Seemae activity. Contact with Sents is forbidden. Maintain distance and do not interfere with Sent evolution. Personal transmissions are strictly forbidden. No exceptions. Protectorate High Chancellor Eesh-Slic*

My mind spun. This was not happening. I must leave Erox immediately. Our family expected me home to attend Aix's Ascension celebration. If personal transmissions were forbidden, I could not contact them to explain what had happened. That was unacceptable. I wanted answers. I needed to know how long I would have to tolerate this awful place.

> *High Chancellor — Leg injury sustained. I lack food and medicine. When can I expect rescue? Please provide information omitted from envelope. Guardian of the Sky EBN-Reyoz-X*

I sent the transmission and returned to the front chamber. My computer *beeped* immediately. The outgoing transmission bounced back. I sent it again, but the same thing happened. I grunted my dissatisfaction. I was quickly losing patience.

Dread and homesickness panged in my gut. I had just arrived and already could not wait to complete this mission and return home, where it was quiet, clean and technology worked.

I re-sent the transmission a third time. When it bounced back yet again, I tossed my computer and weapon onto the table in frustration. Aggravated, I stomped across the chamber, pushed aside the blinds and peered out the patio doors. Night still reigned, but the darkness did not blanket what my eyes beheld. Instead of my footprints tracking across the pale parched soil, a wide trail of orange and gold wildflowers cut across the desert and ended at the barracks' front door.

My stomachs sank to my knees. I raced outside, sprang off the patio, ran alongside the flower path and looked behind me. With every step, golden poppies burst through the soil and sprouted at my feet, carpeting the desert in shades of orange and gold. I may as well have erected a giant glowing sign stating, "Extraterrestrial life form located HERE."

Disregarding my inflamed leg, I sprinted through the field. While I ran in concentric circles and other geometric formations to conceal the path I had inadvertently made between the barracks and the *Surety*, I thought of the black cat and wondered if I had healed it. But that was absurd. I shook my head, confused.

Anger and adrenaline spiked my system. I should have been briefed about these things, especially the flowers. I dashed non-stop until the field between the barracks and the dry riverbed was evenly disbursed with germinating wildflowers.

There was no time to stop or catch my breath; I crossed the riverbed and continued covering ground. The closer I got to my ship the more difficult my task became, not only because of my waning energy but also because of the rising sun. A compromised skin suit exposed to solar radiation degraded quickly because of its organic composition.

The sky brightened to a deep shade of violet, outlining the craggy mountaintops to the east. However I dared not stop to appreciate it, no matter how much it resembled Pharralax's night sky. Whilst I scurried through the foothills, I remembered I had left the barracks without my weapon, a potentially fatal mistake.

Meanwhile, the desert was waking. Twittering birds filled the air with ancient melodies. I arrived at the clearing and found it unrecognizable because wildflowers bloomed everywhere. The Sents with the weapon were gone but they had left the fire burning. I shook my head at the wanton disregard and extinguished the fire by throwing dirt on it.

When I finally reached the boulder outcropping, I could neither sprint nor jog any further. Panting and sweat-drenched, I avoided the crash site but ascended and descended the mountainside in irregular patterns to disguise the path made by my footsteps.

By the time I headed back to the barracks, the sky burned with fiery orange and gold tones underneath a dark blue dome. Rippled cloud layers like filmy purple swaths stretched across the horizon.

I advanced as quick as I could while watching for signs of Sent activity but after re-crossing the dry riverbed for the third time that morning, my injured leg seized. Forced to limp the remaining distance, I wondered what else Eesh had failed to mention. Once again, I thought of those blank pages and questioned their meaning.

The sun peeked over the jagged eastern mountains as I crossed the wildflower field. To my dismay, two young Sents — one male and one female — emerged from the dilapidated brown habitat box. Intent on avoiding them, I hobbled toward the barracks, unaware if they had seen me.

When I ducked under the door and stepped over the threshold, every electrically powered object inside the dwelling turned on like before. Letting out a groan, I imagined the barracks dark and quiet. In an instant, everything responded and shut off.

Before closing the door, I looked out one last time. The litter-strewn field beyond the barrack's patio now blazed with wildflowers and their sweet fragrance masked the stench that turned my stomach.

The black cat lay curled in a ball in one of the reclining chairs. As the door clicked shut, it mewed, stretched a front leg and went back to sleep. To my surprise I no longer felt tired, but my cramping leg felt stiff and sore.

I hobbled into the front chamber, grabbed my computer and limped to the bath chamber, where I drew a hot a bath. I checked for transmissions again. One waited, but it was not from Eesh. It was the outgoing transmission I had sent earlier. Too tired to be angry, I re-sent it for the fourth time.

While I undressed and struggled to fit my long, lanky body into the tiny Sent-sized bathtub, I realized a single decision had altered the course of my life. I could have been killed — or worse, captured.

When Eesh had approached me at the PLEXUS way station and offered the mission, I accepted on a whim. My intuition had fired warnings, but I did not listen. By allowing greed to overrule my intuitive sense, I had acted primitive, like a Sent, and gotten my due. Now I was trapped on their home world. Only one thing felt worse than the shame of my mistake. A terrible, lurking feeling gnawed the pit of my guts.

The hot water felt wonderful against my skin. After the burning subsided, it even soothed my shredded leg. I leaned against the cool bath tiles intending to only rest my eyes, but the moment I lowered my eyelids I slipped into a deep decompression and dreamed of home.

Chapter Two: The Leap

The moment school is dismissed I rush home, expecting to find my older sister waiting for me. Days have passed since EBN's last transmission and I am anxious to see her. Halfway up the grand elliptical walkway, the smells of my favorite meal greet me. I inhale deeply, savoring the aroma of roasted bricsen and plush leaves, prepared the Nadreen way with a tongue-curling, tangy red glaze. On the second floor, pans clatter and liquid bubbles. Otherwise the house stands quiet. I doubt EBN has arrived. I pause at the second floor landing and gaze out the glass wall at the shela.

The pink sandy beaches below have been abandoned since the end of sweltering second summer season. This afternoon was calm, but the first storm of harvest season now brews. Green clouds loom in the distance, growing large and black. They blot out Scyros' rays, change the water's color from aquamarine to gray and swallow Pharralax's celestial neighbors, tiny amethyst Doridaen and the hulking ivory moon, Orioa. The clouds roll in with a sense of foreboding, and the crashing waves churn up an uneasiness I buried when EBN deployed. She promised to be here and she never gives her word lightly.

A flock of thorin soars in a V above the water's surface, wheeling and darting through the wind currents. Remaining in formation, the flock simultaneously dips their heads and dives. When they spring from the pitching water, they clutch fish in their mauve curved bills and fly toward the cliffs our house sits upon, returning to their nests to feed their young.

I wish the birds would fly closer so I can better see the purple undertones gleaming within their green iridescent feathers.

It was a near perfect day and I wasted it indoors at school, I think to myself. My first day at the Conservatory passed quickly, but it wasn't fun. I miss my friends. Although we share some classes, there was no time to socialize with Nyl and Xtarr.

Letting out a sigh, I long for the simplicity of the past and wish to return to the time prior to EBN's deployment. I miss my sister terribly and feel her absence deeper than either of our parents.

Is that the Ascending light Being I hear? Our mother's voice vibrates in my mind and chimes like crystal bells. Her speaking voice is symphonic in resonance but of the many qualities I inherited from her Nadreen lineage, her mesmerizing musical voice was not one of them.

Yes, A-ma, my thoughts resonate back. I walk to the end of the hall, pass under a tall, rounded archway and enter the nourishment chamber. A semi-circular, shiny alloy countertop runs along the back section of the circular chamber and a second, oval-shaped countertop forms an island in the chamber's center. Both surfaces slide open for access to cooking appliances, sinks and storage areas.

Fresh seeded and sprouted edibles and a wide assortment of sundries crowds the countertops. The weekly home delivery of food and household supplies just arrived from the Protectorate.

Come help your elder Being, Preece vibes, glancing up with a smile. For a Being of one thousand and one years old, A-ma doesn't look a day over seven hundred. Her white tunic dress complements her luminous caramel skin, white-blonde hair and Sent-like violet eyes.

I watch her as she places items inside the cold storage bin. Looking at her is like looking in the mirror. Some Nadreens have wings, like my friend, Xtarr, but neither A-ma nor I have them.

I don't mind looking different from EBN or the other men in our family, who hatched with fully developed, blue-skinned bodies that grow younger as they age. My strong resemblance to her sometimes causes me to wonder if Ulem is my biological *A-da,* since EBN favors Ulem, while I do not. After all, Preece descends from the Nadreen Queen, and royal females often reproduce asexually to preserve the bloodline.

43

Happy Ascension, offspring.

Thank you, A-ma, I vibe. *What can I do?*

Prepare the annex for the Eldersberry ceremony, service for five. She turns her attention back to organizing the week's supplies.

I walk into the annex immediately right of the rounded entryway. The annex — like the formal dining chamber — is separated from the nourishment chamber by floor-to-ceiling crystalline partitions that, like the ceiling, can be programmed to change color and pattern. I hold my open palm over the partition and a sapphire sphere interface surfaces.

I imagine the tabletop and five seats rising from the floor. The annex fails to respond, so I clarify my thoughts and sharpen my focus. The second time I envision the floor panel sliding open, a round white tabletop with white disk seats rises from within it. They stop at hip height then hover in a stationary position. Satisfied, I wave my hand over the sapphire interface. The floor panel closes. The interface fades away but the tabletop and seats remain hovering in place.

I turn to rejoin A-ma in the nourishment chamber when Eesh strolls through the chamber's arch, followed by four Protectorate guards dressed in black uniforms. Eesh notices me in the annex and nods solemnly. I smile and nod back.

I feel honored to have the Protectorate High Chancellor attending my Ascension celebration. Almost one Scyros cycle has passed since I last saw him, but I've never seen him in the company of guards before. Eesh speaks to the soldiers. Three of them exit the chamber while the fourth stands at attention at the chamber's entrance. I watch with rapt attention, expecting EBN any moment.

Smells delicious, Preece, Eesh vibes. He stands before her, bows his head and leans forward. She leans forward and touches her forehead to his in greeting. For some reason Preece pulls away and stares at her A-da. Eesh murmurs something I can't hear and pats her arm. Pressing her lips together, she hurries from the chamber. As I watch them, my sense of foreboding intensifies.

Eesh strolls into the annex. His compound gray eyes flash within his youthful face but a shadow lurks in their depths. His white skin no longer holds the blue pigment from his younger years. When he touches foreheads with me, a lock of his silver-blond hair falls forward over one eye. *Happy Ascension.* Eesh's raspy voice vibrates in my mind and he claps me on the back.

Thanks. I wince from the force Eesh uses.

How does mastering your first principles feel? Eesh's gritty vibe wavers with chuckles.

I hesitate before answering. Something feels wrong. Eesh's energy disturbs the chamber's serenity as well as my own. *Growing up seems overrated. School was disappointing. I don't know how one can learn to think in that environment.*

———

45

Are you at least excited about the Sent Studies program? That was all my idea, you know, Eesh vibes with a sly smile and a wink.

Does that mean the Protectorate is extending an invitation for Sents to join?

Eesh's mouth pulls to one side in a half-frown. *Perhaps when Sents learn to live in peace, we can reveal ourselves to them.*

Seemaes have never known one day of peace, yet the Protectorate formed an alliance with them.

Eesh stares into my eyes. *And that is a mistake the Protectorate intends never to repeat. Now, what do you think of Sent Studies?*

It's my favorite subject, but I think it should be taught by a Sent conservator, not a Seemae, whom I suspect dislikes me, I vibe.

What did you do? Tell me you did not hack into the Conservatory's computers again.

No Gran-Ada. Where is EBN? Will she be along soon?

Eesh glances away.

Gran-Ada, what troubles you?

EBN will not be joining us this evening, he vibes in a dry tone.

A flash of disappointment crushes my excitement. *I knew it.*

Eesh's bushy left eyebrow arches up. *Have you spoken with her?*

I frown. *No. Not lately.*

Eesh's gaze locks on mine. Apprehension grips my stomach. *What happened?*

We shall discuss it later, as a family.

Is EBN all right? Is she hurt?

I say nothing of the kind.

I stare at him, angry. *I wish you would say she is well, Gran-Ada.*

Eesh places a hand on my shoulder. *Aix, your Ascension comes at a strange time. Things are changing.* He gestures to the guard positioned at the chamber's entrance. *Society is taking a new turn. As for EBN, worry not. I have personally seen to her comfort and safety.* With a nod of his head, Eesh turns and exits the annex.

Eesh's words do little to quell my apprehension. There is some comfort in knowing EBN has Eesh watching out for her, because EBN isn't always the fastest ship in the fleet. But as I watch our Gran-Ada enter the nourishment chamber, thunder rumbles and shakes the dwelling's walls. Startled, I glance to the right.

Far beyond the terrace lightning flashes, momentarily illuminating the darkening sky. The storm is coming.

The house is quiet except for the sound of howling wind. Lightning scrawls across the sky and reminds me of skeleton bones. My family gathers in the annex. The table glimmers with crystal and silver. Pale blue, heart shaped fruits sit in the center of each plate.

Ulem, Preece, Eesh and I stand in a circle around the hover table. Preece's silver gossamer ceremonial gown sweeps the floor. The fabric catches the colors of the spectrum and reflects them like a soap bubble. Ulem, Eesh and I wear identical white silk robes over our clothes for the occasion.

Preece gives a slight nod. We outstretch our arms and hands but we do not touch. White light pulsates from her fingertips and spreads into a visible ring around us. Her bioluminescence expands until it encases us and fills the annex.

"Tonight we celebrate Aix's pledge to live in accordance with *The Way* and honor him as a light Being," Preece says. The exquisite triple timbre of her voice lulls us. "In honor of this joyous occasion, we begin our feast with the Eldersberry Ceremony." Her eyes fix on me. "However, before partaking of this blessed fruit infused with the memories of ancient ones, we express our gratitude to the Source."

We pray in unison, "He'tah, Them'the, Na'mi Ha'ni, Wi'she." *Thank you great Source for life, love, family.*

We break the circle and take our seats. Eesh sits to my left, in EBN's usual seat. Ulem and Preece sit with their backs to the nourishment chamber, facing us. I glance at the empty seat and place setting meant for EBN and wish she was here.

We follow Nadreen custom and eat our Eldersberries in silence out of respect for the Source.

I pick mine up, take a deep breath, brace myself for what is to come and bite into the succulent fruit. Sour juice squirts into my mouth. My lips and tongue tingle wildly. Soon the fruit's soporific properties take effect. My eyelids grow heavy then droop shut.

Completely relaxed, I float in the black void of space. When I open my eyes I look upon a tiny planet with pale blue skies and blue oceans. I float toward it until my feet hit solid ground.

White clouds fill the sky. Green trees and grass cover the land. I stand near an irrigation ditch at one end of a large, flat field, where blue-skinned Adelian farmers in brown uniforms till the soil. A group of wrinkled Adelian children dressed in white play nearby. Although I'm not eavesdropping, I hear their vibed conversation with perfect ease.

The eldest child, a stocky female with blueberry skin uses a smooth stone to furrow the dark soil. *A-da must plant more crops to feed our new neighbors. Soon more will come and we cannot let them go hungry.*

Jal, I do not like them, vibes a girl with big ears and light teal skin.

Why not, Thela? the plump child, Jal, replies.

My A-da says they are not to be trusted. They look like bugs.

We probably look funny to them, too. They have offered us medicines and technology we do not have, a silver-haired boy with rheumy eyes named Shkoa vibes.

That is right. We would not want them to let us go hungry, would we? Jal vibes.

Thela hangs her head low and says, "No."

A roadway edges the field some distance to my right where an antiquated red vehicle putters. It stops in front of three sphere-shaped buildings lining the road's opposite side. Numerous Adelians mill in and out of the structures on foot.

A gentle breeze caresses my face. As I wonder where I am, a shadow engulfs me. The farmers stop working and stare skyward. Some shout and wave while others point and smile.

"The colonists have returned!"

"Let us greet them."

Dozens of black disks appear out of nowhere, infesting the sky. All of the children except Thela jump to their feet and wave to the ships, welcoming them.

Without warning, orange beams shoot to the ground, striking the farmers and children. I dive into the ditch and cover my head with my arms.

Screams pervade my ears. Acrid smoke assaults my nostrils. Inching my body up, I peek over the top of the ditch. The buildings along the roadway blaze. Orange flames dance in their round windows; black smoke billows from their shells. Adelians run in every direction but none escape the ships' deadly beams.

The ships land on the field. Hordes of identical, armor plated Beings swarm from them, descending upon the land. Each has six spindly legs covered in spiky hairs that extend from segmented, rust colored bodies. Nine eyeballs dominate the invaders' faces. Black mandibles hang from their jaws and black tufts top their large, insect-like heads. Several scuttle past the ditch, carrying a wretched, rotting smell with them.

Terrified, I hold my breath. I've never encountered Beings like them.

The invaders cross the field. As they approach the farmers' corpses, one of the farmers sits up, fires a weapon and blows two legs off one of the invaders. A second invader rears on its hind legs while its black tufts unfurl to form two long antennae. Before the farmer can fire a second shot, yellow laser blasts issue from the Beings' antennae, killing the Adelian.

Trembling in fear, I slide to the bottom of the ditch and close my eyes. It is awhile before I work up the courage to take another peek. When I open my eyes, I'm crouching inside an empty wood paneled chamber with scuffed wooden floors.

Slowly I rise and stand before a round picture window. Hundreds of Adelians huddle together in the town square below, surrounded by invaders. Without a sound, the creatures rear and unwind their antennae in perfect synchronicity. They fire upon the unarmed Adelians and cut them down. The room spins. I lose consciousness.

51

The floating sensation washes over me again and I awaken. I hover over a blackened field covered with thousands of dead Adelians, their mouths agape. Vacant stares fill their still-open eyes. Thick brown haze taints the air. Invaders crawl over the dead, tearing flesh from corpses and feasting on the remains. I gag violently.

Tremendous force yanks me into space, knocking the breath from my lungs. I see the blue planet again from a great distance. Two colossal interstellar passenger ships drift near me. A blinding explosion flashes on the planet's surface. Waves of molten fire roll over the sphere, consuming everything — land, water and atmosphere.

I cry out and drop the Eldersberry onto my plate with a *thunk* that pulls my attention to the present. I look around the table. My family stares at me.

What happened? Preece vibes.

Shaken by the experience, I recount the disturbing images and memories to them.

Do you know what you saw, Eesh vibes.

"I saw betrayal," say I. Thunder rumbles long and low and shakes our home.

And what else? Eesh vibes.

"The End Conflict on Odos[1]? Were those creatures Beligs?"

Well done, offspring, Preece vibes, nodding with pride.

---

[1] Mars

52

Evening nourishment is served and consumed in the formal dining chamber, off the terrace. Eesh and I sit at the ovular hover table and watch the violent storm batter the North Shela through the floor-to-ceiling windows. The oval terrace door rattles in its frame. Rain and debris pelt the terrace wall. My A-da, Ulem, clears the dirty dishes and carries them into the nourishment chamber, where A-ma Preece gathers items for dessert.

Ulem approaches the chamber carrying a polished silver tray. A stack of plates, cutlery, a large slicing knife, a gleaming silver teapot with steam rising from its spout and four teacups crowd the tray's surface.

Still dressed in his Protectorate uniform, Ulem's ivory suit makes him appear taller than his height of six letrs. His compound left eye peeks from beneath a half-drooped lid. The youth of his middle age is undetectable due to the mottled and misshapen skin on his face and neck, which is covered in swollen purple scar tissue. Two small patches of the aquamarine flesh tone he hatched with — one above his compound right eye, the other on his chin — stand out in stark contrast from the rest.

When Ulem enters the chamber and sets the tray down, the partitions darken, dimming the chamber's light. Fireworks shoot across the walls and explode, illuminating the chamber with showers of multicolored, sparkling lights.

I marvel at A-da's abilities. His precise thoughts alter his environment in an instant, eliminating the need to utilize interfaces. I admire his control and hope to master the same abilities someday.

Preece enters carrying a salt-encrusted tahdis cake — my favorite treat. She sets it in front of me and sits down. *Since A-da Ulem traveled here from Nilotic and Gran-Ada Eesh chose us over Protectorate matters, I thought an extra sweet in order,* Preece vibes.

"Thank you, A-ma," I say, smiling wide. I cut the cake into thick slices and glance at the empty seat to my right. I wish EBN were present. Tahdis cake is her favorite too.

Ulem pours Amuscatamus tea from the steaming pot and distributes the cups. While we eat our dessert, the shrieking wind rises and wanes, drowning out the musical clatter of cups, saucers and clinking cutlery.

Eesh finishes first. He empties his teacup and sets it on the table. Instinctively Ulem reaches for the teapot, but Eesh holds up his hand.

Preece rests her utensil on her plate and looks at me. "Tell us about your day, offspring. What classes are you taking?"

I swallow my last bite of cake. "Planetary customs, cultures and civilizations, planetary science, galactic travel theory, math applications, data management systems, information systems design, Sent studies and current events," I tick off the classes on my fingers as I speak.

"You are most fortunate," Preece says. "The Conservatory almost denied you admission after you hacked into their computers to elevate EBN's grades three Scyros cycles ago."

I smile at the mention of EBN's name and chortle. "It's a good thing she doesn't attend now. She wouldn't have taken classes about Sents. She hates them."

"Speak not of hatred, Aix. It is against *The Way*," Ulem commands in his basso voice.

"Yes, A-da," I say, looking down.

"Preece, Ulem, Aix" Eesh extends his arms and stretches. "Thank you for this evening."

"A-da, you must not leave so soon," Preece frowns.

"I apologize, but there is much work to be done."

"Let it wait," Preece pleads.

Gran-Ada shakes his head and sighs.

"What cannot wait? Our time together is too limited these days. What happened to 'Family above all; we are all family?'"

Eesh glances at Ulem and then at Preece. "I am due on Orioa then Nilotic."

Preece glances across the table. "But A-da, planetary alignments favor neither travel nor important decision making. Tui is in direct opposition to Pharralax and Amyx's orbital velocity has slowed," she says.

"The challenges of life still carry on regardless of celestial mechanics," Eesh responds.

"Not more problems with the Protectorate outpost, I hope," Preece says. "Have there been more Seemae uprisings?"

I bristle at the mention of A-da's project on Nilotic. Ulem lives on that planet, overseeing the development of a Protectorate military installation and rarely travels home. Lifting my teacup, I sip the hot, sweet liquid and feel the steam collect on my upper lip. I stare at A-da to see his response. Ever the diplomat, Ulem's expression remains neutral.

Eesh clears his throat and lowers his gaze. "The Seemae dissention is manageable. Their attempts on my life have failed, thanks to Ulem and my escorts."

Preece nods. "I am pleased that our family's sacrifices during the past sixty Scyros cycles have not been in vain."

My forehead furrows. This is the first I've heard of multiple assassination attempts.

Eesh picks up stray crumbs with his fingertip and flicks them onto his dessert plate with his thumbnail. "Other matters trouble me."

His eyes sweep our faces. "Disturbing reports about the Sents. The Protectorate has neglected to watch them closely. This must change." He points his finger at us, sweeping it in a circular motion around the table. "You must never repeat this information," he says.

He speaks slowly, deliberately. "The situation is dire. I am petitioning the Zuma Neway to approve a permanent Guardian presence on Erox," Eesh continues. Outside lightning cracks and casts purple light onto the terrace.

Preece gasps. A delicate hand covers her mouth. "Peace has reigned throughout the Xionin star system for 3000 Scyros cycles. We are not at war," she says.

Eesh's eyebrows raise; he tilts his head slightly. "We could be and soon. Sents have acquired advanced technology and are reverse-engineering it. They intend to use it against us."

"How can you know? Sents don't even know we exist," I counter.

Eesh glances at Ulem then at me. "Too many Sents know of our existence. Pilots from nine different orders of Beings have gone missing. There could be more. Sents tortured and murdered them by experimentation."

My head jerks back. I'm stunned and stare at Eesh in disbelief.

"Never underestimate the brilliant minds among them. Sents are on the cusp of discovering how to make the Leap. We must monitor their progress and be ready," Eesh says. He glances across the table at his daughter. "Preece, I have never criticized Aix's obsession with Erox, however, I wish you would do something about his emulation of Sents' speech patterns."

"With all due respect, Gran-Ada, might you be overreacting?"

Eesh shakes his head. "Their technology has outpaced their morality. They destroy everything they touch. Their polluted planet, atmosphere and space are evidence of this. Sent pollution has grown so extreme that a cosmic junkyard orbits Erox, making those space sectors impossible to navigate. Imagine the damage they would inflict if we allowed them off Erox." Anger blazes in his eyes.

"You can't know that," I argue.

Eesh locks me with his gaze. "If their current course is not corrected, Erox will soon be uninhabitable. Sents will seek new worlds to colonize. Would you have them come here and destroy Pharralax?"

This possibility never occurred to me. Although the idea thrills me, I shake my head.

"This matter has yet to be determined. The Zuma Neway needs more information before reaching a decision," Ulem offers.

"Sent rovers have invaded Odos. They are ignorant of our history and holdings there. We must keep it this way. Sents endanger us all. They are Beings of tremendous gravity and one of my biggest problems." Eesh runs a hand over his face, opens his compound gray eyes wide and shudders.

"A-da, I did not know," Preece says, barely above a whisper.

"Good," he says, nodding in Ulem's direction. He rises to leave.

"Gran-Ada, wait."

All heads turn toward me. "We never discussed EBN," I say in a small voice.

Eesh stares at me as he sinks into his seat. After a long silence he says, "I have held office only a short time, yet I have made mistakes, been careless."

"She's in danger, isn't she," I blurt. It is the only plausible explanation.

"Yes," Eesh whispers.

Enraged, Preece shoots to her feet. "You promised you would keep her safe."

Eesh sighs. "Be proud. EBN is the best pilot in the Guardians."

"How could you?" she cries.

"I had no choice," he counters, raising his voice. "The mission had to be undertaken. We shall get her back."

Preece's eyes bulge. "Get her back? This is all your fault," she hisses and points at Eesh with an unsteady hand. "You never should have encouraged EBN to join the Guardians. After she gave her commitment, I begged you to release her from the obligation, but you refused me."

"This is why I did not tell you," Eesh responds. "I knew you would react this way."

A shrill sound escapes Preece. She whirls and runs from the chamber.

I swallow hard and glance at A-da. Fear and concern fight for control of his disfigured face. Ulem's disfigurement results from an Erox mission gone horribly wrong. He almost died from a disease called entropy.

Eesh stands and lets out a heavy sigh. Ulem and I stand and touch foreheads with him.

"I will escort you and the guards down to the Matter Transference Chamber," Ulem says.

"No need," Eesh replies. He throws a final meaningful glance at me and says, "I will take it from here. Family above all—"

"We are all family," we respond in unison.

Chapter Three: Observations

A sonic boom pierced the sound barrier, rumbling the ground and shaking the barrack's thin walls. I awoke with a start in the bathtub, the freezing water chilling me to my bones. Gritty sand lined my mouth, tongue and chattering teeth and I wretched in the icy water.

I climbed out of the tub, dried off and examined my injury. The tears in my skin suit had widened. They revealed the badly discolored flesh of my lacerated, swollen lower leg. Amber, evergreen and grape blotches surrounded the gashes slicing into my muscle. My leg throbbed and hurt to stand on.

The computer sat on the countertop near the sink. I checked it for transmissions but found none. I let out a heavy, lonely sigh. I missed my family, especially Aix.

The diffuse light entering the frigid chamber through a rectangular window near the ceiling burned my eyes. I glanced out the window anyway. Judging by the sun's position, there were three mangnas left before it reached zenith for the day. I limped to the front chamber and dragged the supply sacks to the bath chamber. Unable to tend my injury, I dressed in jeans, a red and yellow Hawaiian shirt and wrap around sunglasses with iridescent reflective lenses.

The cat appeared in the doorway. It chirped, arched its back and hopped sideways. As I watched its display, I realized I did not know the first thing about cats or their role on Erox.

On my home world, cats were mythical creatures and symbols of fertility in the Loredi culture. For all I knew, throwing bottles at cats was some sort of sacred Sent ritual that I had interrupted. I limped to the nourishment chamber, filled a glass with water and set it on the floor. The cat lapped then dipped its paws in the liquid and licked them.

At the PLEXUS way station Eesh had mentioned the Sents' 'Internet.' It took me only moments to access it. While reading about felines on my computer, the tiny beast jumped in my lap and head butted my chin and hands. I figured it was hungry but did not know how to go about procuring food for it.

On my home world (where resources are distributed and recycled by the Protectorate) I would have placed an order for fresh meat and waited for it to be delivered.

According to my research, Sents frequented places called stores and exchanged currency for goods and services. I located the nearest one, removed the stack of currency from Eesh's envelope and stuffed it into my pocket. As a precaution, I also pocketed my computer and Disintegrator, but hoped I would not need them. My primary concern for this aspect of my mission was to blend in, which would not be easy because of my height.

While consulting my computer, I fished a sombrero out of one of the duffel bags, put it on along with my jacket and checked my appearance in the mirror. I frowned at my reflection, feeling uncomfortable. The outfit looked ridiculous. I longed to wear something familiar and missed the simple, monochromatic uniforms from home. The hat seemed ostentatious, but Eesh had assured me it would be the most effective way to shield my skin suit.

My pulse quickened when I peeked out the patio doors to check the weather. As I ducked under the doorway and exited the barracks, my dry palms moistened.

It was an overcast, gloomy day. A crisp chill and the reek of contaminants weighted the air. I walked to the edge of the barrack's patio. One glance at the field of wildflowers reminded me to stick to paved surfaces. Anxiety-ridden, I took a deep breath, stuffed my hands into my pockets and hurried past the dilapidated brown box next to the barracks.

I hurried toward the red stop sign marking the end of Stellar Way, where the pavement began, stepped onto the asphalt and looked back. Clusters of wildflower blossoms pushed through the sand, marking each of my footsteps. Confounded, I stared at them. This development raised more questions in my mind, but no answers followed.

Underneath my eyewear, I squinted. In spite of the overcast sky, it was far brighter here than on my home world. Endless rainbows filled my vision. Considering the abundant light energy, I did not understand why solar power was not utilized here. On Pharralax, all buildings and vehicles have photovoltaic coating and produce their own energy supplies.

Before coming to Erox, I would have never considered Pharralax a dim planet, but it was by comparison, causing Pharralax's flora to be significantly darker than Erox's. Instead of being green, our vegetation falls within the range of blue, indigo and black.

Fighting the urge to run, I limped at a slow pace along the mobile home park's narrow streets, figuring I would attract less attention than if I hurried. One particular dwelling caught my attention as I approached it. It was the largest habitat box I had seen yet. It had a satellite dish, a wide yellow awning and shiny windows.

As I stared at the wheels set into its base, I finally understood the meaning of the phrase 'mobile home.' A unique aroma radiated from the box. I sniffed the air. To my surprise, the Sent food smelled appetizing.

A wrinkled Sent couple with white hair sat under the awning in webbed chairs. As I walked past them, I forced a neutral facial expression so as not to betray the fear gripping me. They are just Adelian children, I told myself; they are just Adelian children. The statement was not far from the truth. The couple did, in fact, resemble freshly hatched Adelians.

The man — who emitted a wide, sapphire energy field — nodded to me, while the woman stared with her mouth agape. Her orange aura hugged her physical body tight. I returned the nod and kept moving. Despite the loud thumping of my heart in my ears, I heard the woman say, "George, did you see the size of that fellow?"

The entrance to the mobile home park sat on a roadway called Columbia Way. A glowing pink and blue sign that said "Oasis Mobile Home and RV Park" stood next to the driveway. As I turned, I sneaked a glance at my computer to learn the names for things.

Housing developments and vacant lots lined both sides of the street. When I came to a cinderblock wall the color of sand, I stayed close to it because it provided a sense of security. I thought of my younger brother, Aix, and wished I could speak with him.

Sent vehicles spewing toxic fumes passed me going both directions. Some of the vehicles thumped. Others rolled by with music blaring from their windows. I found it ironic that Erox was habitable all solar cycle because the pollution made it unlivable, whereas pristine Pharralax was uninhabitable for certain lunar cycles because of its elliptical orbit around Scryos. If memory served me, the Sent name for Scyros was Barnard's Star.

The vacant sidewalk provided me with a sense of relief, but it reminded me I was alone. This feeling intensified when I checked my computer and found no transmissions.

A moment later, Aix's tenor voice vibrated in my mind. *EBN.*

Out of habit, I almost answered but stopped myself. Hearing Aix's voice felt bittersweet. I desperately wanted to talk to him, but kept my mind clear.

EBN, Aix repeated, his tone urgent.

It physically hurt me to ignore him, but I had no choice. I pressed my lips together in a tight line. Orders were orders.

When the cinderblock wall ended I passed an undeveloped lot strewn with trash. A colorful billboard towered overhead that displayed an image of a scantily clad Sent female with enormous mammary glands. It read, 'Eat at Mike's' and I realized the billboard's purpose was to advertise. I could not help but stop and stare.

I never considered Sents to be attractive, but they were. I resumed walking and looked across the street. Another billboard stood across the road. This one showed a group of scantily clad Sent women with large mammary glands.

By the time I approached 50th Street, I had passed several such billboards. Regardless of what the advertisements aimed to sell, they all contained attractive Sent women dressed in revealing garments. Before now, I was unaware how significant large mammary glands were in Sent culture. I glanced down at my modest chest and determined my small glands were inadequate by comparison.

It was not long before I approached my destination, a non-descript, tan building with no windows. I stood on the sidewalk and stared at it, feeling so nervous my knees shook. Sents were unavoidable. They moved in and out the doors; their vehicles entered and exited the parking lot. I considered turning around and rushing back to the barracks. Instead, I moved toward the entrance with caution.

Cold air blasted my face as I stepped through the automatic glass doors. Music floated through the air, setting my nerves further on edge. I wandered down an empty aisle, baffled at my surroundings. The number of items on display boggled my mind. In my six hundred Scyros cycles I had seen much, but never anything like this.

A myriad of Sents with different colored energy fields roamed the store. I watched them and found them curious.

I stared over the shelves at a group of young females in the next aisle. They huddled in front of a mirror and rubbed colored substances on their faces. One glanced over her shoulder, looked at me and said, "Nice sombrero," in a loud tone. The other Sents turned, giggled and jostled one another.

I located the medical supplies easy enough but gasped once I realized Sents lack organic technology. As I selected boxes of fabric bandages, tape rolls and healing ointment from the shelves, I recalled Aix's favorite Sent expression, 'old school.'

With my arms full of old school medical supplies, I meandered up and down the long aisles, unsure what cat food looked like. Some Sents stared, while others did not notice me. I returned their gazes, unable to focus on my task.

I must have looked lost, because a female with violet energy and billboard-worthy mammary glands approached me. She smelled like flowers, but different from the wildflowers at the barracks. Her pale hair and tan skin reminded me of my A-ma, and a fresh wave of homesickness hit me.

Her green eyes twinkled as she smiled and asked if I needed help. Distracted by her chest—which rose and fell as she breathed—I stared at the tag pinned to her uniform. It said, 'Crystal.'

A stream of impressions flooded my mind because Crystal projected her thoughts in all directions. She was a nineteen-year-old college student who had failed a recent biology exam. Her car needed a new transmission and carburetor. She worried that the cost for the repairs would deplete her savings account and felt angry with her boyfriend for not calling. His whereabouts were unknown and her period was three days late.

"I seek cat food," I blurted out.

She led me to the next aisle. "Here are the cat supplies," she said, with a swooping gesture. "What do you need?"

"I am uncertain. Do they have requirements besides food?"

"I take it you've never owned a cat?"

I pondered the question and squirmed, uncomfortable with this concept. In my culture, ownership never, ever pertained to another living Being. It went against *The Way*.

"No, I have never been a cat steward before."

Crystal gave me a sideways glance, said she'd be right back and hurried away. She returned with a cart and pulled items from the shelves, explaining as she filled it. "You'll need a litter box, litter, food, a collar, toys, treats, a food dish, water dish and a litter box scoop."

I cocked my head and pointed to the box of clay pellets she had called litter. "What do I do with that?"

69

She smiled and explained. After patiently answering all my questions and encouraging me to dump the medical supplies into the basket, she escorted me to the counter at the front of the store. I thanked her for her kindness and sighed with loneliness when she walked away.

As I stood in the queue something unusual caught my eye, a mother and child in a nearby aisle. Silver light surrounded the girl, who sat askew in a motorized chair, her thin limbs, hands and feet contorted. My eyes widened with wonder. Only the most spiritual and highly evolved Beings radiated silver light. The child's mother asked the girl a question. Unable to speak, the girl grunted her response.

Drawn to her silver aura, I felt compelled to help her. Before the thought finished in my mind, the girl's eyes locked mine and a jolt of electricity zapped me. Shivers raced through my limbs, down the length of my spine. Feelings of warmth and acceptance oozed over me, confirming my initial impression. Her name was Melody. I smiled and lowered my eyes out of respect, humbled to be in the master's presence.

"Can I help you," the cashier asked in a loud, scratchy voice. While she scanned cat items, I stole glances at Melody until she and her mother moved beyond my line of sight.

"That'll be ninety-one dollars and seventy-two cents." The cashier's sour breath smelled like smoke.

I removed the Sent currency from my pocket and fanned twenty or so rectangles out on the counter. They were identical; each one had the number 100 printed on all four corners.

The Sent's eyes grew large. I glanced between the currency and the cashier, wondering what I had done wrong. "Take what you need," I said.

She lifted one of the bills off the counter with a puzzled expression and urged me to put the rest away. For some reason she handed me more bills and metal discs varying in size and composition and said something about changing my receipt, whatever that meant.

I loaded my purchases into the cart and stuffed the currency into my pocket. But instead of moving toward the exit, I wheeled the cart down the aisle where Melody and her mother went. I found them at the back of the store, waiting at the counter labeled 'pharmacy.' Melody sat next to a bench, while her mother perused items on sale.

I knew I should stop and exit the store, but I felt powerless over the inexplicable force pulling me toward her. "Leave now," I whispered to myself. "Do not do this."

Disregarding my orders and training, I ambled toward Melody with thoughts of the black cat and wildflowers filling my mind. If my impression was correct and I had healed the cat, then according to *The Way*, it would be a criminal offense to withhold healing from any Being with her capabilities.

Perhaps my ship had crashed for this very reason, so that I could help this child, which would help the planet and multi-verse by extension. Melody's sharp eyes followed my movements as I approached her.

In spite of the nagging sensation in my stomachs signaling me to stop, I reached out, tapped her shoulder and continued moving without looking back. Before I reached the aisle's end, a cry sounded behind me. I glanced over my shoulder in time to see Melody's mother crumple to the floor.

Several Sents rushed to her aid and a call went out over the loudspeaker. Employees, including Crystal, hurried toward the pharmacy. Against my better judgment, I turned the cart around and stood behind the growing crowd.

Distracted by the frenzy, I glanced at Melody's now-vacant chair. I searched the crowd, concerned. In the chaos, I overlooked her standing on straight limbs next to her mother.

She tugged on her mother's sleeve and pointed at me.

"Mommy, Mommy, that's him," Melody said. "He's the one who touched me."

My eyes expanded. The Sents gathered around Melody's mother stared up at me with angry, confused expressions. Before I could react, Melody's mother flung her body onto mine and knocked me backwards a few steps.

"What are you? How did you—?"

Trapped by her tight embrace, I stood rigid, staring down at her in silence. After a long moment I uttered, "I do not know."

"Thank you," she sobbed into my chest.

I tried not to fidget as the woman released her emotions. When I could stand it no longer, I pulled my body from her strong grip, but it was too late. Sents of all kinds had gathered around us. I heard their layered voices.

"What just happened?"

"Should I call an ambulance?"

"I don't know. That lady fainted."

"I heard the little girl say that tall man touched her."

"Are you sure that's a man?"

"Did anyone call the police?"

"It was a miracle," said a stout Sent wearing a wide brimmed hat. He lifted a gold cross from under his red and white checked shirt and touched it to his lips. The Sent's companion nodded in agreement and touched his forehead, belly and each side of his chest.

My eyes darted to a group of whispering employees standing behind the pharmacy counter. The intensity of their stares frightened me, especially the glaring one who spoke into a corded, plastic object. My head spun and terror rushed through me. I had to get out of there.

Except the throng of Sents blocked my cart. With trembling hands, I gathered my bags, the box of cat litter and limped toward the exit. When I stepped outside, I stopped suddenly.

73

Wildflower clusters bloomed from every crack in the parking lot asphalt.

I rushed back to the barracks as fast as I could limp without regard to where my feet landed. As if the wildflower proliferation was not strange enough, they only germinated down one side of Columbia Way, growing between cracks and lining the sidewalk's edges. So many wildflowers crowded my path; there was no room for more to grow.

Returning to the outpost unnoticed seemed impossible. I clutched my purchases to my chest and limped faster, desperate to return to safety.

I had no Being to blame but myself. I had compromised the mission and could never allow it to happen again. Now that I had cat supplies, I vowed to lock myself inside the barracks and not leave until rescue came.

Forming this plan calmed me, but it would not change what had happened. As I recalled the scene at the store, waves of regret churned my stomachs and I could not look behind me, not even give a cursory glance over my shoulder.

I grimaced at the thought of sending my next transmission. I dreaded reporting what had happened, admitting that I had disobeyed orders. There was no excuse. Light Beings did not behave as I had.

By the time the Oasis Mobile Home and RV Park came into view, I slowed my pace because my injured leg ached. When I limped past the mobile home park's neon sign, I finally gathered my courage and looked behind me. A lone figure in a wide-brimmed hat and red and white checked shirt followed several paces behind me. I sucked in my breath.

The Sent had been at the pharmacy.

I moved fast, slipping into the mobile home property and attempted to lose the Sent in the labyrinth of narrow streets. Once I reached the barracks, I ducked inside and locked the door.

The cat waited for me at the door. My hands trembled as I unwrapped the purchases and set everything up in the front chamber. The feline stuck close, meowing and chirping until I filled a dish with food. Then the animal forgot I existed. It ate so voraciously I worried it might burst. After it finished, it jumped into the litter box and left two deposits.

Meanwhile, I hobbled between the barrack's windows and peeked outside. The Sent from the pharmacy was nowhere in sight. It seemed I had evaded him.

The televisions squawked endless chatter. Just as I imagined them shutting off, I heard the words "environmental disaster," and looked at the screens. Both sets played the same news program. Mirror images of black muck spewed from an underwater well. I crossed the chamber and stood before the machines.

"BP executives now say far more oil has spilled into the Gulf than was previously thought. An estimated fifteen million barrels of crude oil have leaked into the Gulf of Mexico since the catastrophic explosion on the Deepwater Horizon drilling rig last month," a Sent said off-camera.

Now I understood why Erox reeked of death. This place was far worse than I had imagined. As I wondered how I could not be allergic to it, something occurred to me. Perhaps my newfound abilities could be some sort of allergic reaction to the environment.

In accordance with Crystal's instructions, I cleaned the litter box right away. While scooping out the deposits, guilt overcame me. What was I thinking, keeping the cat in the barracks? That was never my intention; I only wished to save it from harm. I could not have predicted it would follow and cling to me. Now that I had fed it, there would be no getting rid of it. Not that I wanted to be rid of it. It was my only companion in this lonely place.

After peeking out the windows one more time, I checked my computer. Still no transmissions.

I limped to the front chamber and sat to ease my aching leg:

High Chancellor – I circulated amongst a number of Sents and observed no conflict among them. This area of Erox is not plagued by war or conflict as the Protectorate has led citizens to believe. Still, I am anxious to return home. When can I expect rescue? Guardian of the Sky EBN-Reyoz-X

I stared at the screen, deliberating if I should admit disobeying orders. Unable to decide, I sent the transmission and waited. It bounced back at once. I did not understand why my communication system was failing and dreaded to think what it meant.

The cat slinked into the front chamber carrying a toy mouse in its mouth. It dropped the toy at my feet, batted it across the floor and chased it. The game amused us both. When it grew tired, it jumped into my chair, flopped in my lap and purred. I scratched its head, grateful for the company. I did the right thing last night and felt no regrets. When the Guardians rescued me, I would take the animal home.

I rested, tended my injured leg. After several more glances out each of the barrack's windows, I ventured out again, this time without the sombrero.

The Quartz Hill Public Library was located a short distance beyond the store I had visited. The single story building had a pitched roof and reflective windows spanning the façade. I entered the front double doors. The long counter to my right swarmed with excited, chattering Sent children. Three adult Sents stood behind it, but none noticed as I walked past.

I limped to the back of the building and stood before the last row of bookshelves. I had never seen so many Sent books housed in one location before. Neither Xtarr's nor Aix's favorite museum — the Sent Emulation Center — had as many books in their collections.

Starting at the top shelf, I removed one book, fanned its pages and replaced it in its designated space, reading each volume in seconds. I worked my way down the shelves, book by book and soon had read every volume shelved along the back wall. Not needing to pause to digest the material, I moved to the next row of bookcases and continued reading.

This was a new experience and I thoroughly enjoyed obtaining knowledge this way. On Pharralax, information was recorded and stored on gold plasma cones that glowed and rotated as one absorbed the information telepathically. Feeling the weight of the books in my hands pleased me but what I appreciated most was the books' unique smells. Dust and velum scents rose off their paper pages and tickled my nasal passages.

By mid-day, I had read every book in the library and my head swam with information. As I limped toward the exit, I stopped at a half-shelf, picked up a fashion magazine and thumbed through its pages. My eyes strained at the patterns, styles and designs of Sent clothing.

It had never occurred to me how complicated the act of dressing could be. The variety of choices perplexed me. Perhaps that was why there was no emphasis on fashion in Adelian culture. Anything not involving science or technology was considered superfluous and held little value. Adelians wore monochromatic uniforms according to profession and few deviated from the dress code. Nadreen culture was less stringent. They ruled the textiles and manufacturing industries.

Like the billboards I noticed earlier, the majority of advertisements in the magazine contained sexually suggestive imagery. I intended to read only one or two of the periodicals, but found them so entertaining that I could not stop. Even periodicals designed for women contained sexy images.

When I stepped outside, information exploded in my mind and my brain tingled as I made new connections. For the first time in my life, I felt I understood Sents. They were passion slaves; sex and violence drove them. While I did not agree with Sent choices or behavior, I felt I had gained a rudimentary understanding of them as Beings. I felt so delighted and stimulated by my time at the library that I forgot about my chaotic morning.

While I ambled along Columbia Way, I wondered why the town was so spread out. I had hoped to find the answer at the library, but none of the books I read addressed this topic. I had only seen a small portion of the area, but did not understand why this town sprawled.

On Pharralax, builders utilize vertical space to preserve nature. Entire forests are never clear-cut. Instead, individual trees are selected and cut and whatever is removed is immediately replanted. As outlined in *The Way*, natural resources are protected. This development model ensures pristine air, prevents drought, soil erosion and flooding. It also conserves plenty of fertile land for agriculture.

Of the many subjects I had studied, I enjoyed Sent history the most. Compared to Adelians, whose written history and culture began 750,000 Scyros cycles ago, Sent culture was very young—between 10,000 and 16,000 solar cycles old.

Although I could not be certain, I thought perhaps this explained how the two groups of Beings could share 89.5% DNA, yet differ so dramatically in philosophy and behavior.

A while later I arrived back at the Oasis. As I limped through the community, my wounded leg burned and begged for rest. I looked forward to reaching the outpost and learning when I would be rescued.

When I rounded the barracks' corner, I halted mid-step.

The Sent from the pharmacy — the one in the red checked shirt — stood on the porch next to another Sent slumped in a metal chair with wheels.

Caught off guard, I stood motionless. Had I been able, I would have run away.

The Sent from the pharmacy flashed a nervous smile and touched his companion's shoulder. "She's here, Betty, the miracle worker." Betty raised her baldhead and looked at me with dull, lifeless eyes.

Despite the searing pain in my leg, I spun on my heel.

"Wait," the Sent pleaded. "Please, don't go."

The desperation in his voice stopped me. I turned to face him. His name was Emanuel. For some reason, dark spots patched his pale yellow aura. At once, I distrusted him.

"We don't mean to bother you. I saw what you did for that crippled girl —"

"I did nothing," I said, interrupting him. "You are mistaken and should not be here," I said in an angry tone.

"We need your help—" Emanuel countered, staring up at me.

I held up my hand. I already knew Betty suffered from a Sent disease called cancer. Her body produced no life force. She did not have much time.

"Miss, please. We mean no harm. I spent all morning tracking you down. I'll probably lose my job," he said, wringing his hands.

"How did you find me?"

"The flowers," Emanuel said. "They weren't there when I came to work this morning, but they were after you left. Surely you know about—"

"I know of nothing."

"Don't make me beg. I can pay."

"No," I insisted. "I cannot help you. Go away."

Emanuel lowered his chin and narrowed his eyes. His aura darkened to crimson. "We're not leaving until you help us," he said, squaring his shoulders. "I don't care if we wait all night, you're not getting rid of us until—"

Recognizing the Sent's growing hostility, I reached into my pocket for my Disintegrator. "Do not threaten me."

"I'm sorry." Emanuel glanced down at Betty and stroked her cheek with the backs of his fingers. The crimson energy faded from his aura as quickly as it had appeared.

"We've tried everything, spent our life savings on treatments and hospital bills. I don't know what else to do." His lower lip trembled. "I've prayed day and night, asking God to heal her. We've got four children. They need their mother."

I raked a hand through my hair and looked away. The Sent's words resonated with me. I was someone's offspring too, but I had vowed to follow orders and not repeat my earlier mistake. I wished I were home now, with my family, instead of here.

I glanced at them. Emanuel meant what he said. I imagined worse scenarios unfolding if I refused to help them. I could not risk Betty dying here. Other Sents would come. Emanuel would tell them what had happened; perhaps blame me for her death.

I let out an exasperated sigh. I hated moments like these. "If I help you, you must forget about me and never speak of this," I said.

"Done and done," he agreed.

I limped over to Betty and took one of her cold, frail hands in both of mine. In an instant, time reversed itself. Betty's posture straightened. Strands of sleek, black hair flowed from her scalp down to her shoulders while lush eyebrows and lashes lengthened too. Color flamed her cheeks. Moisture plumped her dry skin, erasing the ravages left behind by the devastating disease.

I dropped her hand and staggered sideways a step. A black curtain dropped over my field of vision and I leaned against the barrack's wall for support.

———

"God bless you," Emanuel exalted. He grabbed my hand and pumped it vigorously.

Betty leapt from her wheelchair. "This is the greatest day of my life," she cried out, embracing me. "God answered our prayers, Manny. He sent us this wonderful girl."

She released me and hugged Emanuel. After giving him a long kiss, she turned cartwheels on the patio.

"Please, stop," I whispered, uncomfortable with the commotion.

Betty and Emanuel stopped and looked at me.

"Miss, are you okay?"

I nodded, still light-headed. "Tell no one," I warned.

"I won't," he answered. Emanuel pulled his wallet from his back pocket and held out a stack of folded bills.

"Keep it ... and your word. Now go," I insisted.

"Thank you," Emanuel said. Betty linked arms with her husband and he pushed her empty wheelchair off the porch. The metal wheels rattled against the unpaved ground.

I entered the barracks and collapsed in the closest reclining chair, exhaustion hitting me like a wrecking ball. Too spent to chastise myself for what I had done, I closed my eyes.

Mangnas later I awoke and checked the computer. No transmissions from Eesh.

84

High Chancellor — Second attempted
transmission today. My outgoing transmissions
are bouncing back and I have received none since
last night. I am assessing geopolitical events and
compiling my report. I have ideas about
expanding our areas of operation and am
anxious to share those. Awaiting further orders,
I look forward to rescue. Guardian of the Sky
EBN-Reyoz-X

From the quality of fading light in the front chamber, I knew it would be dark soon. When I stood and put my full weight on my injured calf, pain bolted up my leg and I shrieked. Once it dulled, I limped to the front chamber, opened the patio blinds and looked outside. Luckily, the patio was Sent-free. While I decompressed, the clouds had dissipated. Now brown haze hung in the atmosphere like a death shroud.

I stared at the field of wildflowers and thought of my childhood more than five hundred Scyros cycles ago, when my A-da had told me stories about his Erox mission.

If I concentrated, I could hear Ulem's rolling, basso voice telling tales of plentiful rainforests, unspoiled desert plains and clear, cerulean oceans teeming with wildlife. Back then birds crowded the sky, not pollution.

From what I had seen, it was difficult to imagine the Erox A-da had visited. Since then, Sent populations had exploded and ushered in an era marked by a sinister disposable mentality that poisoned everything.

Sents were environmental terrorists. As an order of Beings, they had not achieved the requisite evolution entitling them access to the multi-verse. Maybe they would get there in another 500 or 600 solar cycles, but considering their propensity for self-destruction, I predicted life on Erox would go extinct long before Sents evolved.

As I stood at the patio doors contemplating Sents' nature and their place in the multi-verse, a young male Sent with an azure energy field walked past the barracks. Frightened more than ever of male Sents and wary of attracting attention, I snapped the blinds closed. Then, remembering my orders, I wedged a finger between two slats to observe the Sent's behavior.

The Sent was tall, slight of build and long-limbed like me, however he walked with a pronounced slouch. Although his shoulders curved forward, his white hair brushed the collar of his green t-shirt.

In one hand he held an empty plastic bag and the handles of more plastic bags overhung each of his back pockets. I just knew he would allow the bags to fly away.

The Sent combed the wildflower field with a downcast gaze. Not far from the barracks, he stopped, picked up discarded containers, placed them in the bag and continued walking. A few steps later, he retrieved more trash and bagged it.

My head jerked back. There was no mistaking what the Sent was doing. He was collecting, not dumping litter. Somewhat puzzled and curious, I stared at him in order to access his thoughts.

Littering makes me sick. The oil spill in the Gulf makes me sicker. It's a crime against nature and humanity and heads should roll. The Sent bent low, picked up cans and placed them in his bag.

I wish I hadn't gone to school today. I already knew about the garbage islands floating in the Pacific Ocean that are killing the wildlife. They're twice the size of Texas and won't biodegrade because they're plastic. When Mrs. Adams said no one's doing anything about the situation, I got a stomachache. I wish more people cared. The Sent picked up a plastic bottle, bagged it and kept walking.

I'm ashamed to be human. I don't want to be part of the group that's responsible, but I am and I hate it. I wish I were dead. At least that way, I could see Mom again. He stooped down and bagged more trash. *I wish I knew where dad was. Wherever he is, I hope he's safe ...* Then he turned and walked toward the barracks.

Although he wore spectacles with thick lenses that greatly magnified his eyes, he was the most divine expression of a Being I had ever seen. He halted and rubbed his eyes.

87

A moment passed before I realized the Sent was crying. When he moved closer, I got a better look at him.

The angles and planes of his handsome face reminded me of the images I had seen in fashion magazines. Large, almond-shaped eyes fringed with white lashes sat above prominent cheekbones and his square chin stretched into a strong, square jaw line. Everything about him seemed more Adelian, more light Being than Sent and I felt drawn to him. Unnerved, my stomachs dropped to my pelvic floor.

I stood as still as a statue, shocked. I did not know what surprised me more: the Sent's rebel behavior, or my inexplicable attraction to him.

This Sent was nothing like the others I had encountered. For a moment, my heart softened and the corners of my eyes turned down. If only every Sent acted like this one, there might be hope.

The word 'home' lingered in my mind as my eyes opened late the following morning. Still groggy, I grabbed the computer off the bedside table and checked it for transmissions, but there were none. Concern jolted my mind awake.

I sat up and unwound the bandage from my tender left calf. My leg should have healed by now, but it had swelled more during the night. Not even the bruising had faded. My mangled skin lay open; the edges of every cut were maroon and puffy—infected. The medicine I had used seemed useless. If only I had proper supplies.

I rose from the platform and limped to the bath chamber. After I washed, changed the dressing on my leg and dressed in clean Sent clothes — a purple and white Hawaiian shirt and jeans, I limped into the front chamber with the computer, eased into a reclining chair and composed my status report:

FUNDAMENTAL PROBLEMS ON EROX:

1. *Sents lock up the food. There is plenty for all but access is controlled. No method of equitable resource distribution exists.*
2. *Half of Erox's land surfaces have been dramatically transformed by Sents. Over the last 100 solar cycles, the number of vertebrates was halved, while the number of Sents has quadrupled.*
3. *Currently, a toxic substance called crude oil gushes unchecked into the Gulf of Mexico. The Sents responsible for the pollution have no way of stopping the disaster and admit they could have been better prepared.*
4. *War rages throughout Erox over food, energy and other resources. War is a popular method of conflict resolution.*
5. *Sents possess advanced technology and are reverse-engineering it. Sents are working toward interstellar travel and have launched telescopes that search for an Erox analog*

because they have damaged their home world beyond repair.

6. *NASA (National Aeronautics Space Administration) intends to colonize Erox's moon.*
7. *Sex and violence drive Sents.*
8. *Survival has become a political issue.
Despite the fact that the twenty-two warmest solar cycles ever recorded have occurred since 1980, there is little consensus about Erox's climate crisis. Sent leaders waste time bickering instead of taking action.*

Erox is no Pharralax, but I imagine it was once a beautiful planet. After breathing the polluted air and witnessing the ongoing environmental devastation, I am convinced the majority of Sents are destructive Beings of gravity that must be contained on Erox for the continued safety and greater good of the multi-verse. Guardian of the Sky EBN-Reyox-X

Before sending the report, I checked for transmissions. There were none. To make matters worse, my computer's power supply had dwindled to half. I desperately hoped the Guardians were on their way to extract me.

I sent the report to Eesh. A moment later, an alert sounded. A surge of joy rushed through me until I saw it was the status report I had just sent. Disappointment crushed my excitement. This was unacceptable.

I re-sent the report. I needed to go on patrol, check on my ship, assess the damage and charge my computer battery, but not until nightfall. My computer *beeped*. An error message appeared on the screen. The transmission had bounced back again. I felt helpless, confused and afraid.

I glanced at the sleeping cat curled in the other chair and turned on the television to take my mind off the situation. Soon my eyelids grew heavy and drooped shut.

The afternoon shadows stretched eastward as the sun drifted west.

It was early evening before I stirred, coughing and sputtering on account of the fecund air. I checked the computer. Nothing.

Burning, throbbing pains coursed up my leg. I imagined I could survive a few days more without medical attention, but I should have heard from Eesh by now.

As I minimized my computer and pocketed it, I heard strange noises resonating through the barracks. Unable to identify their source, I got up and looked around the front chamber.

The cat sat before the patio doors, looking outside. I limped over, opened the blinds and peered out as well. Countless Sents crowded the barracks patio. My hands flew to the top of my head. I could not believe my misfortune.

Just then, the trash collecting Sent rode past the outpost on a yellow bicycle. I sucked in my breath and stared at him. Today his wide energy field swirled orange and cerise. As he passed, he looked directly at me, glowering.

His hostile expression startled me. Alarmed, I snapped the blinds closed. My feline friend, however, meowed, sat up on its hindquarters and pawed the glass.

My blood pressure spiked; cold sweat moistened my palms. A mob of Sents waited for me outside my hiding place.

Feeling ashamed, I buried my face in my hands and shook my head. The fault was mine; I had brought this on myself. With shaking hands I checked the computer for transmissions. There were none. I winced and maximized it:

> *High Chancellor — Two days have passed. My communications systems are malfunctioning. I have not received any transmissions from you. I regret to inform — I disobeyed orders. Maintaining distance with Sents is impossible. Despite taking preventative measures, I have attracted Sents to the barracks. Please send extraction team. Guardian of the Sky EBN-Reyoz-X*

As soon as I minimized my computer, the transmission bounced back. My anger surged. I re-sent it, re-sent it, re-sent it and re-sent it then flung the computer onto the table. If only I knew what was going on.

In spite of my fear and throbbing leg, I gathered my coat, pocketed my weapon. Unable to think of another solution, I limped to the front door and took several deep breaths. When I opened it, a hushed silence fell over those gathered.

I stepped onto the patio and closed the door behind me. Sents of every shape, size and manner of dress stared at me in awed silence. Based on their serene energy fields, none meant me harm. I had expected them to be monsters, but they were ordinary Beings, just like me. From their vibrating thoughts, I knew they either knew Betty or someone who did, and most were sick or injured.

For the first time since my arrival, I saw myself reflected in their faces. I too was injured and in need of help. Incapable of turning them away, I limped through the crowd, touching hands or squeezing shoulders.

Each of them smiled and thanked me. Mid-way through the group, I stumbled over a glass jar stuffed full of Sent currency. Someone had taped a handwritten sign to it that said 'Offerings." I touched everyone and lingered longest with the sick children, elderly and those confined to chairs with wheels.

Not everyone needed healing. Many healthy Sents accompanied ill loved ones. After receiving my attention, their companions led them away. A few Sents asked to take my picture, but I refused. As they returned to their vehicles, I heard reverence in their voices and talk of miracles. I did not even mind that they trampled the wildflowers under their feet.

Near the end of the procession, another group of Sents arrived in a van topped with telescoping radars. They identified themselves as a news crew and asked to interview me. With as much energy as I could muster, I declined, picked up the glass offerings jar and retreated inside the barracks.

When night darkened the landscape, I exited the barracks.

Cold wind streamed across the desert while rain clouds gathered overhead. The frigid evening air bit at my exposed skin. Behind the gray-bottomed clouds, stars popped against the lavender sky. To the west, a band of orange glowed above the horizon and distant mountain peaks.

As I limped across the wildflower field, I took deep breaths in an attempt to master the pain in my leg. This calmed me, but horned pollen particulates tickled my nasal membranes and I sneezed several times in succession.

For a moment I forgot about my problems because the vision of the lavender sky reminded me of my home world. I savored the wildflowers' floral aroma and pretended I was home.

My sense of tranquility did not last long. Midway through the field, I felt eyes watching me. Shivering against the dropping temperature, I turned and scanned the landscape. At first glance I saw nothing and dismissed the feeling as paranoia.

Then a flash of light popped near the barrack's west wall. A violet-blue energy field wavered from behind the barracks and I saw white hair. It was the trash-collecting Sent, the one I had watched yesterday. The last light of day had reflected off his glasses, betraying his position. Amid the earlier Sent-confusion, I had forgotten about him.

Being the object of Sents' attention was growing tiresome. I hurried to the riverbed, hoping he would lose interest, slid down the embankment, crossed the basin and crawled up the opposite bank. After spotting the largest, widest creosote bush I could find, I ducked behind it and scanned the landscape through the branches. He was crossing the wildflower field on foot. The Sent was following me!

His audacity infuriated me. This was my life—not some silly game. I moved through the foliage, searching for a better place to hide. Joshua trees beckoned, but none offered adequate cover.

I had little time to waste; he was near. A cluster of creosote bushes positioned several letrs beyond the trees looked promising. Gritting my teeth against the sharp, stabbing pains in my leg, I limped to it and ducked down. While I waited for him to climb up the embankment, I thought of my computer and wondered whether or not Eesh had transmitted word about my rescue.

Chapter Four: Stranger

It had been the craziest six months and last night was another one for the record books.

Thirteen-year-old Shale Bice had almost drifted off to sleep when a high-pitched, screaming whistle woke him. He'd lunged toward his bedroom window and pulled back the faded sheet curtain in time to see the tail of a white-hot ball streak across the sky. About fifteen minutes later, the first officials arrived on the scene. Since the episode with his father one month earlier, Shale had been waiting, expecting strange things to unfold.

Now a rumor circulated around the Oasis Mobile Home and RV Park and Shale not only heard it first, he knew it was somehow connected to the weird goings-on. As part of his after school routine, he stopped into the Leasing Office where his seventeen-year-old sister and legal guardian Harmony worked. Ever since he'd become the target of the Oasis' resident bully, Tommy Nutter, Harmony insisted that Shale check in every day before going home.

He could've popped in, waved hello and been on his way except another Oasis resident, Teensy Shaw, was already in the office when Shale rolled his yellow mountain bike inside, so he parked it near the door and waited.

Mrs. Shaw was a slender elderly woman with a long waddle neck and recessed chin. She wore only pastel colors and today her white hair was tinted the same shade of pink as her blouse and polyester pants. Her pink painted lips flapped excitedly as she spoke with Harmony, so involved in her gossip that she never acknowledged Shale's presence.

"This was before I went to the beauty parlor," Mrs. Shaw said in a piercing soprano voice. "George and I had just finished breakfast when this fellow strolled by our space. He was at least seven feet tall and looked as strange as the day is long." She leaned across the yellow countertop and lowered her voice. "He was wearing a sombrero."

Shale smirked but did not laugh. She made it sound like sombrero wearing was against the law. Maybe it was funny hat day at the guy's job.

Harmony kept a straight, concerned face. She listened and nodded.

"What sort of fellow wears a sombrero with ski glasses and a camouflage jacket? If you see him, be careful. I have a feeling he's up to no good," Mrs. Shaw said.

"Did he do or say anything to give you that impression," Harmony asked in a respectful tone.

Mrs. Shaw shook her head. "No, he nodded and kept on walking." She pursed her lips and shook her index finger. "He didn't fool me. Something about him wasn't right."

Shale appreciated Mrs. Shaw's concern. Every Oasis resident knew that their father, Step, had disappeared outside their mobile home last month. It was understandable that some residents might overreact to a stranger's presence.

Harmony raised her brows and considered Mrs. Shaw's warning. "I'll alert our groundskeeper, Nestor. We'll keep an eye out for him," she said.

"I already told Nestor," Mrs. Shaw said. Her sharp tone implied Harmony wasn't doing a good enough job.

"Thank you, Mrs. Shaw. I'll let you know what happens," she said.

Insulted, Mrs. Shaw sniffed angrily. She stepped away from the counter and retreated to the water cooler across the room.

"Hey Shale," Harmony said, glancing up at him. Dark circles hung beneath her jade eyes. She grabbed a stack of contracts from under the counter and sorted them. Halfway through the task she twisted her long, butterscotch hair into a messy pile on her head and secured it with the pencil tucked behind her ear.

When she wore her hair up, she looked like a heavier version of their mother who'd died last Christmas. Shale missed her so much that he hadn't uttered one word since the police notified them of her death.

"How was school?"

He shrugged.

"Got homework?"

Shale grimaced and shook his head.

Harmony looked up from her sorting. "Don't look at me like I'm crazy. You're the only thirteen-year-old high school senior in town. It could happen."

Still grimacing, Shale continued shaking his head.

"Your skin's pink. Did you apply sunscreen today?"

He nodded.

"Detective Alvarez called. He said to tell you there were no new developments."

Disappointment furrowed Shale's brow.

"What are you gonna do now?"

He grabbed a scrap of paper and pencil off the counter, scribbled a note and passed it to her. *Going to look for dad.*

"Don't waste your time, Shale," Harmony said in a sardonic tone.

Shale snatched the note back, flipped the paper over and continued writing. *You didn't see the commotion in the desert last night. Something happened out there. Maybe the cops found evidence relating to Dad's disappearance.*

"I wouldn't hold your breath waiting," Harmony said. She glanced at Mrs. Shaw and then looked at him. "Since you don't have any homework, I need you to ride around the park. If you see an unusually tall man wearing a sombrero, come straight here and get me, okay?"

Shale scowled and shook his head.

"Or you can go straight home, lock the door and wait for me to get there," she said.

As Shale nodded glumly his facial muscles seized and squeezed his eyes closed. He hated his facial tic. He also hated that Harmony aggravated it. He'd experienced only two other tics the whole day before entering the Leasing office. Now that he was mad, though, his face would be seizing all night. He waved goodbye, grabbed his bike and pushed it outside.

A cold wind burst hit his face and blew his hair out of his eyes. The air smelled thick with rain. He zipped his windbreaker against the unseasonably cold May weather. Another tic hijacked his muscle control and clamped his eyes shut. He climbed onto his bike and set off.

Shale understood Harmony's attitude about their father, but he still hated it. Harmony thought their father had abandoned them, but Shale knew better and thought she should too.

Their father would've never done such a thing, especially after their mother's death. Still, Shale didn't want to waste the afternoon riding around the Oasis, looking for some weirdo in a sombrero, but he had no choice.

Since their parents were gone, the Oasis belonged to both of them. The income generated by the property was their only means of support because right after their father disappeared, Harmony's business manager ran off with every dime she'd earned acting on the television show *Wonder Kids*.

Shared responsibility or not, every time Harmony ordered him to do something—which was every day—he missed their parents even more. Most days, he carried his grief on his shoulders like a backpack. Even lying in bed at night he felt the weight of it wedging between his ribs and lungs.

Glowering at his father's watch every few minutes, he rode through the mobile home park and did Harmony's bidding. He patrolled the entire property twice but didn't see any tall dude wearing a sombrero. Luckily, he didn't run into Tommy Nutter either. The only extraordinary thing he noticed was the cars—dozens of unfamiliar cars filled the guest parking area and lined the mobile home park's narrow streets. He wondered to whom they belonged.

After an hour, he called it a day. He rode to the back of the park, turned left onto the unpaved section of Stellar Way and pedaled toward the double-wide trailer he and Harmony called home.

Only three mobile homes sat on their unpaved street. Mrs. Perkins' gray house stood on the corner, directly across from their house and then the white one next door.

All three homes backed up to miles of government preserved land. Although the desert preserve didn't belong to him, he'd always felt connected to it. He knew every landmark, foothill, trail and riverbed in the desert as well as he knew the mobile home property.

But Shale didn't feel like going home, not yet, so he passed the brown trailer and wove through the myriad of cars blocking the wooden barricade at the end of their street. Rain clouds approached from the East, the first hint of rain the region had seen in months. Yet thousands of flowers had sprung up overnight through the cracked desert topsoil.

Shale noticed another oddity as he rode behind the wooden barricade. Thirty or forty people of all ages gathered around the vacant white trailer next door while five children ran through the wildflowers, playing chase. There were lots of senior citizens and people in wheelchairs in the crowd, including a boy a few years younger than Shale. Several people in the group wore surgical scrubs like nurses. Curious, Shale gave the crowd a wide berth and rode his bike through the wildflower field.

When he passed the white mobile home, he glanced at the window. Shale knew the mobile home sat vacant because he'd heard Harmony complain about the lease-holders being behind on their payments, yet a figure stood at the patio doors, looking outside. Because of his height, only part of his head was visible. Shale couldn't see if he wore a sombrero or not, but he wore a camouflage jacket and iridescent ski glasses.

His eyes drifted down to the black and white cat sitting between the man's feet and his heart lurched in his chest. Although he couldn't be certain, it looked like Princess Leah Lucky Buttons, his and Harmony's cat that had gone missing last week. He and Harmony had posted flyers all over the Oasis, but someone—probably Tommy Nutter—had torn them all down. The kitty sat up and pawed at the glass. Princess did that when she wanted outside. An apprehensive excitement swelled in him. It had to be her.

Shale turned his bike and circled back for another look but the blinds were closed. It had to be the man Mrs. Shaw mentioned, but Shale no longer cared about him or his raging old people party. He wanted to know if that cat was Princess. Shale stopped his bike a few feet behind the horde and considered approaching the patio doors, but the sheer number of people intimidated him. Crowds made him nervous.

He glanced at the front door. If he knocked on it and the man answered, then he'd have to say something. It had been months since he'd spoken to anyone. He considered fetching his dry erase board and markers from his backpack but he wasn't sure if he should confront the man or leave it to Harmony. The only thing he knew with any certainty was he wanted Princess back.

Shale knew from experience that grown-ups rarely listened to kids, but oftentimes people assumed he was much older than thirteen because of his height. While he decided what to do, a news van inched down their congested street and double-parked, blocking a bunch of cars. No one noticed, though, because all eyes fixed upon the man who'd just emerged from the mobile home. Except Mrs. Shaw had been wrong. It wasn't a man at all; it was a teenage girl not much older than him dressed in men's clothing.

Bystanders in the crowd murmured things about the girl who'd healed Betty. Another person spoke of miracles. Shale counted seventeen people in wheelchairs, five with walkers, three on crutches and five more with braces worn over their clothing. Peoples' bodies spilled off the patio and formed a semi-circle around the front of the house. Since none of them held cups, Shale decided it wasn't a party after all. He had no clue what was going on.

The girl said nothing to the group. She moved through the mass of bodies, shaking hands and patting shoulders. This occurred for many minutes. Once they'd received her silent greeting, the crowd disbursed in a slow trickle. Near the road, the news crew set up their equipment while a reporter dressed in a red suit applied fresh lipstick.

From what Shale could tell, there was nothing supernatural about the girl. Supermodel perhaps, considering her face and willowy body. He stared at her, captivated. She was gorgeous, but who was she?

When most of the crowd had thinned, the reporter and cameraman approached the tall stranger. They asked to interview her, but she declined. The reporter persisted, shoving her microphone into the girl's face. The girl raised her hands and backed away, saying, "No," over and over in a singsong, velvety voice with a unique accent Shale had never heard before. After the girl retreated inside the house, the reporter and cameraman chased the remaining stragglers, hoping to interview them.

Shale rode next door. It was 5:30 when he pulled his bike indoors and leaned it against the living room wall. Harmony still wasn't home from work yet so he grabbed a warmer jacket and an issue of Astronomy magazine, went back outside and sat at the weathered picnic table on the patio. He opened the magazine and attempted to read, but he couldn't focus. He could only think about his missing pet.

While he flipped through the magazine to kill time, he eyed an image taken by the Hubble Telescope entitled, "Ultra Deep Field," and decided it belonged on his bedroom wall next to another Hubble image, "The Pillars of Creation in the Eagle Nebula." Several minutes passed before Shale heard a door open. He glanced across the street at Mrs. Perkins' home, but she was nowhere in sight.

Leaving his magazine, Shale walked downstairs and around the side of the house. He stood below Harmony's bedroom window, pretended to inspect it and looked south, toward the San Gabriel Mountains.

The girl limped into the desert alone. While Shale watched, the setting sun broke through the clouds and cast slanting rays on her as she crossed the field of golden poppies. A faint, shimmering dust cloud surrounded her. Regardless of her stiff and uneven gait, the girl's posture was ramrod straight. As he wondered why she held her left forearm against the small of her back, he noticed that her large, elongated head seemed disproportionate to her skinny body.

Once she moved out of sight, Shale crept around their house, glanced at the empty driveway and his father's watch. It was 5:45 p.m. Then he sneaked behind the neighbor's white trailer and peeked around the corner. The girl had advanced to the middle of the wildflower field. Shale watched her, curious.

It was going to rain. Not only would it be dark soon, the temperature was also dropping fast. Shoving his hands in his pockets, Shale peeked past the building but the girl had moved beyond his line of sight again. He inched along the trailer's side and slowly stuck his head out.

When the girl came into view, she stopped and turned around. As Shale craned his neck around the building's corner, the sun glared in his eyes, blinding him. His face cramped, pushing his eyes shut. He lost his balance, pitched forward and saw the girl looking his direction. Shale scuttled backwards and hoped she hadn't seen him.

A rush of excitement raised goose bumps on his arms. He hurried around the back of the building and peered out the opposite side. The driveway sat empty, but Harmony would be home anytime.

Shale raced up the stairs and indoors, scrawled a quick note on his dry erase board explaining that he'd seen the person Mrs. Shaw told her about in the trailer next door WITH THEIR CAT and that he'd be home soon. Then he ran out the door.

The clouds momentarily broke and the almost full moon winked large and yellow against the darkening gray sky. The girl was barely visible at the opposite side of the field. Without a second thought, Shale scurried into the wildflower field after her. A minute later, she disappeared.

Shale ran as fast as he could. The cold night air stung his cheeks and burned his lungs as he gulped large breaths. Halfway across the field a stitch pinched his side. He slowed to a brisk walk, hesitated a second and questioned whether he should turn back. Night was fast approaching. It would be raining within the hour. He'd be in trouble if he were out after dark alone. Plus, he didn't bring a flashlight.

Following the girl wasn't his best idea of the day. The vegetation thickened on the other side of the wash. The thought of walking through cacti patches, Joshua trees and dense sagebrush in the dark would not have appealed to him any other time. He turned around and looked back. The driveway still sat empty. He thought about Princess being alone in that girl's trailer and felt his energy surge. He spun on his heel and darted forward.

Unaccustomed to running, Shale's heart knocked against his rib cage like it might explode. When he reached the riverbed, his feet made shuffling sounds as he slid down the embankment. He hadn't seen the stranger climb the opposite bank and wanted to avoid rushing up on her. It was much darker at the bottom of the wash, but he crossed it and climbed up the far side with ease.

Shale ducked behind a large creosote bush. A faint voice in his head told him to turn back, but he was too excited to listen. If he strained his ears, he thought he could hear Harmony's voice calling for him, but dismissed this as pure invention.

The cold breeze landed a fine spray of rain droplets on his upturned head and face. He removed his glasses, wiped the lenses clean and replaced them on the bridge of his nose, all the while listening for footsteps. He heard nothing. He pushed aside some of the creosote's branches and peered through the foliage but saw nothing. The girl had vanished.

Shale knew he should turn back. The desert wasn't safe at night. Nocturnal predators like coyote and mountain lions roamed this area — but did she know that? He considered giving up and going home while he could still see.

While he grappled with indecision, a dark shadow spread over the top of the creosote bush. The hairs on the back of his neck stood on end and a strong cinnamon smell engulfed him. Shale looked up. A silhouette loomed over him, outlined against the yellow moonlight.

The stranger opened her mouth and sneezed. Startled, Shale jumped, gasped and ran. With his heart thumping in his ears, he leapt down the side of the embankment and ran across the riverbed with strength and speed he didn't know he possessed. Then he bounded over the opposite embankment and scurried toward home without looking back.

Chapter Five: Close Encounter

I watched the Sent boy flee and waited until he neared the barracks before continuing.

Regardless of how appealing I found him, I did not appreciate being stalked. There was no question my safety was in doubt now that I had attracted more attention. I also suspected I had not seen the last of him.

By the time I arrived at the crash site, rain fell in a deluge, weighting my clothes and freezing my bones. I found the ship as I left it, behind the outcropping. It was a relief to see the cloaking mechanism still worked.

I reached for my computer to disable the cloaking shield but my pockets were empty. I had left the device at the barracks. Grek. I trudged inside the control deck, disabled the shield and exited the craft, leaving a cold, wet trail behind.

The *Surety* looked anything but good. Engine three on the *out*, or right side of the ship appeared demolished. A hole the size of my hand scarred the ring-shaped, revolving cabin area while a second hole twice the size of my head punctured the torpedo-shaped chamber underneath the control deck.

Ripples of molten bio-metal had gushed from the raw materials storage chamber and hardened into an uneven bulge on the side of the ship. As I determined the best method of removing it, I noticed dirty rainwater streaming down the chamber in thin rivulets and entering the exposed interior.

Since the camouflage jacket was waterproof, I removed it, draped it over the hole and used rocks to anchor it in place. Then I entered the control deck to formulate a plan.

Without a supply of molten bio-metal, the ship's self-repair mechanisms were useless and no form of bio-metal existed on Erox. My only option was to attempt a manual repair.

I searched the ship and gathered items to make repairs: two spare alloy panels, protective gloves, a face shield, alloy rods, my flight-suit, a working torch and carried everything outside. After lighting the torch, I peered inside the damaged chamber. A fair amount of water pooled at the bottom, so I stuffed my flight-suit inside, soaked up some water, removed it, wrung it out and repeated the process.

Once the interior chamber appeared dry, I patched the holes with the alloy panels. While the metal cooled, I chipped away the bio-metal chunk from the ship's exterior. Although the rock proved an effective tool, it failed to remove the smaller bio-metal bumps. I heated these bits with the torch and smoothed them as best I could.

The entire time I worked, I worried about the wet conditions. If I did not seal the breaches properly and the smallest bit of moisture or debris collected inside the chambers, the repairs would fail. To temper my nerves, I pretended this was a training exercise and nothing more.

The whole exhausting process lasted mangnas. When I finished, I grabbed everything, stepped back and admired my work. The chamber and cabin were whole again with discolored patches blending into the surrounding alloy at the points of impact. Otherwise, no indications remained that breaches had occurred.

With the repairs finished, I dumped everything on the floor inside the ship, reactivated the cloaking mechanism and stepped outside to inspect the shield. The shield neither covered nor blended with the repaired areas but the dark silver patches could pass for mineral deposits. However, when I felt the ship's surface to test its external temperature, I jerked my hands away because of the heat. Without external temperature regulation, the *Surety* could be detected using thermal imaging — yet another reason why I had to leave Erox immediately.

Concerned with the results my work yielded, I returned to the control deck, sank into the pilot's seat and placed my hand over the command module embedded in the armrest. At once, the ship hummed with power. A rush of excitement swept from my head to my toes.

According to the systems diagnostic screen, the critical components of the now dual-engine ship appeared restored. Only a test flight would determine if the repairs held. Although the navigation screen flickered in and out, I could fly without it.

Since I forgot my computer at the barracks I could not charge it, but I did not allow this oversight to dampen my morale. I recomposed the status report and transmissions from memory and sent them to Eesh. I waited for several moments. Nothing bounced back.

It took every bit of my control to leave the ship alone instead of powering up all systems and flying out of Erox's atmosphere. The thought tempted me but I could never abandon my four-legged friend at the barracks.

I cut the power, exited the ship and zipped my drenched jacket against the cold. Dense clouds blocked the stars and moon and my breath formed clouds when I exhaled. Drizzling rain fell onto my skin, numbing my exposed head and neck, but not even this could lower my spirits. The prospect of leaving Erox provided all the warmth I needed.

Ignoring the discomfort in my leg, I planned my departure while hiking back to the barracks. I would gather the duffel sacks and the cat and return to the ship tonight. Perhaps I would become as celebrated in the Loredi community as our mother, and hailed a hero for returning home with a live feline. An even better option would be to take a mating pair.

It was not long before I crossed the muddy riverbed, grinding my teeth to offset each painful step. The barracks sat dark, a tiny spec across the wildflower field. To take my mind off the biting pain, I imagined returning to the ship and loading the duffel sacks and cat on board.

While hobbling across the rain-soaked field, I realized I would have to secure the cat for travel. As I worked out a solution for this problem, I noticed movement near the barracks and slowed my pace. The exterior lights were off, but this did not hamper my visual abilities. I watched two Sents round the barracks corner and approach the front door.

My throat dried with fear. I dropped to the ground and lay on the soaked wildflowers. He was back — the Sent who had followed me earlier.

Another Sent stood near him; did they do anything alone? They moved to the glass doors and one of them squatted. I wondered what they sought.

I pricked my ear holes to hear their voices, but it did not work. I stared at their backs and tried to access their thoughts, but the terror in my mind and the throbbing in my leg made concentrating impossible.

EBN, Aix's tenor voice vibrated in my mind.

Disappointment flashed through me but I ignored him.

EBN, can you hear me? Aix vibed. *I need to speak with you.* His voice sounded heavy with distress. I stared at the Sents and thought of the repaired ship. If things went right, I would be home very soon.

EBN, I need to know … are you well?

Please answer me.

I kept my mind quiet. Soon Aix was gone.

I waited until the Sents left before I rose to my feet and approached the barracks, looking in every direction. As I ducked under the front doorway and entered the outpost, every light and object I had not unplugged sprung to life.

When I closed the door, I noticed the cat sitting on its hindquarters in the front chamber pawing the glass patio door. I remembered it doing the same behavior earlier and determined it had something to do with that Sent boy.

I shivered as I gathered items in preparation for my departure. Dry Sent clothes never seemed so inviting, so I disrobed, pulled on dry jeans and fresh socks and left the wet garments on the bath chamber floor. Before I had a chance to select a clean shirt, I heard voices outside. Then someone rapped on the front door. My heart and breathing stopped.

Not again.

I selected a blue and yellow shirt. As I quickly buttoned it, the knocking continued with greater urgency. I limped down the hall to the door, bent low and looked through the peephole.

The same two Sents stood on the patio. Teal energy haloed the boy with the spectacles. He stood next to a female Sent with a considerable body mass and impressive mammary glands.

Although they shared a vague resemblance, the girl's hair and skin held more pigment than his did. Her golden hair reminded me of the sunshine on this wretched planet but the compact, scarlet aura wavering around her concerned me, especially when I noticed how it crackled and frayed at the edges.

The boy looked at the girl. Her lips moved, but I could not make out her words. She leaned forward and banged her fist hard against the door.

These Sents had not come for healing. I waited, expecting them to leave. Then the female leaned forward and eyeballed the peephole. I gasped and pulled back. My heartbeat boomed in my ears.

Had her life force been a more serene color, I might have opened the door, but this was one hostile, maybe dangerous Sent. Between her enraged state and his relentless curiosity, I wanted nothing to do with either of them.

I crossed my arms over my chest. This could be a test of some kind. Was I in danger of falling into some sort of trap? I did not think so. I doubted Sents were smart enough to set one. They had to go away, sooner or later.

Yet they struck the door again.

I looked down at the brass doorknob and thought of Eesh's directives. Only this barrier separated me from further trouble. All I had to do was keep it shut.

The pounding worsened. *Bang, bang, bang, bang, bang, bang.* I backed away from the door, wishing they would go away.

I wondered if they had seen me and knew I was in here. They had already returned once and would return again. When they did though, I would be gone. I pricked my ear holes and listened for footsteps, but the only sound I heard was rain pattering against the roof.

While I waited for them to leave, the cat ran to the front door, stood on its back legs and touched the doorknob with its front paws. It mewed, turned its head and stared up at me with unblinking gold eyes.

It was trying to communicate. I wished I understood it like our mother could. As I struggled to interpret the feline's behavior, I heard a key slide into the bottom lock. I watched in horror as the knob twisted and turned. This left only one choice.

I took a deep breath, twisted the deadbolt and flung open the door.

The stink of wet Sent mixed with mud filled my nostrils, turning my stomach. My narrowed eyes flicked between them as I scrutinized their body language. The girl crossed her fleshy arms over her ample chest. The boy slouched and kept his arms at his sides. He averted my glare by staring at the ground.

From their stances, I suspected they would not attack, but I did not want to underestimate them. I reached for the Disintegrator but both pockets were empty; my weapon remained somewhere in the front chamber. Some Guardian I was. I watched the Sents' hand movements in case they drew weapons.

The female glanced me over and pursed her mouth. "I need to speak with Ash Slick," she demanded. "Is he here?"

I raised one eyebrow and lowered my chin. The last thing I expected was to hear an Anglicized version of Eesh's name drop from a Sent's mouth.

"No," I offered. My muscles tensed with anxiety. "Who are you?"

"My name is Harmony. This is my brother, Shale. We own and manage this property and live next door. Will Ash be available later tonight?"

I thought the girl's name deceptive, since there was nothing harmonious about her. "No, he will not." I watched Shale, who held his head toward his sister. I stared at his profile, but he shielded his thoughts.

"Do you have any way of contacting him?"

I wished. "Not right now," I answered. I glanced at Shale again and regretted it. He glared at me, his pale blue eyes full of hatred. I watched how his eyes wiggled back and forth then looked at Harmony. He had no right to be angry. He had stalked me. Offended by his behavior, my brow creased in bewilderment.

119

Murk shadowed Harmony's aura. "That's a problem," she said, raising her voice. "My office has sent three certified letters to his alternate address. They all came back unopened because that address doesn't exist."

I hardly heard her words because of the images flashing before my eyes: Harmony and Shale with two adult Sents; Harmony, Shale and the adult male dressed in black, standing with their heads hung low at the edge of a deep, rectangular hole in the ground; Harmony preparing nourishment; cleaning house; loading clothes into a metal appliance; working at the Oasis Leasing Office; watching television with Shale in the dilapidated brown trailer; Shale at school; stargazing on their patio; sitting at his computer; riding his bike, picking up trash and rock climbing in the desert.

"Why did you send … letters?"

"Since Ash is the sole lease holder, I can't discuss it with you," she said in a dismissive tone.

"Eesh — Ash, I mean, is my Gran-A — grandfather."

Her eyes narrowed to slits and her eyebrows drew together in confusion. "We can't be talking about the same person. The young man who leased this space wasn't old enough to be anyone's grandfather," she said.

"I will tell him you said so. It will please him greatly," I said.

Harmony's eyebrows rose. "Well, when your grandfather signed the lease agreement in January 2009, he paid the whole year in advance. Now it's May."

"And?"

"He hasn't made his lease payments in five months. I'll give you ten minutes to collect your things and vacate the premises or I'll call the cops and have them remove you," she snapped.

As she glared at me, vermillion streaks flashed within her aura. I stood on alert, watching and ready. Shale retreated a step and looked away again, ignoring me.

"Take your time. We'll wait," she challenged.

While I processed Harmony's words, the cat scurried outside and wound her body between the boy's feet. In a blur, Shale stepped forward, scooped up the animal and held her in his arms.

"Princess," Harmony exclaimed. Her anger evaporated and lightened her life force to a calmer tangerine color. There was something oddly familiar about her but I did not know what or why.

She stroked the kitty's head while the boy rubbed his face into its fur. The feline purred loudly and licked the boy's nose, drooling in ecstasy.

I watched the reunion, envious. At least one of us was reunited with our family. I also envied the cat's close contact with Shale. Behind them, rain fell in a diagonal deluge. It streamed off the awning and into puddles at the patio's edge.

Joy radiated from the trio. When Harmony's eyes met mine, I understood. *These children are alone in this world. This cat is Shale's only friend.*

"This is our cat, Princess Leah Lucky Buttons. She went missing last week," Harmony explained, sniffing back tears. Her arm shot forward. She held out a crumpled piece of paper. The word MISSING appeared at the top in bold letters. Princess' picture cat sat beneath the page heading. A written description and a series of digits ran underneath the photo.

"What were you doing with her," Harmony demanded.

"I rescued her, in the desert," I said, my eyes darting between them. "Two Sen—boys were throwing bottles at her. They were going to shoot her, but I intervened."

The Sents' eyes widened and they exchanged glances. Shale's hands flexed then curled into fists. "Describe them," she said.

"One had copper hair," I said.

Harmony's eyes cut to her brother. "Did he have freckles?"

I did not understand the meaning of freckles. When I said nothing, she clarified. "Little discolored spots all over his face."

I nodded. "Yes. The other had hair like brown string. His name was—"

"Chaz," she interjected. Her green eyes glittered with anger. Vermillion streaks pulsed within her aura again. "How did you get them to give you Princess?"

I hesitated. "I can be very persuasive."

Harmony stared into my eyes. "I didn't catch your name."

She is as suspicious of me as I am of them. "My name is EBN," I said in a low tone.

"What?" she said.

"EBN," I repeated.

"Exactly what was going on here yesterday afternoon? I had residents complaining in my office. This community has very strict rules about guests and gatherings and parking," Harmony lectured, glancing me over.

My body stiffened as my mind blanked. I had no idea what to tell her.

Harmony beamed at Shale and Princess and her demeanor softened. "Listen, Eee-ben. Did I say that right?"

"Yes."

"Thank you for rescuing Princess. You don't have to leave tonight, but unless I get the balance on your grandfather's account by end of business tomorrow, you'll have to go. It's nothing personal. It's business," she reassured me.

I wondered if this 'business' was the information Eesh had omitted from the black envelope. "How much currency does he owe?"

"Two thousand dollars, plus another five hundred for May."

I figured if they were going to attack, they would have done so by now. I relaxed, content to be in the company of other Beings. More than ever, though, I wanted Shale to look at me, but he only regarded his pet.

"I am only a visitor," I said. "My stay should not be long. Please wait here." Not waiting for a response, I pushed the door closed and limped down the hall to the supply sacks. I retrieved the remaining currency from the black envelope, collected the cat food and supplies I had purchased and placed everything in plastic shopping bags. I returned to the door with my arms loaded.

"Your Princess was in bad shape when I found her. They starved her and she had developed mange. I would not allow her to roam outdoors anymore," I suggested, setting the bags, litter pan and box of litter outside the door.

"Oh, we won't," she assured me. A puzzled expression crossed her face as she glanced down at the bags. "What's that stuff?"

"Supplies for Princess. I went to the store," I said in a quiet tone, ashamed of my actions. I pulled a stack of folded hundred dollar bills from my pocket and handed it to her. "I believe this amounts to three thousand five hundred dollars. Please count it."

Harmony's head jerked back and her expression softened. She counted the money, cleared her throat and thanked me. "I'll issue your receipt first thing in the morning. I'd be happy to reimburse you for Princess' stuff and the vet bill," she offered.

I shook my head. Within her serenity, Harmony was charming—for a Sent. "That is not necessary. Seeing her reunited with her family is payment enough."

"You're very kind, EBN. I'm sorry I gave you attitude." She glanced at her brother and tousled his hair. Shale grimaced and stepped away from her touch. "Having Princess back means everything to us. We've been through a lot the last six months."

I waited for Shale to speak, but he remained silent and shuffled his feet on the concrete. His stubborn refusal to acknowledge me piqued my curiosity. I watched him with wonder, no longer afraid, slightly less angry but more than a little insecure. "You are welcome," I said. Perhaps I could bait him. "Did you see her scratching on the door Shale? I did not realize what her behavior meant."

Shale kept his gaze downcast and hugged Princess tight. He acted as though I repulsed him. Well, he had repulsed me first.

Harmony looked at her brother then at me and half-smiled. "He doesn't mean to be rude. He just doesn't talk much."

She resents having to raise her brother as her own, but she does not want him to live elsewhere, with strangers.

Shale's face reddened — she had embarrassed him.

"Oh — and one more thing about yesterday. If you plan to get together with more than ten friends, use the clubhouse, okay? The sign-up sheet is in the Leasing Office. Reserve your dates in advance, though. The calendar fills up fast."

When I least expected it, Shale looked up and fixed his eyes on me. *Sadness. Overwhelming sadness.* The weight of the boy's emotions hit me, squeezing the breath from my lungs.

I gasped for air and stumbled backwards, grabbing the doorknob to steady myself. When my voice returned, I said, "I understand."

Harmony's eyebrows lowered and her forehead wrinkled. "You okay, EBN?"

They mean me no harm and seek nothing.

I nodded. "I must go. I feel unwell."

"We won't keep you any longer," she said, placing a hand on Shale's arm. "If you need anything, we're right next door. Stop by anytime." She smiled at me as she reached for the striped umbrella leaning against the wall. She handed it to her brother, grabbed the cat supplies and said, "Ready?"

Shale nodded, glanced at me, raised his hand and waved goodbye.

At the patio's edge Shale opened the umbrella. They huddled beneath it, stepped off the patio and out of sight.

I closed the door, leaned against it and stared into the front chamber. Except for the sound of rain drumming against the roof, an eerie stillness permeated the barracks. Now that I was alone, the outpost felt even bleaker and emptier.

While I hobbled down the hall to retrieve the duffels, guilt and shame tortured my mind. The ease with which I continuously disobeyed orders and interacted with Sents alarmed me. Before the wreck, I would never have thought myself capable of disregarding orders, yet I had and with frightening speed. I felt terrible about what I had done. Next time, I planned to think before I acted.

But the Sents had come to me. I did not seek them out. I did the right thing by handling Eesh's business and seeing the animal returned to her rightful stewards, had I not? I thought of my A-ma and remembered the words she had spoken before my deployment.

"Wherever you travel in the multi-verse offspring, always remember who you are."

I had failed. I had forgotten who I was, dishonored myself, my family and compromised my future. I worried about losing the rank of Guardian and vowed not to interact with any more Sents. I grabbed one sack, dragged it into the front chamber, slumped into the nearest chair and stared at my computer near the televisions. Afraid to check it, I feared an even deeper pit of loneliness should no messages appear.

I felt physically spent. Besides the heat radiating off my damaged, throbbing leg, I felt a strange illness attacking my system that caused my internal temperature to rise. As I contemplated undressing, chills ran down my spine. My teeth chattered from the cold, yet my skin burned with heat.

It took all my strength to push out of the chair and grab the computer from the table. Suddenly dizzy, I sank back down. There would be no returning to the ship tonight. When the stars cleared from my field of vision, I checked the computer for transmissions but the screen remained dark. The battery was dead.

Too ill to react, I felt the strength drain from my body. A sudden flash of insight accompanied the sensation and I understood the cause underlying the strange illness — my life force was weakening. My last coherent thought before closing my eyes was of returning to my airship.

Chapter Six: Discord

After Eesh and his guards leave, Ulem turns to me.

"I will deal here. Go to your chamber. Do not disturb your A-ma with the use of your computer or any other kind of mischief—"

"I know, I know," I say. "No further disruptions to her sense of Harmony." I approach A-da and stand before him. "Thank you for coming, A-da. I'm sorry for asking Gran-Ada about EBN."

"Their argument had nothing to do with your question."

I stare at Ulem's disfigured face. Our eyes meet and hold. "Did you know about EBN, A-da?"

"I did not," Ulem says. His expression falls with sadness.

Ulem leans forward. I lean forward and touch foreheads with him.

"Family above all," Ulem whispers.

"We are all family," I reply.

The decompression chamber I share with EBN sits at the opposite end of the hall from the nourishment chamber. I enter it through a glass opaque door that raises and lowers with a quiet *whoosh*.

The chamber is an open, tri-level sphere with programmable crystalline walls and a skylight in the high dome ceiling. A black spiral walkway curls up to the loft, EBN's part of the chamber. A second, shorter walkway leads from the mid-level to the sunken, central area where my decompression platform, desk and cushioned hover seats are located.

Since I can't use my computer or watch Sent broadcasts, I cleanse my teeth and lay down. As I wait for decompression, my thoughts return to the argument between Eesh and Preece. In spite of A-da's assurances, I still feel responsible.

The following morning, Ulem departs for his post on Nilotic. When I wake, the house sits still and silent. As I quietly get ready for school, I feel more alone than ever.

A-ma remains in her decompression chamber and refuses to leave. In A-da's absence, I care for us to the best of my abilities. I attend school, complete my assignments, prepare meals and try to get A-ma to eat.

Every evening I carry a tray of her favorite edibles up to our parents' decompression chamber above the nourishment chamber. I knock softly on the opaque glass door, but A-ma never answers, so I leave the tray outside the door. Most evenings, the nourishment goes untouched.

Days pass but there are still no transmissions from EBN. I attempt to reach her through vibing, but she never answers me. This worries me more than I care to admit.

Five mornings after my Ascension, I awake before Scyros. Xtarr's musical Nadreen voice resonates in my head, rousing me from decompression.

Aix, wake up. It's important.

I ignore her vibrating thoughts and roll over. I dreamed I was marooned on Erox with EBN. She was injured and I left her.

Aix, have you heard?

Decompressing, I vibe and yawn.

Aix, wake up, she vibes in an angry tone. *School is cancelled. Seemae separatists attacked the High Chancellor on Nilotic.*

I jolt upright and fly off the platform. *I'll be right there.*

After I dress, I creep downstairs to the *tube,* a sphere shaped corridor connecting all residences in the immediate area.

Because of the early hour, nighttime penetrates the wide passage through the transparent walls and domed ceiling. When the gallery door lifts open, soft opaque lighting clicks on and glows from the floor.

Since walking would take too long, I step onto one of many cushioned ivory pads lining the length of the tunnel. Each footpad generates an electromagnetic field that anchors the feet and stabilizes the body for travel, so that every Being can ride without risk of injury. I wait as the electromagnetic field surrounds me.

Once the sensation of weightlessness encompasses my body, I think of Xtarr, but thinking of her in general or how I feel about her isn't enough. Only when I envision her face with perfect clarity, the footpad moves forward and carries me toward her home.

The footpad floats through the darkness of early morning, down the side of the mountain and under the hanging boughs of the arcandians, the most common of the musical trees and plants on Pharralax, a hardy conifer with swollen triangular charcoal needles.

Mushrooms the size of footstools slide over the forest floor, leaving slimy trails as they suckle nutrients from the tree bases. Their red caps glow in the dark, casting scary shadows in the forest.

I close my eyes and imagine hearing the sounds of early morning. The corridor's sensors respond at once. The symphonic sounds of humming trees and vibrating mushrooms fills the breezeway. Melancholy, sonorous tones in an exquisite four-part harmony rise and fall in perfect synchronicity.

I am glad to be out and away from the constant reminders of EBN's silent absence. It's been too long since I've seen Xtarr outside of school and I intend to enjoy the day in the warmth of her company. Anxious to receive word about Gran-Ada, I consider checking my computer, but decide against it. If I receive bad news, I don't want to be alone.

High above the base of the mountain, the corridor straightens and splits in several directions. The footpad coasts along a skyway bridge extending over the village of Sheltdonic.

From this height I admire the massive white Protectorate Orb sparkling in the distance and the hallowed sculpture garden surrounding it. Rock sculptures resembling the faces of my ancestors not only line the grounds and roadways, but they also form a protective ring enclosing the Orb, guarding all from harm. Dramatic white, green and violet lights illuminate the Protectory Orb and sentinels' faces day and night.

Near the water the condensation thickens and little is visible through the arcade's windows. But as Scyros rises in the sky, the tube runs between the three gigantic pyramids housing the prestigious Adelian Conservatory. The viscous, magenta-bottomed clouds reflect in the pyramids' silver exterior, cloaking the buildings' apexes from view.

With Sheltdonic behind me, the corridor angles up the grade of an adjacent mountainside. It is not long before the high stone masonry walls of Xtarr's family castle come into view. Nestled beneath the summit, the Nadreen Royal Estate stretches for k-mets in every direction. When the woodlands give way to blue, rolling grounds and manicured gardens I know I'm close.

The footpad slows some distance before my stop. When I step off, I notice two solemn-faced Protectorate guards standing before the section of walkway leading up to Xtarr's. As I approach them, Xtarr's personal attendant, a Loredi man named Hsoj, emerges from behind them to meet me.

Hsoj has hair and eyes the color of coal and shimmering bronze skin. He moves with fluid grace as he brushes a tiny spec of dust from his white uniform and bows to me in greeting.

"Sorry to hear about your Gran-Ada, young Aix," Hsoj says in a soft-spoken, baritone voice. He speaks in the customary hushed manner typical of Loredis.

Like Xtarr, I've known Hsoj most of my life. I nod my thanks and follow him up a gently sloping walkway that opens onto a long courtyard. Freezing wind stings my face, hinting that Harvest season will be short this year. Although it's too early, I smell snow.

As we walk under a series of tall archways, I glance through the round openings in the courtyard's walls. Two groups of Protectorate soldiers run drills on the lawn while the first snowflakes drift to the ground. I shiver against the cold and stuff my hands into my pockets.

An intricately carved, round wood door rises at the far end of the courtyard. We walk under it and enter the Main Hall, a round stone building with cathedral ceilings and leaded glass windows.

The Main Hall bustles with Loredi servants, which isn't unusual, but as we near the back entrance to the living quarters, I notice more Protectorate guards standing inside each door. I've never seen guards on the property before and suspect their presence relates in some way to the news about Gran-Ada. I swallow hard to dislodge the uneasy feeling that swells like a lump in my throat.

At the far end of the Main Hall we climb a spiral marble walkway then follow a long corridor to a second grand spiral walkway. Protectorate guards stand like statues before every doorway we pass. Near the top, I hear Xtarr's laughter and relax. Hsoj raises another heavy, wood door carved to resemble Doridaen, Pharralax's second moon and I enter Xtarr's receiving chamber.

The receiving chamber is a two-story, round hall. In spite of large, lead paned windows, little light penetrates the cavernous chamber. On both floors, a number of carved wood doors lead to chambers off the central, receiving area. A spiral walkway at the chamber's opposite end winds up to the second story catwalk overlooking the receiving area below.

Across the chamber, fire burns and crackles within an enormous sunken marble fireplace. The flames illuminate the darkness and cast shadows onto the oversized plum and maroon velvet furniture. Drawn to the warmth, I move toward the fire, figuring I will find Xtarr lounging on her 'throne,' my nickname for the recessed sitting area across from the fireplace.

"Xtarr," I call out.

Her auburn head and the tips of her silver-edged, lavender wings pop into view. She giggles then sinks from sight. As I approach the ramp leading to the sunken fireplace, I see what drew her down—my friend Nyl.

Although she is one Scyros cycle older than both of us, Xtarr looks far younger straddling Nyl, with whom she is play wrestling. Diminutive and bird-like, her radiant smile lights up her delicate features when she sees me. For a moment, my heart stops beating.

"Give it back," she demands in her rich, melodious voice. She snatches her computer from Nyl's turquoise hand and holds it over her head. Without expending much effort, Nyl reaches up and steals it back.

Nyl, like the majority of students at the Conservatory, is Adelian. I met him long ago, when our families resided on the Protectorate Ship *Sanctuary*. Nyl's wrinkled, turquoise skin, bald head and compound cobalt eyes sometimes remind me of EBN — that is, when Nyl isn't rolling around on the floor with the Nadreen Royal Princess.

I watch them through narrowed eyes. I suspected Nyl had feelings for Xtarr, but when asked, Nyl denies it. It is hard to not have feelings for Xtarr. She exudes bewitching charm and grace — but I wasn't aware the two had become so close. At once I feel betrayed and blame myself for introducing them.

Nyl lays on the floor, facing the fire. He cranes his neck backwards to greet me with a smile.

I nod but hold a serious expression. "Nyl. Xtarr. Greetings."

Xtarr climbs off Nyl, rushes to me and wraps her slender arms around my middle. Because of her small stature, the top of her head doesn't quite reach my chest. "I'm so sorry about what happened," she says, squeezing me tight.

"Tell me. I still don't know," I say. I run a hand over the sleek auburn hair that falls past her shoulders.

"You don't," she asks. She pulls away and looks up at me.

My eyes flick to Nyl. Now he stares at me with narrowed eyes. I return his glare with a smirk, but clear my expression before gazing down into Xtarr's Sent-like mahogany eyes. "I'm cut off. I can't even do my current events assignments at home. A-ma's sense of Harmony has been destroyed."

Xtarr's eyes fly open. "Not so close to the holidays," she says. She sinks into the sitting area's cushions and stares at the fire, looking crestfallen.

"Please tell me what happened with Gran-Ada."

The firelight casts an orange glow onto her golden skin. "You better sit down," Xtarr says.

We sit with Xtarr between us. I turn and stare at her perfect profile.

"He was on Nilotic when it happened. The Seemae Rebel Faction ambushed him. The SRF murdered his entire security team. Somehow Eesh escaped," Xtarr says in a quiet tone.

"Where is he now?"

"Recovering at an undisclosed location within the Protectory. Right after the attack, my A-da received broadcasted transmissions from Beings claiming to be SRF. They threatened A-da's life and threatened to abduct me." While she speaks, Nyl's hand reaches for hers but she bats it away.

"Of course, A-da turned the broadcasts over to the Protectorate. The Protectorate publicized the transmissions and temporarily closed the Conservatory to keep students safe."

Nyl's fingertips brush her hand again. She moves her hand again, shrugging from his touch.

I stare at the fire. The uneasiness constricting my throat drops to my stomach and hardens.

After a long pause, Xtarr turns to me. "What happened with your A-ma?"

I tell my friends about the argument between Preece and Eesh after my Ascension celebration. I conclude by describing how the news has impacted A-ma.

Xtarr stares at me in disbelief. "Where is EBN now?"

"On some mission. Gran-Ada didn't provide many details."

Nyl leans forward. "Are you going to tell your A-ma about your Gran-Ada's attack?"

My eyes cut to Nyl's face. My expression is somber.

"I didn't realize it was so serious," Nyl says. "I know nothing about the Nadreen sense of Harmony."

"It's not meant for Adelians to understand," I half-mumble, half-growl.

"It happens to Loredis too," Xtarr adds.

I wince. "It's an affectation with them, part of their Nadreen worship. Loredis don't die from it."

Xtarr's eyes flick to Nyl then to me. Princess or not, it's not appropriate for her to discuss, but that doesn't stop her.

"Generally speaking, a Nadreen cannot survive without an intact sense of Harmony. When the disturbance is small, the sufferer becomes disabled. When Harmony is destroyed, the afflicted dies. That's why my A-ma lives on Doridaen. She can't cope with reality," she explains.

"I apologize for your hardships," Nyl says. "I meant no offense."

His tone sounds sincere. I mumble my thanks.

Xtarr shrugs her shoulder and flips her hair over her wingtips. "Some Beings aren't longed for this world."

I gaze at her in admiration. Xtarr is more like her A-ma than she knows.

"Can she recover in time to lead the Solstice ceremony," Xtarr asks me. Her wings twitch with anxiety.

I shrug. "Time will tell. She may not, in which case the responsibility will fall on you."

Xtarr leans forward and throws her head into her hands. "But I'm not ready," she groans.

"You may have no choice," I reply.

Nyl rubs Xtarr's back. "Don't get upset. Everything will be fine," he says. He glares at me. "What's the worst that can happen?"

"Chaos," I say.

Nyl scowls at me. "Stop exaggerating. You're scaring her."

"Nyl, you really should pay more attention in planetary customs and civilizations class," Xtarr remands, lifting her head.

"Pharralax's true power center does not lie with the wealthy Nadreen class, or even the royal family. Nadreens rely on Loredi fealty and service. That's how it's always been, since long before Adelians arrived. Without their eminent spiritual leader, the Loredi community will fall to disarray. If that happens, Pharralax's power center will shatter."

"It comes down to multi-versal law. Everything depends on everything else," Nyl mutters.

"Exactly," she agrees.

Unsettled, I stand up. "I must go. I shouldn't have left A-ma alone considering what's happened." Even though I don't want to leave Xtarr alone with Nyl, I hurry back to the tube unescorted. A-ma is home alone and vulnerable. If anything happens to her, I'll never forgive myself.

Chapter Seven: Dilemma

Nightmares and hallucinations haunted my decompression. I awoke two days later, confused and disoriented. My body ached from decompressing in the reclining chair and I could not move my leg without whimpering.

I checked my computer for transmissions. The device held no power. Stressed over the severed connection, I ran a hand through my hair. There was not much time. With disease pulsing through my veins, I had to reach the ship.

I stuffed the essential items into one duffel sack and left the rest in the front chamber. I considered leaving everything behind because my leg was so inflamed I could barely stand on it.

Before setting out, I peeked through the patio blinds. Hordes of Sents waited for me outside. I wondered how long they had been there and whether or not Harmony had seen them.

Their presence left me no choice. Using all of my strength, I pushed a reclining chair into the front entryway, opened the door and sat in the open doorway. The crowd surged toward me, anxious to see the reputed miracle-worker.

My eyes swept over the sea of bodies. Sents stood in a neat line, three or four deep. I estimated the group exceeded sixty Sents and those were only the ones I could see. Who knew how many others snaked around the side of the barracks?

I touched them all, one by one. Many bowed their heads as they approached me and some whispered prayers. It seemed that for every ill or infirmed Sent there were three or four healthy Sents who came to receive my blessing or leave offerings. When I refused to accept their money, the Sents dropped it at my feet or tossed it into my lap while the sneakier Sents tossed it over my head, inside the barracks.

After the fourth time it happened, I gave in and set the glass offerings jar at my feet.

With every Sent I touched, I grew progressively weaker. Somehow my healing touch remained unaffected, though.

One after another, the Sents kept coming. The constant stream of bodies seemed endless.

After two mangnas passed, I felt drained. Just when I thought it would never end, the queue wrapped around the barracks corner. As I touched the last Sent in line, I noticed something unsettling. The news van that had been here days earlier sat parked across the street. A male Sent stood across the road, pointing his camera at me. He had recorded everything.

Using my healthy leg, I slid the chair backwards, nudged the offerings jar aside with my toe and kicked the door shut. As it slammed closed, I sank into a deep and dreamless decompression.

I felt no better when I awoke at sunset. I pushed on nonetheless, determined to leave.

With one duffel sack slung over my shoulder, I stepped out of the barracks and into the warm evening. Dry wind gusts pushed against me and whistled in my ears as I stepped off the patio.

I hobbled into the desert, sweating and shivering. Each time I shifted my weight onto my left leg, I sucked air through my teeth.

Consumed by pain, I almost failed to notice the thinning wildflowers. Countless golden poppies lay wilted or dead at my feet. Several patches of beige soil stood out against the surviving blossoms snapping with the wind and few new flowers bloomed in the wake of my footsteps. Soon the whole field would revert to its former bare state. I hoped to never see it again.

I felt eyes watching me and glanced over my shoulder. Shale stood astride his yellow bike in his driveway. I groaned and limped faster.

I reached the riverbed at twilight and pitched the duffel sack across it. Before sliding down the embankment, I turned and scanned the field. Shale approached. He stood in the middle of the field between the barracks and riverbed. I quickened my pace and pressed on.

After crossing the riverbed and hoisting my body over the opposite embankment, I lay in the dirt for some time, resting and listening for Sent sounds but it was impossible to hear anything over the bustling wind. Even though my body begged for decompression, I rose, shouldered the duffel sack and continued the painful trek toward the ship.

When the wind stilled, the desert reverberated with insects. I followed the sandy path through waist-high vegetation. Bones lay scattered everywhere on the trail. My eyes fixed on a stark white spinal column stripped clean by scavengers. A severed coyote head lay further along the footpath. As I stepped over it, I noticed maggots squirming in the eye sockets.

Almost a mangna passed before I reached the *Surety*. Lightheaded and queasy from pain, starbursts exploded in my field of vision as I staggered toward the ship, dragging my left leg behind me. I climbed inside and passed out before the hatch closed.

145

I awoke sometime later on the *Surety's* floor. I looked around, noticed my rumpled flight-suit, torch and bio-metal pieces on the floor, realized where I was and hauled my body into the pilot's seat. When I sat, turquoise backlighting blazed from the console. It reflected off my blue and white Hawaiian shirt and cast a glare onto the windshield.

I rested my hand on the command module, expecting it to respond by glowing with turquoise light, but no power flowed through the ship. I lifted my hand, waited a moment then replaced it. The same thing happened — nothing.
The plan was not going according to plan. My breaths grew rapid and shallow.

"Do not panic. You know what to do. Get it together. Come on, think!"

Except I could not think. I felt sluggish and stupid and kept forgetting things that were second nature. I burned with fever and used my remaining strength to fight off decompression.

I pulled the computer from my pocket. Something was wrong. It should have automatically charged once I entered the ship. I inserted it on the console jack but when the device snapped into place, the console lights flickered and dimmed. In a blur, I snatched the computer off the charger and pocketed it.

I glanced at the systems screen, ran a diagnostic and groaned at the results. Dots blinked over the ring-shaped capsule and within the chamber's interior. Something about the repairs had caused a failure in the operating systems. The ship held adequate fuel. Something must have gotten trapped inside the chambers. But it worked last time.

In all my lunar cycles of training there had not been any scenarios addressing this situation. Reinforcements would have been deployed; a rescue and recovery mission would have been underway, but none seemed to know of my distress.

Not knowing what else to do, I held my finger over the port on the ship's console. Alerts chimed and my vital signs flashed red, confirming my suspicions. I was entropic. Entropy caused the body's fluids to coagulate, leading to organ failure and eventually death. I knew of the risk long before Eesh had warned me during my briefing.

Eesh had also said that should this occur, the pharmaceutical systems would dispense medicine through the port, but nothing happened. I held my finger in place and waited for the pinching sensation as the ship injected my finger with medicine, but no pinch came.

I composed another transmission:

High Chancellor — Mission day four. Skin suit is compromised and degrading. I am gravely injured, entropic and deteriorating. No food or medical supplies. Send rescue medical team please. Guardian of the Sky EBN-Reyoz-X

Seconds after I sent it, the transmission bounced back. I ran a hand over my face, took a deep breath and exhaled sharply.

The bright full moon threw shadows in the darkness while warm, dry winds blew through the California desert, charging the air with static. They knocked against the craft's exterior, rocking it slightly. I listened to the whistling gusts and allowed myself to think about my home world, hoping it would give me strength.

Suddenly a shadow dropped from the sky and landed on the front of the craft. Beyond the blue-white glare, a vulture perched outside the windshield. As I wondered about the efficacy of the airship's cloaking mechanisms with respect to birds' eyes, it bent low, cocked its head sideways and peered through the windshield, staring me down with an unblinking, black eye.

Distracted by horrendous throbbing, I lifted my *in* or left pant leg. Beneath the knee, my lower leg had ballooned, doubling in size. I twisted my leg and examined my torn, gaping skin suit and the suppurating gashes underneath it. My teal skin had stretched taut and was a bright raspberry shade, as if sunburned.

The open wounds displayed my sinewy scarlet muscle tissue. I brushed my fingertips over the cloudy green discharge and winced, feeling the emanating heat. Throbbing aftershocks coursed up my leg and waves of nausea churned my stomachs. Clenching my teeth against the pain, I smelled my fingertips. The malodorous stench curled my upper lip.

I shifted in my seat and assessed the situation again, from the beginning: Although I had repaired the breaches from the wreck, my ship still had issues. At least the ship's diagnostic component functioned; however it confirmed I was entropic. The pharmaceutical dispensary had failed; my primary and secondary communications systems had also failed. I had sent multiple transmissions to my commanding officer, but most had bounced back. Now the computer battery was dead and could not be charged without compromising the dwindling auxiliary power supplies.

My protective skin suit and life support system was damaged beyond repair. I had barely made the trek from the barracks without collapsing and was uncertain if Shale had followed me. If I retreated to my post, would I be able to return to the ship the following night without treatment? Unlikely. I had yet to try a manual start. I took a deep breath and mechanically engaged the *Surety's* operating systems. Please, please work.

Nothing happened.

My pulse quickened. A metallic taste filled my mouth. Cold sweat coated my skin, encasing my body. Still nothing. Struggling to remain calm, I composed another transmission:

High Chancellor — Please send help. Guardian of the Sky EBN-Reyoz-X

I sent the transmission. It bounced back immediately.

I powered the console down and waited. No training modules had addressed this challenge. Help was supposed to always be available. I gazed out the convex windshield. The vulture was gone but another, larger shadow moved through the scrub. Was it Shale? My heart galloped behind my breastbone and I sucked in my breath. Had the cloaking mechanism failed?

The shadow moved closer. It was a coyote. The creature wandered around the boulder outcropping, sniffing the ground where I had walked. A moment later it lifted its head and howled, signaling others. It smelled my sickness and fear. It would hide then ambush me if I exited the ship. For a moment being eaten alive seemed preferable over the slow, painful death caused by entropy. As I let go of my breath I noticed I was trembling.

"Come on, *Surety*," I pleaded, pushing buttons and flipping switches with greater urgency. Power surged through the ship but a series of clicking noises sounded from behind the console — clicking noises I had not heard before. I looked around the control deck, waited for the faint *whrrrr* sound, the slight lifting and subtle vibration, but nothing happened. The airship sat motionless, silent. Sweat trickled down my forehead and into my eye — burning.

Moments ticked by. I strained my ear holes for the slightest sound but heard nothing — even the wind momentarily stilled.

Shifting again in the seat, the rustling of my clothes was amplified against the hideous silence. My breathing came faster, seeming unnaturally loud, as did the sounds of my pulse and blood rushing through my veins.

In a single motion, I disengaged the *Surety's* operating systems and cut the power. I heard the blustering wind, felt the faint rocking motion of the ship. Straightening my back and squaring my shoulders, I slowed my breathing and let my mind drift.

I thought of the vessels I had grown up in, the cramped quarters I had shared with Aix. Our family had only recently obtained a spacious terrestrial home on the planet Pharralax. Constructed of metal and transparent solar panels, our curvaceous home sat on a corniche, high upon the cliffs of Sheltdonic.

I remembered the day I deployed and recalled how Aix stood before me with his troubled expression. I had told him not to worry or be concerned for my safety. What a fool I had been.

My A-da — a former Guardian — had conducted a successful Erox mission with untold bravery and had almost paid with his life. I pictured my beloved A-da's face, disfigured during his time on Erox and my A-ma's beautiful one that stood out because of her angular bone structure and Sent-like eyes. It was hard to envision A-ma and not see Aix also.

Most of all, though, I missed my Gran-Ada's silly laughter and his gray compound eyes that always made me feel safe. I missed his raspy voice. I would give anything to hear Eesh's voice right now, telling me how to get out of this mess. But that was not going to happen. My body quaked with emotion. My whole family was so proud of me.

I was never going to see them again.

I spent the night slumped in the pilot's seat. The problems I faced heightened the menace of my situation and gave me a morbid awareness of my vulnerabilities and the ease with which I had been hurt. I struggled to remember how much time I could survive without a functioning skin suit.

Because of my failing cognition, I could not recall my instruction. Even if I could, I doubted I could calculate the conversation of time increments. There was only one fact of which I was certain: If help did not arrive soon, I would die.

Fueled by rage, I leapt out of the seat and slammed my fists against every non-mechanical surface in the ship. I punched the pilot's seat, kicked the bio-metal lumps across the floor, pummeled the roof, pounded on storage compartments and stomped my healthy leg. Instrument panel casings and storage compartment doors shook in protest. The duffel sack I had secured earlier tumbled to the floor. I kicked it twice with my good leg.

My tirade was brief. When I collapsed on the floor at the back ship, exhausted, I blinked several times in disbelief. I had never experienced such intense emotions before, let alone expressed them. I had behaved like a Sent. Unacceptable. I had shared the same space with Sents, exchanged energy with them and had fallen under their influence. Perhaps this was the reason contact had been forbidden.

Ashamed and embarrassed, I admonished myself for losing control. My eyes scanned the trashed control deck. Every panel casing and compartment door stood open. At the back of the deck where I had unleashed most of my fury, my belongings spilled out of the duffel sack and lay strewn about the floor.

The black envelope from Eesh lay near the pilot's seat. Seeing it impressed upon me what I faced. I was alone, far from home and unable to contact the only Being that knew my whereabouts. My leg was killing me. It would be awhile before I could tolerate putting weight on it.

As I crawled about the deck, collecting objects and setting things right, I noticed two shadows at the back of what I thought was an empty storage compartment. I reached inside and pulled out a dark box—an old, unopened medical kit. Inside it I found several packets of pain medicine and antibiotics and swallowed them dry. This medical kit was twice the size of standard issue kits distributed to Guardians and held far more supplies. However, it held no entropy solution.

I removed the second object—a battered metal box—from the storage compartment. It contained several bottles of expired Re-breather formula and two sealed boxes of entropy solution. Expired Re-breather formula was toxic and could not be consumed, but it could still be used to boost oxygen in the air. I cracked open one of the bottles and set it nearby. Wisps of white smoke wafted from the top and gave me an idea.

I slid the metal box across the ship's floor, closed the top and used it to elevate my injured leg. Then I positioned the open bottle of Re-breather formula directly under my wound. The lacerated area tickled and itched as the oxygen vapors licked my damaged, infected flesh.

When the bottle of Re-breather formula was empty, I fished through the medical kit and found tubes of antibiotic ointment and fresh synthetic skin bandages. After swallowing a second dose of pain medicine, I carefully cleaned and redressed my wounds. The swelling had already gone down and the skin surrounding the affected area had faded from raspberry to Doridaen-pink.

I tore into the entropy solution. It too had expired, but I was willing to take the risk. Perhaps ingesting poison would bring a faster, more merciful death than the slow, agonizing suffering entropy caused. Without glancing at the directions, I ripped open two silver foil packets and swallowed the contents. The thick orange gel tasted sour and gritty but I did not care.

At once my energy surged. My head cleared as I pulled myself upright. My body tingled and pulsed as the medicine worked through my system. It was not long before a potential solution to the ship's mechanical problem entered my mind.

I returned to the pilot's seat, ran a diagnostic on the whole ship and isolated the problem at the repair sites. Trapped moisture or debris had to be the cause. Provided I could survive another few days and the weather cooperated, the chamber would likely dry and I could leave. If that failed, I could attempt to reopen the panels and troubleshoot from there.

With a greed I had never felt before, I drank a third packet of entropy solution. Walking no longer seemed impossible. I glanced out the windshield. The sky was lightening. The sun was rising.

I prepared to trek back to the barracks. There was no other place for me to go.

Chapter Eight: Omen

Five minutes before the last bell of the day sounded, Shale slid his schoolbooks and folders into his backpack and waited. And waited. He tried to sit still, but his legs jumped to some irregular beat. It had been a crappy day and all he wanted to do was go home.

When the bell finally rang, routine pandemonium ensued. Students raced for the door and poured into the crowded hallway. Shale wove through them, keeping his eyes lowered, careful not to make eye contact with anyone. His face clenched over and over as he dodged the bodies blocking the halls and exits.

Shale hurried to the bike rack, unlocked his ride and pedaled away fast. The instant his tires cleared the chain link fence enclosing the bike compound, he felt free. The sun bore down on his head and back, warming his body.

Maybe today would be the day the oil spill ended. B.P.'s executives said they were close to a working solution. Shale wanted to believe them, but whom was he kidding? It was more likely he'd find his dad.

While he pictured their joyous reunion, Santa Ana winds pummeled him from different directions. The force almost tipped his bike and set his nerves back on edge. The Santa Anas were a bad omen. Nothing good ever followed them.

He zipped down Enchanted Way. Peach stucco homes with orange tile roofs sat to his left and the school's baseball and soccer fields lay on the right. Two blocks ahead the road t-boned. Stop signs marked each of the corners but the intersection stood empty. Instead of stopping like he usually did, Shale turned wide and blew through the stop sign. As he rode through the quiet residential streets, he let out a sigh of relief, unaware he had been holding his breath.

Today had started out good, but it turned horrible at lunchtime. He'd been sitting alone at the far end of the football players' table where he always sat, finishing his calculus homework and minding his own business when something hard smacked the back of his head. His hand flew to the spot and he whipped around to see what had happened.

Tommy Nutter and his followers (who Shale thought of as the 'Loser Crew') sat laughing hysterically two tables back. Tommy grinned wide and waved like they were friends. Shale glanced down. A milk carton with one smashed corner lay on the floor gushing milk. Shale turned and looked at the teacher's table at the front of the cafeteria. Mrs. Darling and Coach Heaps sat there, engrossed in conversation. As usual, they didn't see what happened.

He turned around and glowered at Tommy, who clutched his sides, howling with glee. He'd picked the perfect moment and had gotten away with it. That's why Tommy did it. Tommy antagonized him because he knew Shale wouldn't tell on him.

Shale wasn't a rat. For that reason, Shale avoided the nurse's office in spite of the sore, golf ball sized welt that rose on the back of his head. He figured he'd ice it when he got home and imagined Harmony would say it was a good thing he had a thick skull.

The harsh, unmistakable stink of wildfires blew past him and returned his attention to the present. To the south, twin pillars of white smoke billowed over the San Gabriel Mountains like mushroom clouds. Shale squinted against the glare of the sun, made brighter by the smoke and ash in the air.

The increased number of wildfires worried him. When he was little, wildfires happened every few years. Now wildfires raged throughout California every year. The sharp, bitter-tasting haze burned his lungs, making it hard to breathe. Feeling his face tense, Shale thought about his new obsession—the mysterious neighbor, EBN.

Ever since meeting her, he'd thought of little else. Each day started and ended with him wondering when he'd catch sight of her again. Several days had passed since the afternoon when he first saw and followed her into the desert.

Shale didn't know what came over him that night to cause him to act the way he did. He blamed curiosity, but desperation played a large role too. He wanted to find his father so badly that he was willing to investigate any lead.

But that night, he hadn't felt desperate. At the time he'd been excited … captivated even, until she'd scared him. Then he ran home like the boogeyman was chasing him.

Shale shook his head, embarrassed he'd acted so childish. The next time he saw EBN, he planned to do something manly to erase that moment from her mind. He'd kept an eye out for her, but hadn't seen her in two days.

Not since night before last, when he watched her limp into the desert at sunset. Shale wondered where she was going and what she carried in the black bag. EBN wasn't very friendly and kept to herself. Even though the girl had rescued Princess, Harmony was still suspicious. She'd said, "You stay away from her until I say it's okay. The last thing we need is more problems."

There was definitely something interesting and unique about EBN, but nothing bad. She was the tallest and most beautiful girl he'd ever seen. It was only a matter of time before some agent discovered her and turned her into the next mega-famous supermodel.

But his fascination resulted from more than just lust. Shale felt comfortable around her and he didn't feel that way around most people. He hoped EBN was okay and not lying on the floor dead inside the mobile home.

He stopped at a traffic light to cross Columbia Way then turned off the paved road and cut through the desert. Dust clouds plumed behind his tires while hot wind lashed his cheeks and stung his eyes. The air tasted of smoke. Ash dried and cast an annoying tickle at the back of his throat.

On the trail ahead, Shale spotted a black-tailed jackrabbit before it dashed away and disappeared into the brush. As he rode along the unpaved ground and pumped his legs harder, sweat beaded on his forehead. Soon he was within sight of their trailer.

As Shale looped around the front of the house and hopped off his bike, he thought EBN could be either Swedish or Dutch and about fifteen-years-old. He noticed the empty driveway. Harmony's car wasn't parked on the street either. She hadn't mentioned anything except taking today off work. Maybe she'd been called in at the last minute.

He considered riding by the Leasing Office to cover his butt in case she was there, but decided against it. She said she'd be home. Maybe she went to the store or something.

When Shale removed his house key from his backpack and slipped it into his front pocket, he noticed a Mohave black-collared lizard sunning itself on the wooden patio railing. It watched Shale approach then scuttled out of sight.

Shale tightened his grip on the bike's handlebars and climbed the stairs to the deck. He was almost to the top when he heard gravel crunching behind him.

An unsettling feeling in the pit of his gut told him it wasn't EBN and his mouth twitched when he spun around. Tommy Nutter stood in the driveway, near EBN's mobile home, his copper hair glinting in the sunlight. Shale's stomach lurched at the sight of him and his face cramped three times in back to back spasms.

"Hey there Casper. Long time, no see," Tommy said, smiling disdainfully.

Shale tried to relax but he couldn't control the spasms squeezing his eyes shut. He raised a hand to shield his eyes from the sun but his bike slipped from his grasp and clattered loudly down the stairs. It landed sideways in the driveway, back wheel spinning in the air.

Tommy sauntered toward him, crossed the driveway and lifted the bike off the ground. Shale had never seen so many freckles on one person's face.

"How's your head feeling," Tommy asked with an evil smile. "Come get your bike."

Shale's face tensed and twisted into a grimace. When he didn't move, Tommy contorted his own features into a similar expression and flapped his hands. "My name is Shale," Tommy tormented in his 'special' voice, the one he used when he harassed the special needs kids at school. "Grow a pair and quit acting like a retard."

Shale was used to Tommy making fun of him and didn't care. But Tommy's mimicry of disabled people offended him. Deep down, Shale wanted nothing more than to beat the disrespect out of Tommy.

Shale's face flushed with anger and his eyes involuntarily clamped shut. Harmony had ordered him to ignore Tommy and he did. Tommy, however, never ignored him.

"Come on, Powder, don't be scared. I won't bite," he said.

Yeah, right. Tommy was mean as a snake and everyone knew what snakes did. Still, he needed his ride. Reluctantly Shale walked down the stairs.

Tommy looked Shale's bike up and down like it was a big-screen television or a fine sports car.

"Nice bike, whitey. Your other one was stolen, wasn't it?"

Shale's mouth fell open. The only people who knew about the theft were Harmony and the police.

A glob of saliva appeared on Tommy's lower lip. He sucked it into his mouth, pushed it onto his lower lip, sucked it inside his mouth then shot it at Shale's feet. Shale jumped to the side and dodged it just in time.

Tommy threw Shale's bike and it clattered as it hit the ground again. Shale's face clenched twice. Tommy stepped over it and stood in front of him.

"Say something, albino boy," Tommy taunted.

Shale glared at him between spasms.

"I said answer me, you fucking freak of nature."

Shale held his arms and head rigid. *Do not make the first move. Stand your ground. Let him throw the first punch.* His facial muscles clenched; his eyes squeezed shut.

"I'm just fucking with you, man. Chill-ax," Tommy chided, laughing. He turned and stepped away then spun around and lunged at Shale.

Startled, Shale flinched and stepped back. His foot caught on the bottom step and he fell backwards.

Tommy grabbed Shale's t-shirt, twisting it in his fist and yanking him upright. "What did you say?"

Shale heard his shirt tear. Harmony would be furious with him.

Tommy pulled him close to his face. "Are you accusing me of stealing your bike? Those are big words when your whale of a big sister isn't around to protect you," he said in Shale's ear.

Shale shuddered, creeped out more by the sensation of Tommy's hot, wet breath on his ear than the psychotic episode. Tommy's words infuriated him but Shale was determined not to speak. He'd never give Tommy the satisfaction. His facial tics fired in rapid succession. He looked down and kept his eyes fixed there; *do not make the first move – whatever he says.*

"Say something, dummy."

Tommy's breath smelled rotten. Shale's nose wrinkled in disgust. He imagined heaving on Nutter's shoes but the image made him want to laugh. Fighting to keep a straight face, he focused instead on the dirt smell rising off his blue t-shirt. He'd never been in a fight before and didn't know if it was normal to have the giggles right before getting your butt kicked.

Shale heard a door creak and listened closely as his eyes squeezed shut again, but the only sound he heard over Tommy's breathing was the wind blowing across the desert. He wished Harmony would come home. He really needed her right now.

"Look at me when I talk to you," Tommy shouted. "Oh, I forgot. You can't hold your eyes still. Maybe this will help." He jerked Shale's glasses off his face and threw them over his shoulder.

Shale gasped. He was blind. Even though Tommy stood inches away, he was a non-descript blob. Shale tried to twist free but Tommy maintained a firm grasp on his t-shirt.

"I've done you a favor — you look like an owl, only uglier. Next time spend a few dollars and get some contact lenses," he cackled.

Shale focused on his blurry feet and braced himself. *Just get it over with. If you're going to hit me, then hit me.* His face cramped again and again and again.

"What's the matter brainiac? Why don't you say something?" Tommy demanded, raising his voice.

Shale's body twitched. He wondered how bad it was going to hurt. He felt Tommy tighten his hold on his shirt and braced himself. It was coming. Any second now, Tommy's fist would smash his face.

Chapter Nine: Innocents

My nightmare continued with no end in sight.

Two days had passed since my attempt to leave Erox. I should have been home by now, or at least back at the PLEXUS way station. Instead I stood in the front chamber, applying duct tape over the window and patio doorframes.

When I finished, I sat down and stared at the televisions with my face set in a grim expression. Live footage of the oil disaster in the Gulf of Mexico played on one screen, while the program *Whale Wars* played on the other.

I never imagined Erox's environmental situation could worsen, but more than one lunar cycle after the explosion on the Deepwater Horizon drilling rig, oil still contaminated the Gulf and Sents proved powerless at stopping the flow.

To make matters worse, enormous wildfires burned in close proximity to the barracks — the Angeles Crest National Forest and San Gabriel mountains. A toxic cloud of smoke and ash hung over Lancaster. Sents were urged to avoid the hazardous mess by remaining indoors. Schools cancelled outdoor activities including physical education classes and after school sports.

Regardless of my efforts to seal the barracks, my eyes and skin burned from the dry, smoky conditions. I blamed inadequate Sent construction. It not only caused energy inefficiency, but also allowed the ash and smoke to seep indoors.

But as much as I disliked the fires, they proved useful in one respect — they kept Sents away from the barracks.

During this time, I found comfort in my 'otherness.' Since I was not a Sent, my actions neither caused nor contributed to the disaster in the Gulf, but after a smug glance around the front chamber, I realized that every day I remained in-terra, the barracks used electricity supplied by oil. This made me guilty by association.

Anger and frustration swelled in me. I should have been rescued by now. I had no business contributing to Sents' problems and wished I had never been exposed to these abominations. But I was a Guardian of the Sky and Guardians followed orders without asking questions. I was just doing my job, albeit poorly. Maybe my inability to follow orders was the reason I had been left to die here.

Unable to relax, I muted the volume on the set showing the oil spill and turned the volume up on *Whale Wars*, a show about a group of volunteers aboard the Sea Shepherd Conservation Society vessel *The Steve Irwin*. The Sea Shepherds patrolled the Antarctic Ocean and attempted to end illegal whaling by sabotaging Japanese whaling ships.

Well aware this program would not lift my mood, I stared at the television screen anyway, engrossed. At this point I welcomed any distraction—anything to keep from thinking about my situation.

Except it did not. In the Nadreen language, the name EBN means 'whale' or 'Holy One' after one of the most popular Nadreen deities, EBN the Whale God. In my mother's culture, whales symbolize innocence and purity, as the deity EBN played a key role in defeating evil in the epic Nadreen creation story, *Sanoj-etan*. Whales thrive in the protected shelas on my home world, but none are as massive as the species found in Erox's oceans.

I liked these Sea Shepherd Sents and deemed them worthy Beings. I cheered the tacticians when they deployed a rope overboard that tangled in one whaling ship's propeller and slowed it to a stop. The victory, however, was short lived. A second ship appeared on the horizon. I gripped the chair's armrests in horror as it harpooned a whale and pulled it aboard for processing.

I sagged in my seat and my throat constricted. When my eyes welled and chin quivered, I wiped away the tears and vowed to be tougher and stronger. I would have to be if I were to survive this mission.

Six days had passed since I crashed on Erox. The application of oxygen vapors to my wounded leg accelerated the healing process, but it also accelerated the deterioration of my skin suit. Below my knee, the organic material hung loose and flapped with my movements under my jeans. It would not be long before the damaged part disintegrated and left my teal leg exposed.

If I were not rescued, I would die soon. With a heavy heart, I watched the Japanese whalers butcher the slaughtered whale. As the magnificent creature's blood stained the deck and whalers' boots red, a horrible thought occurred to me. If I were captured, Sents would butcher me, too. I shuddered and pushed the thought from my mind. I would throw myself into the wildfires before I would allow that to happen.

I turned the televisions off, got up and limped to the decompression chamber. The fatigue and hunger I suffered did not compare to my overwhelming loneliness since I had no other company than my own mind. I eased my body onto the nearest decompression platform, curled into a ball to keep my legs from hanging off the end and closed my eyes.

Time passed so slowly here yet an entire season had passed on Pharralax. It would soon be Freeze season back home. Preparations would be under way for Beings to hibernate or evacuate before perpetual darkness fell over the planet's surface.

I imagined the forests of Sheltdonic blanketed in snow and icebergs floating in the shela. I imagined standing on the snow-covered terrace of my family's home, admiring the clear icicles hanging from the carved stone veranda railing and feeling the frigid air on my skin.

In honor of the Nadreen holiday Dim, peace rituals would be performed and gold and silver candles would burn in each chamber of my family's home. I wondered how Aix was getting along at the Conservatory. I imagined my younger brother excelling at school and going about his days without a single care.

A loud clanging sound disrupted my serenity and pulled me back to the present. My eyes snapped open and I sat up. The noise sounded close, right outside. I peeked out the window blinds.

Two Sent boys stood outside the brown habitat box next door. I recognized them both, even though the Sent with the copper hair and murky energy field stood with his back to the barracks window. My eyes narrowed. I could never forget him.

The copper-headed Sent lifted a yellow bicycle off the ground and held it upright, while Shale stood frozen on the stairs, his ruby aura rippling with emotion. Regardless of his apparent distaste for me, my feelings for him had not changed. That was untrue—my feelings had changed. They had intensified, so much so that it hurt to watch him. I watched their interaction anyway, unable to turn away.

171

The copperhead said something unintelligible. There was no mistaking his sharp, confrontational tone. Shale slowly descended the wood stairs. He stepped onto the driveway but moved no closer as if repelled by an unbreakable physical law.

The copperhead uttered a guttural noise then leaned forward and spat at Shale's feet. Shale jumped sideways—his only response. I waited for him to act, but he did nothing, said nothing and just straightened his backpack.

The bully threw the bike down, stepped over it and stood nose to nose with Shale. Shale stood taller than the copperhead and could have easily dominated him.

It was obvious what the copperhead intended to do, but Shale stood there cowering. Sensing Shale's terror, I wondered what was he waiting for? Confused, I scratched my head. To the best of my knowledge, Shale's atypical behavior was neither known nor documented in Sents.

"I said answer me, you fucking freak of nature."

Fearful for Shale's safety, I rose to my feet. My heartbeat echoed against my eardrums. I failed to understand why Shale took the abuse instead of defending himself.

I silently urged him to do something. Sents fought all the time; it was their nature. But this one refused to engage. I remembered the first time I had seen Shale demonstrating strange behavior. He picked up trash others had dumped in the desert, something I would never believe had I not seen it happen.

Copperhead lunged forward. Shale flinched and fell backwards. I clenched my fists, cutting half-moon impressions into my palms. Shale's inaction urged me to intervene, but I remained rooted in place. Whatever I witnessed, I must maintain distance and let things unfold. Having already disobeyed orders countless times and vowed not to do it again, I withdrew a step and turned away from the window.

But it was not so simple. If it had been simple, I would never have disobeyed orders in the first place. In actuality, not a single day had passed on Erox without me disobeying orders. In a society so far removed from *The Way*, all choices led to regret.

After a quick glance over my shoulder, I returned to the window, wedged a finger between the blinds and peeked outside. Something tugged at my insides when Copperhead grabbed Shale's t-shirt and pulled him to his feet. I had to act. Eesh's raspy voice sounded in my head. "This is not your battle to fight. Do not interfere."

I had compromised my own safety too many times. Shale was not defenseless. If only he would protect himself.

173

"Fight back," I urged, startled I had whispered such words. "Do it."

Yet Shale did nothing.

I disliked observing. My chest muscles tightened and a strange sensation bubbled behind my breastbone. For a moment I wished I had never discovered a thoughtful, non-violent Sent on Erox. Shale would be hurt and I must allow it. An image flashed in my mind of the slaughtered whale on television and my face puckered. I shook my head as I stepped away from the window. Disobeying Eesh's orders was no longer an option.

But nothing about this situation was right. My stomachs churned and twisted. It was not supposed to be like this. A highly evolved Sent deserved protection. He was the only hope this distressed planet had.

Feeling miserable and unsettled, I let out a heavy sigh. As I limped away from the window, the pressure inside my chest swelled, threatening to halt my heart.

Unable to stop myself, I fled the chamber. After all I had endured, I could spend my few remaining days living with dishonor. Better to live in disgrace than allow an innocent to be brutalized. I would not have it on my conscience.

When I darted outside, burning cinders caught in my throat and I seized, doubling over, coughing and choking. The sizzling wind lashed across my skin, stinging like a whip. My lungs contracted as I struggled to inhale oxygen where there was none. Water pooled in my burning, stinging eyes and streamed down my cheeks.

174

Black smoke stacks rose over the distant mountaintops. Against my better judgment, I forced myself upright, rounded the corner of the barracks and stopped at the edge of the neighbor's driveway just in time to hear Copperhead demand, "Look at me when I talk to you."

I stopped behind the downed bicycle while Copperhead gripped Shale's shirt in his fist. With his free hand, he snatched Shale's glasses off his face. The boy gasped. My eyes narrowed as my anger smoldered. The copper-headed Sent threw the boy's glasses over his shoulder. They landed near my feet.

I glanced down at the spectacles. *There is still time to retreat. Remember what Eesh said. Jeopardize your honor and things will never be the same.*

I bent down and retrieved the glasses. No longer aware of the burning in my throat or the squalid air, I crossed my arms over my chest, glowered at the back of the bully's head and cleared my throat. I was not going back inside. I would not allow this boy, this human Being to be hurt, whatever the consequences.

Copperhead glanced over his shoulder. When he saw me, he relaxed his fist and let go of Shale's t-shirt. "'Sup?" he said with a nod, leering at me. He gave Shale a hard shove and jabbed his forefinger in his face. "This isn't over."

The copperhead puffed out his chest and swaggered backwards. Except he stepped through Shale's bike frame without realizing it and when he turned to go, his foot caught between the bars. Tommy sprawled forward, dragging the bike with him. His face hit the gravel drive and a loud *crack* sounded along with a string of muffled curses. His fingers flew to his bloody mouth as he jumped to his feet.

"You broke my tooth, asshole. I'll get you for this," he hissed before disappearing around the side of the house.

Shale lowered his head and searched the ground.

He looked so vulnerable I thought my heart might melt. I skirted the fallen bike and limped toward him. The driveway gravel crunched under my feet.

"I think you lost these," I said. I reached for his hand and pressed his glasses into his palm. When we touched, electricity passed between us, pinching my skin. I wanted to hold his hand and comfort him, but knew no good could come from it, so I dropped it instead.

Shale slid his glasses onto the bridge of his nose with unsteady hands and his eyes expanded into a wide stare. I wondered if the spark had stung him too.

I gazed at him, wanting the moment to last. I wanted to tell him not to be embarrassed but held my tongue, since I knew it would only cause him further embarrassment.

Shale looked me up and down then sank onto the steps. His face twitched and clenched, squeezing his eyes shut. After a moment, his aura lightened to the same pale blue shade as his wiggling eyes. At least he no longer disliked me.

"Are you hurt?"

He shook his head.

I nodded. "Take your belongings and go inside. He will return another day, but not tonight."

Shale did as instructed.

I stood guard and did not move until he was safe inside his home. When I heard the door lock click, I turned and limped back to the barracks in a daze. To my surprise I felt no regrets, only an odd sense of calm earned by a duty well done.

Chapter Ten: Sent Emulation

In the days following the assassination attempt on the Protectorate High Chancellor, several suspected Seemae separatists are captured or killed, easing the citizens' minds. Normalcy returns and classes at the Conservatory resume. Between caring for A-ma and keeping up with school assignments, I have little time to worry about EBN.

Preece's health shows gradual signs of improvement. I keep the house as quiet and peaceful as possible. Solstice ceremony starts in three days.

Mangnas before the holiday, Preece leaves her decompression chamber, eats a full meal and announces she is well enough to conduct the ceremonial feast. Then she goes to the Nadreen houses of worship to hold vigil.

It is the last day of school before classes are suspended for the onset of Freeze season. Unable to focus, I sit in current events class and stare out the frost-blurred window. The overcast gray sky drops frozen precipitation, reflecting my somber mood. I dislike the five-week long Freeze season when Pharralax plunges into perpetual darkness and temperatures plummet several hundred degrees, making the surface uninhabitable.

This year I dread it more than usual, even though A-ma and I are boarding a passenger airship for an interstellar cruise. I try to think of it as a vacation of sorts, but all the preparation falls on my shoulders since A-ma still isn't herself.

Chimes sound, signaling the end of class. I file into the hallway where my face stands out amid the crowd of blue ones. A sea of bodies dressed in black and white uniforms moves about the seventh floor hallway.

The crystalline walls display images captured during first summer season: tropical sandy beaches under clear, violet-blue skies. They show nothing of Pharralax's second summer season, when the planet's surface becomes blistering hot because her elliptical orbit brings her dangerously close to Scyros.

I duck into the exit corridor at the end of the hall, rush down the spiral walkway to ground level and sprint outside, where Xtarr's transport vehicle known as a *pert* waits. Sleet splatters the metallic, bubble shaped vehicle parked outside the main entrance. I dash through the freezing cold and climb inside it.

179

Dark tinted windows and white cushiony seats ring the circular passenger compartment. The warm interior feels amazing after being outdoors. I mumble my greeting and slide into the seat nearest the door, positioned across from Xtarr. I glance at the driver's compartment and greet Hsoj, also. Unable to bow, Hsoj inclines his head in greeting.

Xtarr snaps her wings to shake the slush from them. She stares out the window, undoubtedly looking for Nyl. I feel annoyed and jealous, but settle back into my seat, determined not to betray my feelings.

She sighs and turns to face me. "Greetings Aix," she says in a wistful tone. She runs her flattened palms over her head, smoothing the moisture from her hair and flips it over her shoulders. "Shall we go then?"

"What about Nyl," I ask.

The corners of Xtarr's mahogany eyes droop. I can tell from the set of her shoulders that she feels unhappy. While I'd never say so, I've had enough Nadreen unhappiness to last a lifetime.

"He's not coming," she says. Her gaze falls to the floor. "His parents pulled him from school already. They're commanding one of the passenger ships."

"Really," I say with a little too much enthusiasm. My mood improves instantly. Now I won't have to endure their hanging all over one another. "Did he say which one?"

"No," she says and sighs again. "Where shall we go on our last outing of the season," Xtarr asked.

"Care to venture to the Sent Emulation Center," I ask. I hope the suggestion will make her smile, but it doesn't.

She leans forward and speaks to Hsoj in a soft voice. The pert pulls away from the Conservatory pyramids and drives toward the thick woods lining the main roadway.

The city's central industrial district lies well beyond the school grounds. Tightly clustered skyscrapers with solar paneled exteriors tower over the dark coniferous forest. The vehicle turns onto the white roadway that cuts through the woodlands and leads to various retail, residential and recreational complexes.

"How are you spending the Freeze," I ask. I don't anticipate Xtarr's reaction and regret asking the question.

She slumps in her seat. "A-da's dragging me to Doridaen," she groans, rolling her eyes.

I half-smile. Nyl, being Adelian, would not be welcome on Doridaen, Pharralax's pink moon. Doridaen is a place of great myth, magic and mystery. Besides being home world to the Nadreen Royal Family, little else is known about Pharralax's smallest moon. Not even the Zuma Neway, the Protectorate's legislative body, knows much about Doridaen and that is exactly how the Royal Family wants it.

"At least you're not staying here," I say. "You'll see your A-ma."

181

"I know," Xtarr grumbles.

"It will go fast. You'll have an enjoyable time," I offer.

Xtarr snorts. "I'd rather hibernate with Hsoj and his family. My parents are pressuring me about my Declaration Ceremony and future path. I feel like they want me to be someone I'm not. Why can't they just accept me for who I am?"

I smile. This is perfect and exactly what I want to discuss with her. "Have you given much thought to how you'll declare?"

"Too much," she replies. "I feel unprepared to make a decision I'll have to live with for the rest of my life. What if I change? What if, in the future, I hate the path I've chosen? It's a stupid tradition and unfair too, for Beings as young as we," she says, stamping one foot and throwing her hands in the air.

"So what choice will you make," I ask in a quiet voice.

She looks out the window and shakes her head. "I've meditated on the question endlessly. I intend to relinquish my title and all that goes with it."

I lean forward. "Perhaps you should consider further meditation on the question."

For the first time Xtarr smiles at me. "Your concern touches my heart," she says, batting her long eyelashes. "But I have no desire to give up my worldly life on Pharralax for life on Doridaen. An arranged marriage would not make me happy."

"But you have other choices," I reply. "You could follow a path similar to my A-ma. You could be a spiritual leader or a politician."

Xtarr wrinkles her nose in distaste. "Not for me. I want an easy, carefree life."

"Then maintain your position as Princess. Life will not be carefree if you relinquish your title. What does Nyl think?" I brace myself for her answer.

"Nyl has not influenced my decision, although I am anxious to explore our relationship further."

"Are you certain that is wise?"

Xtarr glowers at me. "Now you sound like my A-da."

I look away. Xtarr has no future with Nyl but I know better than to say so. "Xtarr, you're in the same position as my A-ma, when she was our age. She relinquished her title, was banned from Doridaen and never saw her Nadreen family again because she chose an Adelian life partner. Based on how easily her sense of Harmony is destroyed, I think she's deeply unhappy. She's never said so, but I think if she had the decision to make all over again, she would choose differently the second time. You remind me of her in many ways."

Xtarr reaches out and pats my knee. "It's something to consider."

My knee warms from Xtarr's touch. I long for her and wish she felt the same way. "I know you'd be very unhappy if you relinquished your title and crown. Once it's gone, you can't get it back."

"I don't want to talk about this anymore," she warns with a firm nod. "How is Preece doing? I'm sorry for not asking sooner."

"She's improved somewhat, but her sense of Harmony is still not restored."

"And where are you spending Freeze? In hibernation?"

"No, we're going to the ships. Maybe I'll see Nyl," I say. Nyl is rather popular with the girls at school because of his chiseled features and muscular body. Maybe during Freeze he'll meet someone else. I hope so, for Xtarr's sake.

"Have you heard anything from EBN," Xtarr asks.

"No." I glance out the window.

"Do you suspect something's happened to her?"

"I don't suspect it—I know it with every fiber of my being. I just don't know what can be done about it. I wish I knew how to help her."

"Aix, you forget she's a Guardian. They know how to take care of themselves."

I lock her gaze with mine. "Imagine how you'd feel if it were your sibling. You would do whatever was necessary to help them if they were hurt or in danger."

She considers this. "You're right. I would."

We drive past the columnar skyscrapers in the district known as Middle Sheltdonic and approach a small, tree-lined park. Ice coats the trees' branches. The tips of blue grass blades poke out from under the accumulating layer of slush and ice carpeting the ground.

Xtarr leans closer and touches my arm. "I'm sure you'll hear from her soon, Aix. She's probably just busy and lost track of time."

I respond to the caring in her eyes and place my hand over hers to prolong my enjoyment of her touch. I feel disappointed when she pulls her hand away. "I hope so," I say.

"The holidays are fast approaching. Surely she'll contact you for Dim."

I say nothing and stare out the window.

Once we pass the park, we enter the museum district. Of the countless museums in Sheltdonic, the Sent Emulation Center is the smallest. It operates independently from the Protectorate and relies on the support of fans and patrons to stay open.

"I love this place," Xtarr sighs as the pert turns down the narrow side road where the center is located. "When was the last time you were here, Aix," she asks.

"It's been too long," I mumble.

"I can't wait to see the latest Sent fashions," Xtarr says. She runs her hands through her damp hair again. "I'll see that exhibit alone if you're not interested. I hope they have some new music, too. I'm so tired of everything in my collection."

There is no other building like the Sent Emulation Center in the whole of Sheltdonic and I like everything about it. In keeping with the theme, the Center resembles the type of edifice many Sents live in. Housed in a tiny, purple, square wood structure, the two-story building has green painted trim, a pitched green roof, square windows and stairs on the inside.

Besides displaying poor reproductions and loose interpretations of famous Sent works created by Xionin citizens, the Center contains the largest private collection of genuine Sent artwork in the entire star system. The Center also features exhibits in fashion, literature, films and my personal favorites, television programs and Sent music recordings.

As the pert slows to a stop before the building that looks strangely out of place compared to the cylindrical skyscrapers surrounding it, Xtarr and I exchange glances. The Center looks dark and foreboding.

"How divine," Xtarr quips. "We'll have the whole place to ourselves."

Xtarr asks Hsoj to wait before we climb out of the pert and run toward the entrance. The building appears empty too. I try lifting the door, but it fails to open. I cup my hand against a square window and peer inside. No Beings move about the interior. Xtarr moves to the side entrance and tries opening it, but it won't budge either.

"Look at this," she says, pointing to a notice posted inside a window.

I walk over and read the notice aloud. "Closed until further notice under orders of Eesh-Slic, Protectorate High Chancellor. We apologize for the inconvenience."

Confused, I back away from the window and almost step on Xtarr's feet. "Gran-Ada closed the Center. But why?" I mutter.

"How could he? Now what are we going to do?" Xtarr demands. She plants her curled fists on her tiny hips and snaps her wings loudly in anger. "Doesn't he know how important this place is? Beings travel great distances from all over the galaxy to see it. For many, it's the closest we'll ever get to Erox."

"I don't understand what this is about." I turn to Xtarr. "He said . . . some harsh things about Sents the last time I saw him," I explain. The full measure of the Center's closing hits me and my expression falls.

"Don't be disappointed, Aix. We'll do something else fun."

I shake my head. "Let's not," I mumble, disinterested. I turn away from the entrance with my head hung low and drag my feet as we return to Xtarr's waiting pert. "I wanted to hear some new music and see if there were any more episodes of *the Wonder Kids*."

We climb inside the vehicle. "You mean you haven't seen the final season," Xtarr asks. "It was so great. In the last episode, Debbie gets captured by—"

My eyes cut to her. "You're ruining it for me."

She claps a hand over her mouth and utters an apology. "So what now?"

"I want to find out what's going on," I say in an angry tone. I remove my computer from my pocket, expand it and search for news bulletins. Xtarr slides over the seats and sits next to me, resting her head on my shoulder. Her breath warms my neck, sending chills down my spine. My eyes scan the computer screen but nothing comes up regarding the Center's closure.

"I can't find anything about it," I say.

"We could go to the Hall of Records and find out what happened," Xtarr offers.

"We have nothing better to do," I agree.

My somber mood is contagious. We ride in silence, staring out the windows.

The oldest settlements lay outside the city in an area known as Lower Sheltdonic, where the blue boreal forest gives way to expansive farmlands. Through the stands of trees lining the road I glimpse one of many Loredi communities nestled between frozen freshwater lakes. Frozen fields and bare fruit orchards encircle communal thatched huts.

We cross the long channel of the sparkling Ionnis River. Ice edges the riverbanks while steam rises from the river's spring-fed surface. Ancient Nadreen houses of worship stand along the waterway's banks. It isn't long before the community Records Hall comes into view.

Built on a hillside, the massive silver orb glitters despite the dreary conditions. Hsoj stops the pert and connects it to an energy terminal while Xtarr and I hurry toward the entrance to escape the cold.

We bustle past two reflection pools lining the white marble walkway. When we approach the wide circular glass door, it lifts open for us. We step inside and stand in an enormous, unfurnished hall. It is warm and welcoming yet eerily quiet and still. Soft white light streams down from skylights positioned in the towering ceiling.

A thin, shimmering screen hangs suspended several paces ahead and a grid of white, diamagnetic footpads sits on the floor beneath it. I approach the screen, step onto one of the pads, think of the Sent Emulation Center closure and the pad moves beneath my feet. It carries me through the shimmering screen and into the main hall. I glance over my shoulder. Xtarr passes through the screen a moment later.

The floating pads hover the length of the expansive main hall and stop before another wall-sized shimmering screen. Once we're in place, a broadcast originally aired on the Xionin Network appears on the screen. An attractive Nadreen with amber eyes and golden wingtips peeking over the tops of her shoulders stands in front of the purple building. Behind her, Beings enter and exit the Center.

"Sad news today, for fans of the Sent Emulation Center. Protectorate High Chancellor, Eesh-Slic, ordered the museum closed during a speech delivered moments ago in the chambers of the Zuma Neway."

The broadcast cuts away from her and switches to footage of Eesh. He sits on the dais behind the Zuma Neway's bench, surrounded by the other legislators. He wears a high collared slate-gray suit the same color as his compound eyes. Ulem sits in the seat to Eesh's left.

"Citizens of Pharralax and the Xionin star system," he says, speaking directly into the camera. "It is with great regret that I announce the permanent closure of the Sent Emulation Center. Due to the deterioration of Sent culture and the cessation of Sent evolution, I feel it necessary for the safety and longevity of all Beings in the multi-verse to unplug from Sent persuasion.

"Sent influence is pernicious. In order to preserve our own society and culture, I cannot allow our youth to celebrate nor emulate a dead culture and dying people.

"For these reasons I also prohibit the importation of goods from Erox. Any Being found in possession of Sent items acquired after this day will be subject to arrest. Beings in possession of Sent items acquired prior to this ban will be required to show documentation proving the dates of acquisition for the items in question.

"In coming to this decision I have considered the possibility that in the future I may be judged harshly and criticized for these preemptive measures. Nevertheless, I invite these consequences over failing to act and in so doing, propelling all Beings toward a far worse fate. Thank you —"

I turn away from the screen and look at Xtarr with a miserable expression. "Let's go home," I whisper.

Chapter Eleven: Touched

It was my seventh day in-terra, known to the indigenous as "Friday" and almost midnight according to the chronometer on the microwave. To keep my mind occupied, I stood in the nourishment chamber, counting provisions.

Three silver packets of entropy solution sat in a neat row on the counter next to five cans of Re-breather formula. I decided to cut the provisions in half to make them last longer but did not know if doing so was wise. I had consumed all the pain medicine and antibiotic ointment from the medical kits. I felt much better, but the gashes on my leg still had not healed. The wounds looked and felt the same as they had after my encounter with the soldiers.

I wished I had someone to talk to, to help me make sense of what had happened, especially Gran-Ada. No matter how complicated a scenario, Eesh had an uncanny ability to make sense out of anything and he always knew what to do.

So far, I had failed miserably at my mission. I had failed to obey orders and to find signs of Seemae activity. I shook my head, remorseful. If I made it out of this, I would have to answer some hard questions. I dared not imagine what my family would think of me. I was not setting a good example for Aix.

I opened a drawer and swept the packets into it with my forearm. As I returned the cans of Re-breather to the cold storage bin, a smile curved my lips. Aix would laugh until he cried if he knew his Sent-hating sister was living among the enemy. Out of everyone, Aix was the one Being I did not have to worry about. Aix would understand my predicament, loneliness and the temptations I faced. I hoped I lived long enough to tell him about my experiences.

I glanced out the window over the sink. Shale's silhouette blocked the light spilling from the dirty windows next door. While I watched him, I heard Harmony's lilting voice in my head, "If you need anything, we're right next door. Stop by anytime."

Just then Shale looked up and smiled at me. Reluctantly, I smiled back.

"If you need anything, we're right next door..."

I exited the nourishment chamber and limped into the front chamber. The computer sat on the table next to the camouflage jacket. I grabbed both and out of habit tried to turn the on computer. Then I remembered the computer's battery was dead.

I dreaded going out for my evening foot patrol. Like the oil spill, the wildfires still raged out of control. Breathing the poisonous air would exacerbate my entropy symptoms.

Nevertheless, duty called.

I pulled on my jacket and exited the barracks. When I stepped off the patio I surveyed the landscape. The bald patches of topsoil marking the once lush field of California wildflowers had grown in size. As I limped toward *the Surety*, I estimated more than half the flowers were gone. Of those still bathing in the moonlight, most were wilting and dying. After crossing one bare spot, I turned and looked behind me.

Not a single wildflower bloomed in the wake of my footsteps.

A sickle moon hung in the hazy, smoky sky. Hot, acrid winds whipped through the desert, crackling with electricity. I crossed the dry riverbed, hiked through the foothills and negotiated the canyon without much trouble from my leg but it was hard to breathe.

When my shirt proved ineffective as a filter, I shrugged out of my jacket and held it over my nose and mouth. This helped, but I still gasped and gulped. By the time the boulder outcropping was within sight, I felt dizzy. Each time I exhaled, a wheeze rattled my lungs.

I reached the front of the outcropping and leaned against a boulder to rest. My leg throbbed from the rigorous activity, but the discomfort was tolerable. I had endured far worse.

Once I caught my breath, I pushed off the boulder and trekked toward the back of the outcropping. When I reached the ship's location, I stopped.

The *Surety's* cloaking mechanism had failed.

I raced inside the ship to identify the problem. The *Surety's* interior was roasting hot and pitch dark except for the lights flashing from the console. Two faint alerts reverberated through the vessel as well, warning of the failed cloaking mechanism and low fuel supply.

At first, I did not comprehend. The ship held adequate fuel before; I had not flown anywhere. Then I realized the compromised cloaking mechanism must have drained the power levels to the degree that the ship accessed fuel reserves.

I crawled into the pilot's seat, placed my hand on the command module and visualized enabling the secondary auxiliary power system. The ship failed to respond.

I opened my eyes and scanned the console but I could not recall the necessary sequence. I never had to use it before and my training seemed like a lifetime ago. I panicked; sweat poured down the sides of my face.

In a frenzied series of movements, I opened a panel on the console, pressed buttons and flipped switches until I managed to activate the secondary and last auxiliary system. When the alerts ceased and the familiar turquoise backlighting glowed on the console, I composed:

High Chancellor — Mission day seven. Am gravely injured, ship is disabled. Cloaking mechanism has failed. Computer is dead; have no supplies. Please send rescue team. Need entropy solution. Little time left. Guardian of the Sky EBN-Reyoz-X

My pulse quickened as I sent the transmission and waited to see if it bounced back. After a few moments, I pulled the computer from my pocket. The illuminated screen indicated the power supply was charging. Although the transmission had not bounced back, I could not relax. My life depended on this single transmission.

Moment by moment, my outlook became more hopeful. If both auxiliary systems charged to full power, I could attempt to start the ship. I did not care that daylight was only mangnas away. I sensed this was my last chance. I intended on taking it.

The transmission had yet to bounce back. My heartbeat raced. If nothing else worked, at least it had gone through. That was a result!

Chimes resonated from the console signaling the auxiliary systems were charged. According to the systems screen, the main systems were attempting to charge as well. I waited a long while, holding my hand just above the control module. When I could stand it no more, I lowered it. Power surged throughout the craft and the console's backlighting flickered. Alarmed, I jerked my hand off the module and waited. The flickering stopped. I pulled my computer from my pocket. It remained on.

A moment later the cabin blackened. Immediately I cut the power and glanced at my computer. The screen was dark too. I pressed the start button but it would not power up.

Ignoring the savage pain in my leg, I rose and exited the ship.

There was no time to berate myself or stare dumbstruck at the thick film of gray ash coating the undisguised ship. I sprung to action, limping frantically through the desert, gathering armfuls of creosote branches, sagebrush and Sent trash to cover the ship.

The collection process took longer than I expected. Each passing mangna brought more fear and pain than the last. To avoid stripping whole areas of vegetation, I limped farther into the desert than I had been before. Even though the ship was small, it took all night to hide from Sent eyes.

I worked until my hands were cut and bloodied and the searing pain in my leg became unbearable. Confident I was alone but in too much pain to care if I was not, I untangled part of the debris shield, entered the ship and sealed myself inside.

I returned to the pilot's seat, slumped down and closed my eyes. I did not want it to come to this, but I had exhausted every other option.

I visualized my Gran-Ada's face. *Gran-Ada,* I vibed.

There was no response.

Gran-Ada. I visualized my thought energy shooting through the multi-verse along the intricate web of ethereal silver cords connecting all Beings.

Gran-Ada, I vibed.

Silence.

Gran-Ada, please answer me, I begged. *I need you.*

I imagined myself in spirit form, a white-hot ball of light traveling the length of the silver cord as I vibed Eesh. I followed the cord's length until I came to the place where it split four times. I knew not to follow the divergent cords because I needed Eesh right now, not Aix or our parents. Concentrating on the vision of Eesh's face, I followed the pulse of light.

Gran-Ada, I vibed. Just as the word left my mind, I reached a broken, frayed cord end floating in the blackness of space. It should have been attached to an ethereal image of Eesh. However Eesh was not there.

_____

198

My eyes popped open. There had to be a mistake.

Undeterred, I closed my eyes and started over. Once again, I imagined the network of ethereal silver webbing connecting all Beings throughout the multi-verse.

Gran-Ada, I vibed. *Eesh-Slic.*

The pulse of blazing light bulleted through the web at warp speed, but it ended at the same place. It could only mean one thing.

Eesh was dead.

At first I could not believe it. I refused to believe it, but it explained everything.

Shock numbed my body and lingered for some time.

When feeling returned, grief descended on me. My expression puckered. The corners of my eyes fell and a piteous mew trailed from my lips.

The thin, high-pitched sound resonated through the ship. My chest swelled and caved as I swallowed deep breaths. I rocked in my seat, humming a sad melody that changed to a sonorous moan. Soon my cries turned to body quaking sobs.

Eventually everything went black.

Stifling heat woke me. Daylight poured through the windshield. I squinted, unable to recall slipping into decompression. Outside, a fiery red sun hung over the land, burning like an ember in the rosy tinted sky. A brown and beige hawk with one leg glided through the air. It rode the air current, darted toward the ground and vanished from view.

My hands felt grimy, stiff and sore. I glanced at them and jumped, startled by the sight. In my rush to conceal the ship, I had shredded the palms of my skin suit. The tattered, organic material hung in ribbons from my teal hands. I shrugged out of my jacket, pulled off my t-shirt, tore it into strips and wrapped my hands with the makeshift bandages.

Physically spent and wrought with pain, I faced the truth. Disregarding the daylight, I exited the ship and limped toward the barracks in a daze. Along the way, my grief dissipated and a strange sense of calm enveloped me. Finally liberated from uncertainty, there was a sort of freedom in knowing how my remaining days on Erox would unfold.

Returning to the barracks presented a tortuous struggle. The desert was red-hot and bone dry. Gray smoke still plumed over the mountains. Soot browned the sky while ash drifted and spun in the air like snowflakes.

Each time I took a step, I sucked air through my teeth because needle sharp pains stabbed the length of my injured leg. My progress was slow. I wanted to give up and fall to the ground, but I had to return to the barracks; it was my only hope. If Beings came to rescue me, I had to be there.

I did not know how long it took me to reach the front side of the boulder outcropping. I only knew I dragged my left leg behind me. I eyed the lichen-covered stones where I had rested the night before and stopped to rest again. I leaned against the hot sandstone and lifted my face toward the red sky. Three buzzards circled high overhead. My stinking, infected flesh had drawn them to the outcropping.

Distracted by the birds of prey, I failed to notice Shale riding his bike up the trail. I heard a high-pitched, squealing sound and lowered my gaze. Shale brought his bike to a stop and stared at me.

"What are you doing here," I said, my face tense with pain.

Shale's smile faded and his features drew together in concern. He pointed at me and made the 'ok' sign with one of his hands.

I shook my head. "I need help. My leg..." my words trailed off.

Shale nodded, lifted his bike and turned it around so that his back was to me. The wire baskets suspended over the back tire contained plastic bags filled with trash, of course. Shale lowered the bike's kickstand, pointed to me then patted his bike seat. When I did not move, Shale gestured at me and patted his seat again.

I looked at the carrion eaters circling overhead and pushed myself off the warm rocks. I limped over to Shale's bike, pointed at the seat.

"You want me to sit here?"

Shale nodded vigorously.

I straddled the seat and lowered my weight onto the bike. As Shale raised the kickstand and began pedaling, I lifted my legs and rested my hands on Shale's shoulders. Once we found our balance, we rolled down the mountain and toward the barracks at a faster pace than I could have walked.

Branches and bushes brushed against my legs until the trail widened. Shale followed a bike trail through the foothills that skirted the canyon and clearing. He masterfully navigated the terrain as well as any desert dwelling creature could have done.

Soon we reached the dry riverbed. Shale rolled to a stop, lowered the bike's kickstand and stood. With some effort, I lifted my body off the bike. Before I realized what was happening, Shale sidled up to me, swung my arm over his shoulder and hooked his other arm around my waist.

Electricity sparked between us, but I felt too ill and weak to react. Shale, however, flinched and I knew he had felt it too. I stared straight ahead, refusing to acknowledge our chemistry. From the corner of my eye I noticed that his head cleared my shoulder, which I thought unusual considering his young age.

As we crossed the dry riverbed, I thought of my first day of military training known as *Purification*, when a frightful-looking Obe named Phryss had helped me out of the jungle and saved my life. Now Shale was saving me. Touched by his actions, I felt my heart swell.

Once we reached the top of the opposite embankment, Shale pointed at me and made the 'ok' sign again. His face, neck and arms were as red as the sun. Sweat streamed down his head and neck.

"Yes," I said, coughing against the smoky air. "Are you all right?"

He nodded, pointed at me again and held up both hands, palms facing me. Unable to understand his gesture, I accessed his thoughts and understood he wanted me to wait.

"I will wait here," I said.

Shale nodded and slid down the embankment to retrieve his bike. While I watched him scramble up the opposite embankment, moisture welled in my eyes and a single tear rolled down my cheek. Embarrassed, I wiped it away with the back of my bandaged hand.

When Shale delivered me to the barracks' patio, I limped under the patio awning to escape the sunlight and asked him to join me.

His shoulders hunched from slouching. Shale raised an arm and pointed at my hands. I lifted them.

"They are fine. No cause for concern," I said.

Shale scowled, shook his head and motioned for me to follow him. I stared at the boy and his thoughts vibrated in my mind.

You should come over, have Harmony look at your hands. She's good at first aid.

"Let us not disturb Harmony with this matter," I answered. "It looks worse than it is, I assure you."

Shale's head jerked back. He stared at me with large, round eyes. I watched him, puzzled at what I had done.

Did she just read my mind?

"Please wait here. I will return," I said. I limped into the nourishment chamber, retrieved a glass from the cabinet and filled it with ice. As I stood at the sink, filling the cup with water, I chastised myself for answering Shale's unspoken question and blamed myself for everything that had gone wrong.

No wonder I had been left here to die. I was a failure and unworthy of the title Guardian. If I could no longer make a difference by serving the Protectorate, then I would make a difference by helping the mute and anti-social human who had saved my life.

204

I returned to the patio with the glass of water and handed it to Shale. He accepted it and gulped the liquid. I waited for him to finish before speaking.

"Thank you for helping me today," I said, staring at him. "I owe you a tremendous debt."

Shale wiped his mouth with the back of his hand and smacked his lips. He shook his head in disagreement.

"Yes, I do," I corrected. "Where I come from, reciprocity is *The Way*. It is critical to our evolution."

Shale stared at me and cocked his head slightly.

I stared back at him and it occurred to me that I had not seen his face spasm. I wondered if Shale had noticed it too. "To satisfy my debt, I feel compelled to teach you defensive maneuvers so you can protect yourself from that Sen—boy who hurt Princess."

Shale's eyes widened. *You'd teach me to fight? But you're a girl.*

I glanced at him sideways and pretended to study him. "But if you are not interested…"

Shale straightened his posture, smiled and nodded eagerly.

My eyes drooped from exhaustion. "Then it is agreed. Come back this evening, at sunset. Harmony is welcome also."

Shale radiated joy, which I felt with every cell of my Being. I watched him ride away before retreating inside the barracks. As I collapsed into a reclining chair inside the cool and dark front chamber, I worried about being rescued and breaking my promise to Shale.

Then I remembered that Eesh was dead.

I was on my own. No one was coming to take me home.

Chapter Twelve: Changes

Stained and burned avocado shag carpeted the low wood paneled living room of Shale and Harmony's mobile home. The stale odor of cigarettes rose from every green fiber. Noise from the television set blared throughout the house.

"Shale! Get out here!" Harmony yelled above the din.

Two dry erase markers poked out from Shale's hip pocket as he skulked down the narrow hallway with his dry-erase board clutched in one hand and a cold grape soda in the other. He stopped where the hall opened onto the living room and stood by the window.

You don't have to yell, he thought as his facial muscles contracted in a spasm. Harmony knew that yelling at him made his facial tic worse but she did it anyway. He hated her disregard for his tic almost as much as the actual spasms. He sipped his soda and relished the cool burn of the sweet, fizzy liquid as he swallowed.

"Shale!" Harmony yelled again, not looking up from the deafening television set.

He glared at her while she sat in her pajamas on the threadbare, second hand sofa and his facial muscles cramped again. It was late afternoon. She hadn't showered or brushed her hair and Shale suspected she hadn't gotten off the couch all day except to use the bathroom. Now she was so absorbed in her television program she didn't notice him. It was her day off and she was entitled to relax, but it still irked him.

What annoyed him most was the program she watched. He understood some people liked to watch their favorite shows over and over, but most people weren't actors *in* their favorite shows. She'd memorized every script and either moved her lips or recited the actors' lines with them. He wondered if all actors were as self-absorbed as Harmony, wasting their days off watching themselves on television. He wanted to shout that their trailer was not a movie set. There was no star on the door with her name on it. There was just their address on Stellar Way.

A lot had changed since Harmony's acting days.

Almost two years ago when *Wonder Kids* ended production, their family had been intact. Their father, Step, usually stayed in Lancaster to run the Oasis while their mother, Linda, shuttled him and Harmony between Lancaster and Los Angeles. Those had been good times. Shale had friends back then and wasn't burdened with public school. He was tutored alongside Harmony and the other actors and even though he was the youngest of the group, he was the smartest.

A commercial break interrupted the show. Shale glanced at Harmony, who finally saw him and started.

Harmony's hand flew to her heart. "Stop sneaking up on me," she said in an ugly tone. "And for the fiftieth time, stop slouching. Don't make me tell you again," she scolded.

Shale scowled in protest but straightened his posture just so she'd leave him alone.

"Did you take out the garbage?"

Shale nodded and glanced down at his dry-erase board. Maybe now wasn't such a good time to talk to her. Ordinarily, he would've left her alone and allowed her to hog the television in peace, but strange and inexplicable things had happened this morning. He'd found EBN in the middle of the desert, more than two miles from the Oasis, and not one spec of dirt clung to her clothes or boots. It seemed impossible to hike that far without getting dirty, but Shale knew what he saw.

EBN had needed help, which he gladly provided although he felt a little guilty. Last night, as he lay in bed waiting to fall asleep, he'd imagined himself rescuing EBN from a similar damsel-in-distress scenario, but he never imagined it would happen.

He'd given EBN a lift home and when they'd reached the Oasis, Shale could've sworn she'd read his mind. It could've been a coincidence or his imagination, but the absolute weirdest thing happened after he left EBN's. As he rolled his bike home, he felt different. For the first time in months, he felt strong, capable and calm. The fog of depression had lifted off him and magically vanished as if it had never existed at all.

"All of it? The recycling too?"

Shale nodded again, more vigorously this time. Harmony glanced at the board in his hands, frowned and let out a loud, exaggerated sigh intended more as a warning than exhale. Shale heard it so often that he'd nicknamed it 'dragon's breath.' However, to his surprise she muted the television set. She reached for her pack of cigarettes, lit one up and released a long stream of smoke. "What's on your mind?"

Shale crossed the living room and sat at the far end of the sofa, away from the disgusting smoke. It didn't matter though. The moment he sat down, the trail of carcinogens shifted direction and drifted straight toward him. His face twitched, squeezing his eyes shut. He selected the green marker from his hip pocket, scrawled on the board and handed it to Harmony.

Graduation is less than two weeks away.

She took the board, read the message out loud and handed it back. "And?"

Shale used the tail of his t-shirt to erase it and wrote another message. He handed it back to her, took a deep breath and braced himself for her reaction.

I want to apply to Caltech.

She read the message, threw her head back and scoffed. "I don't want to talk about this now, Shale," she said, staring at the ceiling.

He stared at her, erased the board and wrote his message in big letters without looking down. Then he pressed the board against her arm.

I do.

Harmony took a deep drag off her cigarette before reading Shale's response. When she uttered the words he'd written, her forehead wrinkled and her eyebrows drew together. "I know you do," she said, crushing her cigarette butt in a full ashtray. "But I have to stay here to run the business and you're too young to live without supervision."

She handed the board back to him, pressed the volume button on the remote and turned her attention to her show like everything was settled.

Princess appeared at the far end of the living room as if she'd sensed her presence was required to dispel the tension between them. She sat in the open hallway and licked her paws, but moved no closer. Like Shale, Princess disliked cigarette smoke.

Shale felt angry. The television volume blasted him like a slap in the face. Anytime he wanted to talk about important things like his future, she dismissed him or tuned him out with the television. He erased the old message, wrote another and shoved the board back at her.

Hire someone to run the Oasis. We'll go back to L.A. I'll go to school. You can act.

While Harmony read what he wrote, Shale grabbed the remote, pressed the mute button and slid it under his leg.

Harmony glowered at him and dropped his board on the sofa. "If I could get work like this, I'd say let's go. But no casting director will hire me until I lose forty or fifty pounds."

He reached for the board, scrawled another message and handed it to her.

So lose the weight.

Harmony read it and rolled her eyes. "This business is all we have, Shale. I'm not going to leave it for someone else to manage and risk having it stolen the way my business manager stole all my money."

Shale grabbed the board and erased it quickly.

What about me? My potential?

"What about you," she demanded, raising her voice. "You're thirteen years old! Most people don't go to college until they're …older. College can wait another year. You can wait another year. Where's the remote?" She snatched her pack of cigarettes and lit another cancer stick.

Shale scribbled another message and held the board up.

I'm 14 next month. Let's hire an attorney to get your $$$ back.

Harmony uttered the words and laughed. "Attorneys cost money, Shale. College costs money—lots of it. Look around," she said, making a sweeping gesture with both arms. Her cigarette dangled between her lips as she spoke. "We're not exactly rolling in dough."

Shale shook his head and narrowed his eyes. Another tic seized his face and clenched eyes closed. She was afraid and making excuses like usual.

"What," Harmony demanded in a shrill voice.

Shale shrugged and shook his head. The board in his hands was too small for everything he wanted to say. He wished he could be sure Harmony had his best interests at heart. He wanted to do something with his life, something important to help people and the planet and he couldn't do that by staying at the Oasis and wasting his potential. To become a scientist or an environmental attorney, he'd have to go to school for many years.

It wasn't fair. Their lives had taken a tragic turn the night their mother was killed and another one when their father disappeared. One minute he'd stepped outside to smoke a cigarette and the next he'd vanished. It amazed Shale how each detail in life could matter so much. Their lives would have been so different if only their parents had been non-smokers.

"Give me the remote, now," she growled.

Shale handed it to her. When the sound came on he threw her a look and she turned the volume down some. He grabbed the blue marker from his pocket, wrote another message and nudged her leg with the board.

If I got a paper route and saved $$$ could I enroll in community college in the fall? I'll memorize the bus schedule so you won't have to drive me.

Harmony's expression softened as she read his words. Red spots blotched her cheeks while tears swelled in her eyes. She nodded and pressed her lips together. "I'm sorry I'm not better at this, Shale. I'm doing my best. Neither of us asked for this. I think about Mom and miss her every single day," she said, her voice cracking as she spoke.

Me too, he scrawled on the corner of the board.

"I wasn't going to tell you this," she said, sniffling. Tears flowed down her cheeks. "I've been saving my residuals for your college. You get that paper route, though. You'll need books, supplies and who knows what else."

Shale dropped the board, wrapped his arms around Harmony's neck and hugged her tight. Although he felt much better, he cried too while Harmony sobbed. He wished he could hug her and write on his board at the same time, but what he had to say could wait.

Once she calmed down, she playfully pushed him away and told him to go get her a soda. He ran into the kitchen, grabbed one from the fridge and brought it to her. As she popped it open and lit another cigarette, he scrawled the words he'd wanted to say on the board and handed it to her.

As long as we're together, everything will be okay.

She read his message and swallowed loudly. When she looked at him fresh tears glistened in her eyes.

"Everything is already okay," she whispered. She put her arm around his shoulders and pulled him close.

Instead of retreating to his bedroom like usual, Shale remained on the sofa next to his sister and watched the episode of *Wonder Kids* even though he'd already seen it dozens of times. When the show ended, he wrote another message on his board for Harmony.

You need to get ready. EBN invited us over at sunset, and I know how long it takes you to get dressed.

She read the message and eyed him suspiciously. "Why?"

You'll see, he wrote. He couldn't help but grin.

Chapter Thirteen: Lessons

The sound of knocking broke the blackness of decompression. I opened my eyes and looked around the dark front chamber. "Slow your molecules," I called.

When I opened the front door, Shale stood nearest, holding two folding metal chairs. I had to look at him twice because since our morning encounter, his dimensions had changed. He appeared taller, more muscular and broader in his shoulders.

I stared at his black t-shirt stretched tight over his sculpted chest and felt my heart flutter. Harmony stood behind him. It was obvious from her pinched expression and mustard-brown energy field that she was annoyed.

"Hi EBN," she said in a strained tone. "Are we bothering you?"

"No," I said, peering outside. The sun burned like an orange ember over the western horizon. The air quality had improved some, but the sky still held a reddish-brown tint. I flipped on the patio light, ducked under the doorway and stepped outside, closing the door behind me. "I told Shale to bring you."

"Do you mind telling me what this is about?" She jerked her head in Shale's direction. "You know how he is."

217

Shale glowered at her as he unfolded the chairs and set them on the patio.

"I offered to teach Shale defensive techniques so he can protect himself."

Harmony's head snapped toward Shale. "What happened and why didn't you tell me about it," she asked sharply.

"He did nothing wrong," I said. "The man-child ambushed him. Shale refused to fight back. I watched the whole thing unfold. That—"

"His name is Tommy," Harmony interjected.

I tilted my head. "He intended to hurt Shale, just as he intended to shoot Princess. I prevented it, but will not be there the next time it happens."

"I don't want Shale fighting anyone. Our social worker was very clear. If he gets in trouble, authorities will remove him from my care and place him in a foster home," Harmony said.

I turned to him. "You understand the difference between fighting and defending yourself, right Shale?"

Shale nodded.

Harmony pulled a candy bar from her pocket, tore the wrapper and took a big bite. "I don't know," she said with a full mouth.

I lowered my head and peered at her over the top of my glasses, directing my energy at her. "I give you my word. Shale will not start fights. He will only defend and protect himself from harm. He must settle this matter himself. There is no other way."

Harmony considered my words. As quickly as a light switch gets flipped, her energy changed to a dazzling shade of lavender. She shrugged and nodded in agreement.

I placed one of the folding chairs near the sliding glass doors and gestured to it. "Please sit here, Harmony."

She shuffled past me. When she plopped down in the chair, her back brushed against my bandaged hands. All of a sudden disgust contorted her face and her chewing slowed.

She glanced down at her half-eaten candy bar and twisted the wrapper closed. "Where's your trash EBN? This candy tastes gross."

"If you set it by the door, I will dispose of it later," I said.

When Harmony got up, I stole a glance at Shale. I watched how the late afternoon sunlight played against his white hair, making him look divine.

My attraction to him was not my fault. I was maturing and had reached the age when my people sought mates. But I had no right being interested in him — he was neither Adelian nor Nadreen, he was too young and worst of all — he was human. He was so handsome, but could never be mine.

Harmony sat down again, pulled a cell phone out of her pocket and flipped it open. "How long is this going to take?"

She is angry. She would rather be at home watching television and feels resentful because she neither knows nor trusts me.

"That all depends on Shale," I said, smiling despite the incessant throbbing in my leg. I stepped near the front door and pointed to the wall space next to it. "Come stand as straight as you can with your back pressed against the wall, Shale."

He followed my instruction, but his shoulders fell forward. When he glanced at me from the corner of his eye, his eyes did not wiggle and the force behind them disoriented me. My heart was overruling my brain. I looked down as the corners of my mouth curled.

"To be an effective fighter, you must have a solid stance. The foundation of a solid stance is good posture."

Shale stood straight as a pole. His facial muscles contracted and pushed his eyes shut.

"Excellent. Hold that position. Is it uncomfortable?"

Shale nodded.

"Then you are doing it right," I said. "Place your hand on your belly, like this." I demonstrated, placing my bandaged hand over my stomach.

Shale copied my movement.

"Squeeze your abdominal muscles for five counts. Focus your attention on those muscles. Contract and hold ... hold ... hold ... release and inhale."

While Shale practiced, his shoulders rolled forward.

"Shoulders against the wall," I instructed.

Shale straightened his posture.

I glanced at Harmony. She smirked, flipped open her phone again and glanced at the time.

"Good," I said. I picked up the second folding chair and moved it to the edge of the patio, so that it faced Harmony. I sat down then lowered my body onto the concrete by holding onto the chair's frame. "Now come over here and lay down, facing me."

Once Shale was situated an arm's length away, I said, "A strong midsection is very important. Do you perform abdominal exercises?"

Shale frowned and shook his head.

I demonstrated the Sent exercises known as prone and side planks. While I explained the proper form, I felt his eyes on me and glanced up.

He stared at me and flashed a bold, flirty smile. Although I was not trying to read his mind, his thoughts flew into my head.

She's the most beautiful girl I've ever seen. What's she doing here all alone? Where is her family? I love her cinnamon smell and velvety voice. I could listen to her speak all night long.

I felt my face flush, looked away and blurted, "Your turn."

Shale's face clenched and twisted as he performed each exercise. "Keep your tummy tight. Hold it. Remember to breathe," I said. I counted backwards each time, observing and adjusting his form as needed. Toward the end of the third set, every muscle in his body shook, but he did not give up. When he finished, his breathing sounded ragged. I told him good job and to rest.

Shale sat up and looked at me. "No offense, EBN, but this is crap. When do I start training—for real," he asked.

I chuckled and glanced over his shoulder at Harmony. Her mouth fell open and she dropped her phone. It landed on the concrete with a *clack*.

"Spoken like a true warrior," I said. "Stand up." I raised my arms. "Please help me up?"

Careful to avoid my bandages, Shale pulled me up by my wrists. I expected his touch to send sparks shooting through my body, but I was unprepared for my blood to evacuate my addled brain and rush to my reproductive organs. As I inhaled deeply to clear my mind, I realized I could no more control how I felt than with whom I fell in love.

"Each lesson will build on the one before it. One must master basic moves to build strength and prevent injury. I was not going to show you fighting stance until tomorrow, but I will, provided you agree to complete a homework assignment."

Shale nodded vigorously.

"Then we will begin with strike techniques tomorrow." I smiled and glanced at Harmony again. Her aura turned midnight blue and her lower lip trembled. She wiped at the corners of her eyes.

"Stand up straight, feet hip width apart. Which is your dominant hand—the one you write with?"

Shale raised his out hand.

"Take one step forward with your in—I mean, left foot."

Shale did as instructed.

"Not quite that far," I said. I slowly crouched down and adjusted Shale's foot to the correct position. "Bend your knees. Gently bounce up and down. Hold that position. Now, put your hands on your hips and without moving your feet, twist side to side from your waist, keeping your tummy tight." I winced as I rose. In a blur, Shale's hands shot forward and helped me to my feet. My knees buckled and I swooned against him.

"Are you okay, EBN?"

I drew a deep, slow breath and nodded, finding my strength. Then I got into my stance and demonstrated the action.

"Like this," Shale asked, twisting slowly from side to side.

"Exactly," I said. "Keep your back straight. Now count to forty."

As Shale counted off his side twists, I limped over to Harmony. "Louder," I called over my shoulder, "keep your back straight." I looked down at her. Her face was puffy and tear-stained. "Are you all right," I asked in a low voice.

"Nineteen...twenty...twenty-one...twenty-two...twenty-three," Shale called out.

She nodded. "Thank you," she whispered. Tears flooded her eyes. "That's the first time he's spoken in over five months. The doctors warned me he might never ... Thank—y-y," her voice cracked with emotion.

I gave a single nod, raised my bandaged hand to my lips and patted her shoulder with my other hand. Harmony cleared her throat and took a deep breath.

"Twenty-nine…thirty…thirty-one…thirty-two."

I limped back to Shale and stood in front of him. "Well done," said I.

Shale beamed at me. He rubbed his stomach and felt his sides. "My stomach hurts," he said.

Pain blasted up my injured leg. Suddenly dizzy, I sank into the folding chair. "You will feel sore at first, but this shall pass," I advised. "Warriors endure much pain. The question is, can you handle it?"

Shale grinned and nodded.

It was easier to concentrate with some distance between us. "Very well. Your assignment for tonight is three-fold. Practice standing straight, practice holding your stance and perform five additional sets of planks like I showed you."

Shale groaned.

"Warriors neither groan nor whine," I said in a quiet yet firm tone. "Understood?"

"Yes," Shale said.

"That concludes your first lesson. Shall we continue tomorrow?"

"Definitely," Shale said with enthusiasm.

I yawned and held out my bandaged hands again. "Would you help me up?"

"What happened to your hands, EBN?

I cleared my throat. "I ... um ... fell onto a cactus," I lied.

Shale pulled me to my feet. I folded the chair and handed it to him. I found their presence comforting and did not wish to send them away, but I needed rest.

"See you tomorrow then," he said.

"Okay."

Harmony handed me the folding chair upon which she had been sitting. "Why don't you hang onto this," she suggested. Then she gently nudged Shale with her elbow. "What do you say?"

"Thanks for the lesson, EBN," Shale said. Harmony wrapped her arm around Shale's waist and squeezed.

"You are most welcome," I said before ducking inside the barracks.

In spite of the heroic efforts of firefighter crews from all over the United States, the wildfires continued their path of destruction. I rested in a reclining chair and watched the news footage until decompression overcame me.

These fires were the largest in California's history and had been named "The Station Fire." Witnessing the devastation first hand confirmed my suspicions about climate change and Sents' survival on Erox. It saddened me to share something so terrible with my new friends. Neither of us had much time left.

The next afternoon, there was a knock on the barrack's door. Expecting it to be Shale, I opened it and found Harmony standing alone on the patio. There was a familiarity about her face and smile that still bewildered me.

The black silk blouse she wore complimented her amber energy field, glowing skin and shining hair, which hung in loose spiral curls. It was the first time she had worn make-up and styled her hair. "Where is Shale?"

Harmony's full glossy lips spread into a gorgeous smile. "He'll be along in a second," she said, barely above a whisper. "I wanted to talk to you before he got here." She stepped closer and embraced me.

"What is it?"

"He's talking, EBN, like he never went mute," she whispered incredulously as she released me. "You must understand, he hasn't uttered a word since our mother died, but last night, after your lesson, he was a total chatterbox.

"He told me about finding you at the boulder outcropping. He knew you were in trouble and was so excited to help, especially after what you did for him." Her tone rose in delight at the end of the sentence.

"Do you know why he went to the rock formation?"

Harmony's mood darkened and her expression fell. "He was probably looking for our father. Now that he's speaking again he'll probably tell you all about it," she said with a roll of her eyes.

I nodded although I did not fully understand. I shifted my weight to my left leg and pain rocked my whole body. I sucked in my breath and grasped the door by the handle.

"I don't mean to over step my bounds, but Shale told me that you'd injured your leg. If you need to see a doctor I'd be happy to drive you," she said.

"That will not be necessary," I said. I heard footsteps and Shale appeared around the corner of the barracks. In the overnight hours, he had grown even taller and more muscular. We were almost the same height now. I wondered if Harmony had noticed and what she thought of her brother's rapid growth.

"Hey bud," Harmony said, chipper once again. She reached up and ruffled his hair.

"Don't," he said, scowling and ducking away from her hand.

"I'll leave you two to it," she said, smiling and walking away.

Suddenly I worried how I might behave in the absence of our chaperone.

I grabbed the metal folding chair from inside the front door, opened it and sat down. "How is the young warrior?"

227

Shale smiled. "Fine," he said. Out of habit, his shoulders rounded and slouched forward but he quickly corrected himself and straightened his back.

I nodded my approval. "Very good. Every time you notice yourself slouching, correct your posture, like you just did."

"I did my homework last night," Shale said, pushing his hair out of his face. "My muscles are still sore."

"Like I said yesterday, there is never growth without pain, Shale."

Shale laughed under his breath.

"And when life presses your back against the wall, always remember to stand straight and meet your challenges head on."

Shale nodded.

"Enough philosophy," I said. "Time to warm-up. Give me thirty jumping jacks, thirty push-ups and three sets of planks," I instructed.

A pained expression formed on Shale's face.

My eyebrows arched over my sunglasses. "Or, we can forget the whole thing and you can go home," I warned.

Without protesting, Shale performed the warm-up exercises. By the time he was done, he was breathing heavy but he stood straight and waited for more instruction.

"The techniques I will show you require proper form. The practitioner must have a strong stance. Like I mentioned yesterday, you cannot achieve a strong stance with weak posture. There is also another reason to practice good posture. Do you know what that is?"

Shale shook his head.

"We communicate with our bodies. Our bodies' language transcends verbal language. Standing straight says a Being is confident and self-assured. Slouching, on the other hand, broadcasts insecurity and attracts bullies, like that man-child. You study physics, Shale?"

Shale's eyes widened. "How did you know?"

"Suspicion. By incorporating physics into defensive techniques, one has the advantage over their opponent."

Shale's eyes narrowed. "But Tommy outweighs me by twenty or thirty pounds."

I shrugged. "Weight has its advantages, but height is an even greater advantage. Your arms are longer. He will have to move closer, which makes him more vulnerable.

"By using the elements of surprise, speed and ferocity in attack, you can overcome any opponent, regardless of size or weight. Now get into your stance and raise your arms."

Shale did as instructed. "EBN, how do you know this stuff?"

"I learned, the same as you."

I appreciate what you're doing for me, EBN. Someday I hope the world won't have people like Tommy Nutter in it."

"We can never control what is in a person's mind or heart, but we can hold them accountable for their behavior." I slowly stood and got into my stance facing Shale.

I should have known better standing less than an arm's length from him. The air between us crackled with electricity. Our eyes met and held. Before I knew what was happening, he leaned toward me and I toward him. For a moment, all my cares fell away as our lips brushed in a tender kiss. And another.

Until guilt intruded upon the moment's pleasure and gnawed at my stomachs. "Stop," I whispered. I placed my hand against his chest and gently pushed him away.

Crimson flamed his cheeks; he slipped his hand over mine. "I'm—I'm sorry," he blurted. His brow furrowed in confusion.

"We must not do that. I have broken too many rules already," I said, retreating a step and pulling my hand from his.

I felt terrible as Shale's expression changed from confused to sad, but we were growing too close and my feelings scared me. Soon I would have to avoid him, for fear of saying or doing something telling. But for now, I pushed those thoughts from my mind.

"Watch me," I said, shaking my head to clear it. I raised my arms and made fists with my bandaged hands. "When you strike your opponent, your objective is to hit them with the force of your entire body behind your strike. If I do this," I said, pulling my arm back and thrusting it forward in slow motion, "it is not as powerful as if I do this." I pulled my arm back and thrust it forward again while simultaneously twisting my torso and hips.

"What did you mean when you said that you'd broken too many rules already?"

I closed my eyes a moment, disgusted with myself. "I cannot discuss it, Shale."

"Why not?"

"Do you want to learn self-defense or not?"

"I do."

"Then pay attention. I am going to do it again," I said. "This time watch my foot." I demonstrated the punch once more. "See how I raise my foot and pivot on my toes? Only your heel should come off the ground."

"Let me try," Shale said.

I stood beside him and watched him practice the striking technique. It was not long before Shale mastered the move. I felt pleased that he learned at lightning fast speed.

I demonstrated the same move using my opposite arm and instructed Shale to do the same. As he practiced, I kept a safe distance and evaluated his form.

"You never answered my question," he said with a sideways glance.

"In my culture, things are done a certain way."

"What culture is that?"

I smiled and shook my head. "You are persistent."

"You have no idea," he warned.

I laughed. "Oh, I think I do." I studied his movements. What were you doing in the desert yesterday, Shale? Were you looking for me?"

"No. I was collecting trash and looking for my dad," he said.

"Why were you looking for him in the desert?"

"One night last month he stepped outside to smoke a cigarette and never came back. Didn't take anything with him except the clothes on his back and his wedding band. He left his wallet, keys, everything.

"There's been no activity on his credit cards or bank account since. There was no sign of a struggle, and there were no footprints or tire tracks in the sand. He just vanished." Shale switched arms and continued practicing. "Days before it happened he told me about a vortex he discovered out there, except he called it a door. Anyway, I've been searching that whole desert for signs of him ever since he disappeared."

I sank into the folding metal chair and stared at Shale with wide eyes. "That is terrible. Have you found anything?"

"No, but I'm going to find him. I know it."

"Then I am certain you will. Tell me more about this door. Did he say where it leads?"

Shale frowned. "He didn't know that."

"Did he show you where this door is located?"

Shale shook his head. "He never got the chance."

"Oh," I said, dejected.

"I found it since, though — at least I think it's the same place," Shale offered.

I perked up and straightened in my seat. "Would you take me there?"

"Sure," Shale quipped. "Wanna go tomorrow, after school?"

"Yes, I would," I said.

We practiced all afternoon until twilight. Before sending Shale home, I gave him another exercise intensive homework assignment. Then I limped inside the barracks to decompress before tomorrow's journey.

Chapter Fourteen: Rings

It is the Nadreen New Year, also known as Rings. The holiday occurs during Rainy season, when the icebergs melt and shelas rise to normal levels.

Although the Conservatory is a secular institution, the liquid crystal hallways shimmer with images of two enjoined gold rings and green and white twinkling lights in honor of the occasion.

I fidget in my front row seat in Sent Studies before slumping down and letting out a loud sigh. It will be another holiday season without EBN. I stretch my long legs and pretend to read the assignment on my tabletop computer, a scholarly article entitled, *Arrests Continue in Response to Protectorate Bans,* but my concentration falters, my eyes drift up and I look around the class chamber.

The students' seats are arranged in concentric circles with ramped aisles dividing the chamber into four sections. I watch Conservator Faux's back as the reptilian Seemae lumbers up one of the aisles.

Her scaly, green-brown skin reminds me of mold, partly because she smells like moist soil and rotting leaf litter. Red vertical slit pupils divide her yellow eyes. Her nose is small and flat. She has no hair, only two bony ridges rising from her brow. Dents on the sides of her head serve for ears.

Her clawed hands have three fingers and an opposable thumb. I haven't seen her feet but imagine they are equally ugly. A long tail with bony protrusions trails behind her. She holds it high, never letting it touch the ground. When she's irritated, she lowers and swings it back and forth, often tripping distracted students.

I have no Seemae friends and Faux is my first Seemae conservator. Seemaes do not possess the ability to vibe. However, they possess an extraordinary talent neither Nadreens nor Adelians possess. Seemaes shift shape and I admire this quality. They also project their thought energy toward enemies when threatened. I know very little about this defensive measure and hope to never learn about it first hand.

Under the desktop, my fingers trace the outline of my computer in my pocket. I compulsively check it but refrain for now, rather than risk losing it permanently to Conservator Faux.

I attempt re-reading the article's opening paragraph, but I forget what it says as soon as I read it. I miss EBN. Two seasons have passed since my Ascension. So far, no one has heard from my sister, and I can't help but think the worst. I know she is busy but her silence makes no sense.

Conservator Faux's soprano voice yanks my attention back to class. There was an assignment due today but I forgot about it until I entered the chamber. It's my first missed assignment in an otherwise flawless academic career and if my inability to concentrate continues, it won't be my last.

When class ends, I file out with the other students and head down the hallway with my thoughts still on EBN.

Deep in thought, I rush from the Pyramid II building to Pyramid III, the research building. My lab partner, Tibnor-Styr, arrived first and sits at our station in the back of the chamber. Tibnor usually studies or completes his assignments prior to class, but today his aqua face and dark, compound eyes stare at the door. Tibnor is also of mixed heritage and one of the few Adelian students who ages backwards, like Sents. I suspect this is the reason that the math applications conservator assigned us to the same team.

I walk over, sling my favorite, Sent-style blue backpack on the hover table and sit down.

"Tibnor."

"Greetings, Aix," Tibnor says. His smile lifts his aqua cheeks and the corners of his coal-black eyes.

"Why so happy," I ask in a flat tone.

"I'm Matter Transferring home early today. I meant to transmit last night, but I've been so excited I forgot," he says.

My eyebrows draw together. "What's the occasion?"

"My brother is coming home on leave to celebrate Rings." Tibnor minimizes his computer and slips it into his trouser pocket. "I'm leaving now, but wanted to tell you before I went home. Sorry to leave you alone."

"Don't be," I say, shaking my head. "I didn't realize you had a brother in the Forces. Where's he stationed?"

Tibnor stands up and pushes his floating seat under the hovering lab table. "He's a Guardian, stationed on PLEXUS." He removes his computer. "Look at this holograph he transmitted." Tibnor maximizes his computer and sets it on the table.

"My sister, EBN, is a Guardian of the Sky, too," I say.

Tibnor's eyes widen. "Isn't that strange? We've been lab partners for lunar cycles and never knew that about each another." His fingers fly over his computer's interface and a holograph appears on the computer's screen.

The holograph shows a group of thirteen uniformed pilots assembled in two rows. Six pilots kneel in front while the remaining seven stand behind them. A few pilots smile and make silly gestures; others wear cold, serious expressions. I recognize their black uniforms with iridescent undertones—it's the same uniform EBN wore the last time I saw her.

"Which one is your brother," I ask.

Tibnor points to one of the pilots in the first row. "That's Roshlend."

I nod as I lean closer to the computer screen and scan the other pilot's faces. Twelve are Adelian. There is only one Obe among the group. EBN is not among them. "How many pilot groups are stationed on PLEXUS? Do you know?"

Tibnor nods. "Just theirs. Can you believe only thirteen pilots are responsible for patrolling all the space sectors surrounding PLEXUS? Of course, that will change once the station is fully operational, but at the current rate of construction, who knows when that will be."

My stomach clenches. "Only thirteen pilots," I repeat despite the constriction in my throat. "When did your brother deploy?"

Tibnor minimizes his computer again. "Last Scyros cycle. What about your sister?"

I swallow hard. "The same. Does he send you lots of transmissions?"

Tibnor nods. "Several every lunar cycle." He glances at the chronometer on the chamber wall. "I've got to get to Matter Transference Chamber, or he'll get home before I do." He pockets his computer. "I already submitted my portion of our lab work. Until tomorrow's light, Aix."

"By tomorrow's light," I say. I watch Tibnor hurry out of the chamber. As I wait for class to start, I calculate the likelihood of finding EBN at home, waiting to surprise me after school.

Something tells me the odds aren't very good.

I struggle to pay attention during math applications lab and am thankful when the nourishment chimes sound. I meander to the seventh floor of Pyramid I to meet Nyl and Xtarr. It's a long walk between buildings. Not that it matters. It gives me time to think and thanks to my conversation with Tibnor, I have much to think about.

I enter the expansive nourishment chamber and scan the student's faces. Xtarr's wispy plum dress stands out against the other students' black and white uniforms. She and Nyl sit on the patio underneath the retractable windows, which are closed due to the pouring rain. As usual, they're in the middle of an argument, but they stop when I approach. I set my backpack on the hover table and sit down.

Xtarr frowns and glances at Nyl. "You don't look good, Aix," she says.

"What's wrong," Nyl asks, shoveling vegetables into his mouth.

I glance past them and look out the window. Thick fog veils the view of Sheltdonic. "I failed my math applications lab," I mutter. I fold my arms on the table and rest my head on them.

Xtarr's mouth falls open. "No."

Nyl chews on his upper lip. "You ought to go home and rest."

"It won't help," I say in a low voice. "I can't decompress."

"Still no word from EBN," Xtarr says in a sad tone. She reaches out and squeezes my arm.

I raise my head and rest my chin on my arms. "No."

"Go get some nourishment," Nyl suggests. "You'll feel better."

I shake my head. "I can't eat." I tell them about my conversation with Tibnor. Xtarr and Nyl watch me intently and listen.

When I finish speaking, Xtarr asks, "What are you going to do?"

I shake my head and shrug. "I don't know. I can't talk to A-ma. When A-da visited us on the ships, I tried talking to him, but he's distracted by Protectorate issues on Nilotic. I think he's unwilling to see the truth."

"I wish there was something we could do," Xtarr says quietly. She glances down at the table looking miserable.

"What was the assignment for class," I ask.

Nyl glances at Xtarr with a worried expression. "You didn't read the article? Aix, you've got to get it together."

"That's my point, Nyl. I'm useless. I can't focus, I can't eat, I can't decompress," I say. "I'm sorry to burden you." I know my reliance on my friends is wearing thin, but I don't know what else to do, except hack into the PLEXUS mainframe and search for answers there.

"Don't be so hard on him." Xtarr maximizes her computer and slides it across the table. "Just reword your answers, so suspicions aren't raised."

"Thanks, Xtarr," I say, smiling wistfully.

240

"You're not helping him," Nyl grumbles.

"If it were one of us, he'd do the same, wouldn't you?" Xtarr says, scolding Nyl.

"Of course."

Nyl rolls his eyes.

"How dare you?" Xtarr scoffs. "Stop acting jealous," she shoots him an angry look.

"I'm simply stating the obvious since you didn't notice," Nyl says, scowling at her before looking at me. "Keep some originality in mind with respect to this assignment," he warns in a low voice. "It's got multiple parts. There's a presentation due next lunar cycle based on your answers."

I smile gratefully at each of them. "Thank you both. I don't know what I'd do without you right now." I hesitate then turn my attention to the assignment. There is so much more I want to say, but I can't bring myself to utter the words. Discussing my feelings won't change a thing for EBN, or the dangers she faces — wherever she is.

At the day's end, I decline Xtarr's invitation for a ride home and Matter Transfer home instead. Although there are several Matter Transference Chambers in each of the Conservatory's pyramids, student use is not permitted without an approval code, issued either by a conservator or a student's parents. For this reason I'd hacked into A-da's computer when we were on the ships and stole his parental code, in case I ever needed to use it.

I linger after class until the brightly lit corridors of the seventh floor are empty, then I walk to the end of the hall where two Matter Transference Chambers are located. I stand before the titanium door, sweep my open palm over it and the door raises open. I step into the Chamber, enter my destination's coordinates and A-da's code into the sequencer panel.

An automated voice confirms my destination and the door lowers. Before I can blink, I'm thrust into blackness.

Just as quickly, it's over. A high pitch rings in my ears, piercing my eardrums. My teeth chatter and my body pulses with fierce tingling.

The Chamber door lifts open. As I step out of the Chamber in my family's home, I notice a change in the gathering chamber's decor. Three Sent relics—Dogon tribal masks from the West African Republic of Mali—hang on the wall opposite the Chamber door. Voices carry from the second floor, but I can't make out words. Has EBN come home? My heart jumps at the thought.

The smells of evening nourishment waft through the house, stimulating my appetite. I creep silently through the gathering chamber, foyer and up the grand elliptical walkway to the second floor.

Near the top of the stairs I recognize Gran-Ada's raspy voice and my excitement falls into disappointment. Gran-Ada hasn't visited in many lunar cycles. I wonder what occasion brings him here. Dread tightens my stomach. I hope he hasn't come with bad news. Although eavesdropping is a serious offense, I listen from the hallway instead of joining them.

"Preece, you must take action now. You said yourself he's not like other Adelian boys his age — he's highly emotional, his studies are suffering and it's only going to get worse," Eesh says. "There are special schools that address these kinds of problems."

I move closer to the entryway and see Eesh standing in the nourishment chamber with A-ma. Eesh watches her over the rim of his teacup as he sips.

"He attends a special school," Preece contradicts. "The prestigious Adelian Conservatory, or have you forgotten, A-da?" Her eyes narrow and she crosses her thin arms over her chest. "If you think I am going to let you send both my offspring away then you have forgotten who I am," she says.

"Preece, whatever do you mean? I haven't forgotten where your offspring goes to school, but these symptoms require immediate attention," Eesh says, stepping closer to her. He sets his teacup on the counter and rubs her arms. "I only want what's best for your family."

I peek into the nourishment chamber again, but it is empty save for Eesh and Preece. Where are Eesh's escorts? The Seemae Rebel Faction, or SRF, still transmits threats through the media. Why is he unprotected? And why is he emulating Sent speech patterns when he abhors casual speech? I hope he's not ill.

"A-ma, Gran-Ada," I say casually as I enter the stark white chamber. I bow, touch foreheads with my elders and throw my backpack on the floor.

Anger rages in Preece's eyes. "This conversation is over, A-da. I have a ceremony to conduct this evening," she says and exits the chamber.

"Aix," Eesh says, clapping me on the back. "I thought I sensed another's presence." He glances down at my backpack. "Is that a Sent relic I see?"

"No Gran-Ada. All the backpacks in my collection are Adelian-made imitations." I open cabinets and drawers, looking for snacks.

Eesh smiles. "That's an excellent imitation. You're expected to follow the law, like anyone else," he says. "No special priority for family of Protectorate Council Beings." He leans closer to me and lowers his voice. "Although if it were my decision to make, you would get special priority," he says, winking.

"Gran-Ada, is EBN well? Where is she?"

Eesh's gray compound eyes glitter. "The Guardian fares well. I believe she returned to the PLEXUS way station and is being debriefed."

"Oh." I give Eesh a weak half-smile and am happy when Preece reenters the nourishment chamber. "A-ma, when's evening nourishment going to be ready," I ask.

"Not long," she answers. "Staying for nourishment A-da?"

Eesh pulls on his hat and coat. "No, duty calls," he says. He turns to me, leaning forward. "Family above all—"

I touch my forehead to his and look into his close-set, gray compound eyes. Beady eyes. "We are all family," I reply.

Eesh turns and exits the chamber. Preece follows behind him.

When Preece returns, I'm waiting for her. Her white silk gown with emerald trim brushes her slender ankles. I lean against the countertop and stare at the simmering pot of plush leaves on the cooking surface. "A-ma, what's the story with the African tribal masks hanging in the gathering chamber?"

"Those were a Rings gift to A-da from Gran-Ada," she says, adjusting her emerald hood. "Why?"

"You have to give them back. We could be arrested."

"I will do no such thing. They are a gift to your A-da and it is his decision what to do with them—not yours and certainly not mine."

"Gran-Ada questioned me about my backpack. He asked if it was a Sent relic."

Preece looks at me. *What is on your mind, Aix,* she vibes.

Don't you find that an odd gift, especially since the Protectorate has banned Sent relics?

Preece shrugs. "I am certain he procured them before the bans went into effect."

Did he provide the necessary documentation proving the date of acquisition?

She regards me with a steady, measured stare. She is losing patience.

"I overheard part of your conversation when I came in," I confess. "How can he talk about sending me away one moment, and then moments later, when we're alone, tell me that if it were up to him, family members of Protectorate Council Beings would receive special treatment?"

"He is concerned about you," she says. "I ought to punish you for eavesdropping."

"I don't understand Gran-Ada's change in attitude. And did you notice his speech? He's never used casual speech before," I say.

"Aix," Preece says, lifting the lid off a simmering pot and stirring the contents, "we all change. He is getting older, and being the newly elected Protectorate High Chancellor ... he has greater responsibilities now."

"But, wouldn't that make him stricter?" I shake my head. "Something doesn't feel right."

"Perhaps your discomfort stems from something else?"

I consider her words. "What do you mean?"

"You have changed too, since EBN deployed."

"I have?" Her mention of EBN's deployment surprises me.

"Certainly. You're serious now. I haven't heard you laugh since before she left. I miss the sound of your laughter." She reaches out and strokes my cheek. "It is the Eve of a new Scyros cycle. Accompany me to the Ceremony. Xtarr will be there."

I consider it but shake my head. I have something else in mind for the evening. "Thanks, but I've got a pile of homework." I pick up my backpack, shoulder it and head down the hall.

I enter our decompression chamber and sit at my desktop computer. I open several screens on the surface before removing my computer from my pocket. After maximizing it to full size, I use both computers to hack into the Protectorate's mainframe on the PLEXUS way station. It doesn't take long to locate and access the personnel files for the Beings involved in the station's operations and defense. With a series of sharp thoughts, I write an encrypted computer program designed to search for information on EBN. Then I run it.

I wait and wait and wait some more until the prompt, 'no information found,' appears on the computer screen. Puzzled, I repeat the search but receive the same response, so I glance through my program. It contains no errors. However, before attempting the search again, I erase the name EBN-Reyoz-X and enter Tibnor's brother's name, Roshlend-Styr. Immediately several new screens pop open on my desktop, displaying every piece of data on Guardian pilot Roshlend-Styr.

Bile rises in my esophagus and burns the back of my throat. Eesh lied to me. EBN is nowhere near the PLEXUS station.

Chapter Fifteen: The Door

I awoke early on my tenth day in-terra. While I showered, large pieces of skin suit peeled off my injured leg and slipped down the drain. I stared at my teal left leg, now exposed from hip to toe, as were both of my four-fingered hands.

A numb feeling came over me as I dried myself and bandaged my leg. Infection raged through my body but there was no medicine or entropy solution left. There was nothing else I could do except wait. As I dressed in Sent clothes and bandaged my hands to hide my skin, I felt exhausted yet also relieved that my end was drawing near.

Wildfires continued to scorch the surrounding mountains but news reports stated they were contained and would soon be under control. That was more than could be said about the oil spill in the Gulf. Without health advisories urging Sents to stay home, I anticipated more would visit the barracks and seek me out.

In spite of my ill and weakened state, I limped to the front door. When I opened it, a mound of stuffed animals and cellophane wrapped flowers fell into the entryway, rolling over my boots. Sents had adhered greeting cards and handwritten signs to the front door. Another pyramid of cards, flowers and stuffed animals leaned against the sliding patio doors. Burning sticks of incense and white religious candles lined the patio's outer edges; some candles sported gold chains draped around their glass containers.

With the offerings crowding the patio, the Sent queue extended into the desert. I limped outside and greeted those assembled by shaking their hands.

At the queue's center, I encountered a bespectacled Sent waiting in a wheelchair. He smoked a hand-rolled cigarette that gave off a pungent odor. As I neared him, I unintentionally inhaled a smoke plume and staggered sideways, suddenly lightheaded.

The Sent's name was Herb. Underneath the rosy aura haloing him, a black bandana covered his silver-white hair. Colorful tattoos sleeved both arms. Chunky silver rings winked in the bright sunlight near knobby knuckles. Herb stroked the length of his snow-white beard and flattened it against his barrel chest.

When I touched Herb's hand, the man jolted as if electrocuted. His aura pulsed while his body reconfigured its circuitry. In a flash, his energy field changed to the color of moss. Herb relaxed into his seat and bowed his head.

"Thank you, Messiah," he murmured.

I smiled sadly. "I am no Messiah," I replied.

Herb looked up. Sky blue eyes peered over the rims of his round, mirrored glasses and met my gaze. "Then what are you?"

"I am Being—the same as you."

Herb scoffed under his breath and shook his head. He scooted to the edge of his seat, lifted the chair's metal footrests and placed his feet on the ground.

"In 2003, a motorcycle accident left me paralyzed from the waist down. I underwent surgeries, saw every specialist in the country, but none could restore my legs." Herb slowly rose from the chair, took an uneasy step and swayed forward. I caught his arms and steadied him.

"Until today," Herb said, his voice thick with emotion. He took one more step, then another and shrugged out of my grasp.

"I CAN WALK!" Herb yelled, thrusting his arms overhead. He tossed his wheelchair aside. "Who needs that little rabbit when I can ride a HOG!"

The Sents queued behind him broke out in whispers and applause.

A wide smile stretched across Herb's tan face. He jerked his thumb in my direction and said, "Who needs universal healthcare with this girl around, eh?"

And with that Herb strutted off, leaving his wheelchair behind.

After tending to the sick and injured, I returned to the barracks, pushing Herb's wheelchair before me. When I reached the patio, I placed Herb's chair in the corner in case he returned for it, collected the offerings and tossed everything inside the front chamber. Then I collapsed in the nearest reclining chair.

At 3:00 p.m., I answered the knock at the barracks door. Harmony and Shale stood next to four stacked white chairs and a matching plastic table.

"Hello," she said in a cheery voice. Shale nodded his head.

"Hello," I replied, noticing Shale's straight posture and muscled physique. He grew more and more irresistible every day. I tore my eyes away, committed to controlling myself. I stepped onto the patio and closed the door. It was hot and hazy outside.

"We brought you a gift," Harmony chirped. "Patio furniture."

I looked at her, then at the furniture. A thin layer of dust was visible against the white surfaces. "Where did you get it?"

"It belonged to a very sweet couple renting a lot on Hematite Drive — Neil and Laurie from New Jersey. I'm sorry to see them go, but they've got asthma and can't breathe with the smoke and ash in the air."

I nodded and coughed into my hand. I knew exactly how the couple from New Jersey felt.

252

"They came to the office this morning on their way out of town and asked me if I wanted this patio set. You were the first one I thought of," she said, lifting her chin and smiling at me.

"Why don't you keep it," I said.

They shook their heads. "We already have some and never use it. Besides, with this fabulous awning, your patio is perfect. We want you to have it."

I cocked my head and pressed my lips together. They had given so much yet asked for nothing in return except friendship.

"Thank you," I said in a quiet voice.

"You're welcome," she said, obviously pleased I had accepted. "Shale, help me get her set up." She looked down and dragged her shoe across the patio. "Disgusting wildfire ash."

I nodded in agreement.

"Do you have a broom? I'll sweep it up for you."

"I do not," I replied.

"Shale, will you go next door and grab our broom please?" she said.

He nodded and turned to go.

I shook my head. "That is not necessary Harmony. It is fine." I covered my mouth and let out a steady procession of coughs. Feeling weak, I leaned against the closed door.

"I don't know if you've been watching the news, but if the winds shift and those wildfires jump down here, we'll have to evacuate," Harmony warned. She glanced at Shale and back at me. "If that happens, you must come with us."

253

"I will not be here much longer," I muttered as stars twinkled in my field of vision. My knees buckled and I swayed sideways.

When I opened my eyes, I sat in the dark and cluttered front chamber in my recliner. Harmony and Shale stood on either side of the chair looking down at me.

"Are you okay," said Shale.

"You gave us a scare," Harmony said.

"I am fine," I said in a hoarse voice. "Just tired." I pushed out of the recliner and slowly stood. "I stayed up too late watching wildfire coverage."

Harmony and Shale exchanged a long glance then looked at me.

"If you say so," Harmony muttered. She glanced at her watch. "I've gotta go to work. You two have fun and be careful." She walked toward the door then turned and looked at Shale. "Don't let EBN overdo it today, okay Bud?"

"I won't," Shale said.

Shale's third lesson exceeded my expectations. After we finished, I asked if he was ready to go.

"You should wear a hat," Shale warned. He pulled a camouflage boonie hat from his back pocket and put it on.

I nodded and entered the barracks. I returned a moment later wearing the sombrero.

254

Shale burst into laughter.

I frowned and touched the sombrero's wide straw brim.

"I'm sorry," Shale said. He forced a neutral expression but could not contain himself and snickered. "You can wear one of mine," he said and disappeared around the barracks' corner.

I tossed the sombrero inside and secured the barracks.

When Shale reappeared, binoculars hung from a strap around his neck and rested against his chest. He held a second, identical camouflage boonie hat and gave it to me. "Try it; make sure it fits," he said.

I put on the hat. It fit like a new skin suit. "Let us go," I said.

Shale led the way and I limped behind him. Heat baked our backs while we crossed the field beyond the barracks. I glanced across the desert expanse. Only three wildflowers bloomed throughout the entire field.

Neither of us spoke until we neared the dry riverbed. "Time passes so slowly here," I said.

Shale wrinkled his nose. "You mean in Lancaster?"

"Of course," I answered. "What else would I mean?" I coughed into my bandaged hand.

We turned and walked east along the riverbed banks, toward an old couch someone had dumped. I eyed it as we passed.

"This hat belongs to your A-d—father, doesn't it," I asked.

"Yep," Shale said.

I stopped to catch my breath, bent forward at the waist and launched into a spastic coughing fit. Shale rushed over and stood nearby. I looked around for something to rest against, limped to the couch and motioned for Shale to follow. Gasping for air, phlegm rattled in my chest.

Shale squatted low beside me and placed his hand on my back. "You should see a doctor about that cough."

I leaned against the couch arm and nodded. His concerned look touched my heart. After I caught my breath, I said, "What do you think happened to your father?"

"I think he was taken."

"By whom?"

"Aliens."

I winced and coughed for a long time. When the attack subsided, I said, "Distasteful word, that one is — Alien," I blurted in an accusing, malicious tone. "I realize you speak of extragalactic entities, but I am fascinated at the way Americans differentiate and discriminate." I coughed again. "Where I come from —," I stopped speaking and felt my expression pucker.

I looked up, turned my head this way and that as if searching the air for words. "What I meant to say was that word — alien — has a negative connotation, largely because of your country's obsession with citizenship. Just because something is different, that does not make it bad. Can we agree to refer to non-native entities as 'Beings,' as in extragalactic Beings?"

Shale nodded. "I can do that."

256

"Good," I said. My eyebrow arched over my sunglasses. "Now what makes you think extragalactic Beings abducted him?"

Shale lowered his voice. "Can you keep a secret?"

If only he knew. "Yes."

"You can't tell anyone, especially not Harmony okay?"

I nodded. "You have my word."

"Have you met Mrs. Perkins? She lives across the street from us, next to the stop sign."

"No, I have not."

"She's a really nice lady, but she doesn't go out much. She's got agoraphobia and is scared to leave her house. Anyway, the night my dad went missing, Mrs. Perkins was in the back of her house, getting ready for bed. Out of nowhere, her dog Henry jumps off her bed and goes tearing down the hall, barking like crazy. Mrs. Perkins thought someone was breaking into her house, so she got her baseball bat for protection.

"When she stepped into the hallway, the brightest light she'd ever seen was shining into her living room windows. Keep in mind that it was after midnight, there was a new moon that night and all the lights in the front of her house were off. Meanwhile, Henry was standing at the front door in the living room, barking and whining like someone was beating him, so she looked out her windows to see where the light was coming from.

"She saw a cone of light shining onto our patio, with my dad inside it. She couldn't see what caused it, though, because the light source was invisible. My dad's body floated straight up into the cone then disappeared, like the light sucked him up and swallowed him. Then it went dark and Henry stopped barking.

"When she woke up the next morning, she had no memory of going to bed. She thought she'd dreamt everything until she looked down and saw she was wearing the same clothes from the night before and the bat lying next to her in bed."

"What did she do?"

"She called Harmony and found out he went missing. By then the cops had already come and gone. She told me what she saw a few days later, when I delivered her groceries. She swore me to secrecy because she knew nobody would believe her."

"And nobody else saw this cone of light," I asked.

Shale shook his head. "If they did, they aren't talking."

"I am sorry he is missing," I said.

"I wish you could meet him. He's super intelligent and a great storyteller. He told me all kinds of stories about aliens ... I mean, extragalactic Beings."

"Such as?"

"He believes in the ancient astronaut theory, that Earth was visited in the distant past and the extragalactic visitors helped our ancestors build the pyramids and stuff. He also thinks the universe is populated by thousands of different races of Beings."

"Is that what you believe, Shale?"

Shale smirked. "I think most unexplained aerial phenomena and strange lights are military craft, but I've seen some video footage that would make your head explode. Both times the camera operators were taping something else, like airplanes taking flight, but when they went back and watched the footage later, unexplained craft appeared on the tape—craft that were invisible to the human eye. That's all the proof I need," he said. Excitement danced in his eyes.

I nodded, put my hand over my mouth and coughed.

"Maybe we should go back," he said. "I should've brought my canteen."

I shook my head. "I am fine," I said and stood up. "Is it much farther?"

"Kinda." Shale removed a compass from his pocket and showed it to me. I watched the primitive device's dial rotate and point to the letter N. I nodded and Shale returned the compass to his pocket.

We walked parallel to the embankment with me limping behind Shale. I was uncertain what bothered me more, my leg or what Shale had told me. At the PLEXUS way station I had heard rumors about Sent abductions but had dismissed them as invention or fantasy. Then again, I had not believed Sents possessed extragalactic technology, either, until I had secured the proof.

As I pondered these things, a terrible thought came to mind and the blood drained from my face. I never considered what would happen to me after I expired in this strange land. All of a sudden I felt quite ill and scared. I stopped abruptly and stared over the embankment's edge. The riverbed bottom was dry except in one area, where a small pool formed. Two birds perched at the water's edge, bathing and preening. I envied their freedom and ability to fly. I desperately wanted to go home.

"You okay EBN?"

Shale had doubled back to check on me. I coughed, nodded and we resumed our hike.

We walked around a rocky patch blackened by desert varnish before turning onto a trail that led down into the sandy creek bed. Shale spotted a zebra-tailed lizard laying on a rock at the bottom of the wash.

"Look at that," he whispered and pointed. The lizard did push-ups with its front legs. I coughed and the lizard scuttled under a small bush.

"EBN, there's something I want to ask you."

Apprehension knotted my stomachs.
"Yes?"

"Next week, I'm graduating from high school. I was wondering if, you know, you'd come to the ceremony and see me walk?"

I hesitated. I would no longer be alive then. "I will," I said. "If I am still here."

Shale smiled.

I let out a worried sigh and wondered how I was going to spare him from my impending death.

The trail led us up the opposite embankment and toward distant foothills nestled at the base of a snow-dusted mountain. As we hiked, my breathing grew more labored and I coughed more frequently.

We followed the trail for some time. Eventually it led us through a pass then into a gully thick with creosote bushes and sagebrush. To avoid the dense flora, we inched along a narrow ledge above the vegetation toward a dark cave mouth.

The sun, now invisible, sheltered behind rolling, milky haze fogging the air. I was not sure how much farther I could limp.

At the cave entrance, I sensed a subtle energy field. Shale entered the darkness, seeming not to notice. I followed, somewhat hesitant and felt relieved when I saw a bright spot of light at the other end.

Near the middle of the tunnel, I whispered Shale's name and told him to stay behind me. I crept toward the bright light with my back pressed against the rocky wall. When I reached the end, I peered out of the shadows.

The tunnel opened onto a ledge high above a wide, isolated canyon scooped from the mountainside. Vertical walls reached far overhead, making the area impassible without special equipment. This tunnel seemed to be the only route in or out on this side. Shale moved past me toward a narrow trail winding down to ground level, but I caught his arm and held him back. If he felt fear, I could not sense it, but I felt enough for us both.

At the basin bottom, two concentric circle formations sat in the center of the sandy floor. I counted nine quartz obelisks enclosing a ring of six vehicle-sized meteorites. Homesickness twisted my stomachs because I recognized a bas-relief of my ancestors' faces — the original Guardians of the Sky — staring down at us from the canyon walls. Chills ran down my spine.

The carving, although faint, resembled those found in the sacred rock sculpture garden surrounding the Protectory Orb on Pharralax. Seeing it made my blood run cold.

Shale nudged me and removed his compass from his pocket. The dial spun one direction in rapid rotations. Then it slowed and whirled the opposite direction.

"Stay here," I uttered. I dropped to my belly and elbow-crawled to the edge of the ledge.

262

A strong electromagnetic field bubbled around the meteorite ring, indicating a vortex. While I determined its dimensions, several figures appeared inside the wavering magnetic cloud. I wished my computer were working so I could record what I saw and what Shale's human eyes could not see. A group of extragalactic Beings — one Seemae and two Doug-ms entered the Erox realm. I stared, speechless in disbelief.

"What do you see EBN," Shale asked, squatting at my side. He peered at me through the thick lenses of his eyeglasses.

"I thought I saw something," I said, "but it was nothing … just dust and heat waves."

The Seemae emerged from the vortex and lumbered toward the obelisk ring before two slightly built, bipedal Doug-ms. Humanoid in appearance, the transparent, non-physical Doug-ms advanced in their non-linear fashion. They alighted in one place then several paces ahead without crossing the distance between.

The Seemae wore a hooded suit the color of sand that emitted infrared energy, camouflaging it from human eyes. The Doug-ms, though, wore traditional garments, fitted, pale gray tunics and pants. I found the whole scene very odd and disconcerting.

"I don't see any dust or heat waves. What do you think those people are doing down there?" Shale indicated with a chin nod.

My head snapped toward him. "What did you say?"

"Don't you see them, by those pillars? Let's go talk to them," Shale suggested. He moved to get up, but my arm shot out and pulled him down.

"Hey, what are you doing," he said.

"Shale, we must remain hidden for our safety," I whispered.

"But what if they know something about my dad? What if they have him?" He squirmed under my grasp.

I shook my head and opened my mouth to speak but nothing came out. How had he seen those Beings? Human eyes were incapable of seeing non-physical forms and objects in the infrared spectrum … unless … he and his father were not entirely human …

Shale struggled to get up but I held him down. Before he could overpower me, I distracted him the best way I knew how, by crushing my lips against his. My head spun as we kissed. Giving in to my desires felt divine and when Shale pulled me on top of him, I did not resist. I kept my eyes open though, and watched the Beings turn and re-enter the vortex.

After they disappeared, I pulled away. "Your father is not here. This terrain is unsafe."

Shale sat up and glanced over the ledge. "Where did they go, EBN? What's going on?"

My face clouded. "Nothing," I lied. "Let's go back. I need to rest my leg."

Chapter Sixteen: Evasions

"You didn't see where those people went?" Shale asked.

"No. I do not know."

Shale stood and helped EBN to her feet. Even though he distinctly felt like she was lying, he let it go because her kiss left him spellbound. But as they moved through the tunnel, several things bothered him, including EBN's cryptic warnings about the terrain. Who were those people, and why was she scared of them? She definitely knew more than she was telling.

"EBN, why do all those people come to see you and bring you gifts?"

"Because they think I am special."

He thought about kissing her again. "You are special."

She coughed for several seconds. After a long pause, she said, "Does Harmony know about the people?"

"Oh, yeah."

"Is she angry?"

"No. She's been acting really strange. Ever since I started talking again, she's been super calm and uncharacteristically nice, maybe because she's exercising—which is also weird, because she hates exercise. She even quit smoking."

"Really?"

265

"Yeah. She lost interest and stopped cold turkey. She says it's a miracle."

He stayed close while they crossed the narrow ledge and helped EBN climb through the foothills. She seemed exhausted, leaning against him at times so he walked alongside her, not minding that she progressed so slowly.

Moving slow meant more time and physical contact with her and that's what he wanted more than anything. But the farther they walked, the worse EBN's cough sounded. It worried him.

"You should see a doctor," Shale said when her coughing quieted.

"So you and your sister have said," EBN said. She bit at the dry skin flaking off her lips.

"E, what were you doing in the desert Saturday when I brought you home on my bike?"

EBN grimaced and looked out across the desert. "I went for a walk," she replied in a flat tone.

Although Shale couldn't see her eyes behind her sunglasses, he knew she was lying. "You went for a walk with that limp? What's wrong with your leg anyway?"

"You ask too many questions," EBN said, leaning forward and coughing. "I injured it."

"How?"

"I told you, I fell into a cactus."

Shale's brow creased. "You said that was how you'd injured your hands."

"My leg too."

"How come you don't work?"

EBN sighed. "I had a job but they terminated me. I was—expendable."

"Where did you work?"

"Many places."

"Where are you from?"

"Far away."

"I knew that from your accent. But where?"

"That is a discussion for another time."

They crossed the sandy creek bed, walked around the blackened rock formation and headed west along the riverbed toward the Oasis. Shale could tell he was making EBN uncomfortable but there were so many things he wanted to know. He was about to ask what EBN did for work when a loud, unpleasant growl sounded from her.

Shale started and his eyes widened. "What was that?"

EBN's face reddened; one hand flew to her belly. "I have risked your displeasure. I apologize," she said.

"Don't apologize," Shale said. "I'm fine. Are you okay?"

EBN's face twisted in discomfort and she passed gas—a long, drawn out squishy sound. "Please forgive my intestinal disquiets," EBN said. "I have a digestive disorder."

Shale laughed. "Dude, blow all you want," he said. "I'm not offended." To emphasize his point, he lifted his leg and released a loud, trumpet-sounding fart.

"Oh no," EBN said. She feigned a frightened expression and farted again, another noisy, long one. She laughed a little.

267

Shale giggled and a toot escaped him.

EBN pointed at Shale and farted. Shale cackled and gripped his sides.

The hilarity continued for some time. He'd never had this much fun with a girl before and couldn't remember the last time he'd laughed so hard his belly hurt. Without trying, he tooted again and chuckled harder. Tears formed in his eyes but he blinked them away, still snickering.

EBN was quickly becoming his best friend. She was perfect in everyway. Not even her farts grossed him out. He felt so safe around her that his tic vanished when she was near. Shale hoped they stayed friends forever, well, more than friends actually.

The foggy haze reflected the sun's light, amplifying the desert heat and drying the vegetation. They walked in silence until they reached the abandoned couch they'd passed earlier.

"Stop a moment," EBN uttered. She looked around the desert floor, located a stick and picked it up. She limped to the couch and used the stick to pry up the couch's cushions.

"What are you doing," Shale asked.

"Making certain nothing lives here," she said. "Grab these cushions and we will go."

"Why," Shale said. His nose wrinkled at the thought of touching them.

"For your training," EBN said in a flat tone. "So you can practice hitting."

"Why didn't you say so?" Grinning from ear to ear, Shale grabbed the cushions, turned around and looked at EBN. His smile melted into a frown and his forehead wrinkled in concern. EBN looked frightfully pale; her skin had an unmistakable bluish cast to it.

"Are you sure you're okay? You don't look good—no offense."

EBN smirked. "You have not offended me," she panted in a raspy voice. She cleared her throat and coughed.

"You don't sound too good either. Let me take you to a doctor."

EBN shook her head. "Not possible. Rest will suffice."

"Why isn't it possible? You obviously need medicine."

She coughed and shook her head.
Shale was not dropping the subject. "If it's because of money—"

"That is not the reason."

"Then what *is* your reason?"

"It goes against my religion," EBN said. "Medical treatments of any kind are strictly forbidden."

Shale's jaw fell open. His expression was a mix between horror and bewilderment. "What religion are you?"

"I cannot tell you."

"Why?"

"My religion and culture are secretive, to protect us from persecution," EBN said.

Not sold on her excuses, Shale turned his head and gave EBN a sideways glance. His family was not religious, but he'd never heard of anything like that.

A Frisbee-sized tarantula the color of coffee beans crawled across the desert floor on the path ahead of them. They watched it until the spider sensed their presence and scurried into a burrow.

"Let me ask you something," EBN said.

Shale eyed her suspiciously. "Go ahead."

"What would you do if you were out here, looking for your father and you encountered an extragalactic Being?"

They approached the field. EBN's trailer was within sight. Shale scratched his chin with his shoulder. "Just one Being or a group of Beings?"

"Just one," EBN answered.

"Is he or she armed?"

Although EBN's expression was serious, she chuckled. "Of course he is armed, but he is intelligent enough not to use his weapon unless you point one at him first."

"Just checking," Shale said. "I suppose I would try to communicate with him."

EBN leaned against Shale's shoulder. "I am not certain your answer would have been the same had I asked you this question last week."

"You're wrong," Shale said, kicking a rock. "I would have communicated using hand gestures. It worked with you."

EBN halted mid-step and studied Shale with a slow, measured gaze as she let out a long string of barking coughs.

270

Shale pressed his lips together. He waited for her to finish and catch her breath. "EBN, you said something earlier today that worried me."

"What was that?"

"You said you wouldn't be here much longer. What did you mean?"

EBN glanced down but didn't answer the question.

They crossed the field in silence and Shale braced himself for EBN's answer, for it was sure to come sooner or later.

Shale was glad when they reached EBN's trailer because she was hobbling now. When they stepped onto the patio, EBN collapsed into one of the patio chairs he and Harmony had brought over.

He sat across the table, watching her. In the golden light of early evening, EBN's face looked gaunt and her skin definitely held a greenish-blue tone.

Tiny blisters swelled on her lips as if she'd been sunburned, but clearly she wasn't. On the contrary, she looked frightfully pale. Neither the blue skin tone nor the blisters had been there an hour ago, when they'd kissed. Shale felt the corners of his eyes sag. He worried about his girl.

"I am not up for much else today, Shale." EBN's voice, normally velvet smooth and melodious, sounded hoarse and breathless.

Shale shrugged. "Me either. We can just hang out."

EBN nodded. She put her hand over her mouth and coughed.

Shale jumped to his feet. "Can I get you some water? Would it help?"

EBN nodded, still coughing. "Get one of my drinks in the cold storage, please," she said, wheezing.

Shale went into the kitchen and searched the cabinets for a water glass. The cabinets held no dishes, only mismatched cups and glasses that looked like they came from a thrift store. He filled a glass with water for himself then opened the refrigerator. The inside was completely bare except for one plain silver can.

There weren't even any condiments. Shale grabbed the can and examined it. It wasn't a soft drink can, nor was it the sort used to pack canned goods. There was no label or brand or markings of any kind on it and the tab and opening at the top were a weird oval shape. Shale returned to the patio, cracked open the top for EBN and passed it to her.

"Thank you." She took a long drink, gripping the silver can with her bandaged hands.

Shale sank into the plastic chair. "You didn't answer my question."

EBN finished her drink then stared at Shale across the table. "That too is a conversation for another time, but we shall have it very soon."

Shale gulped his water and set his glass on the table. "Then tell me something else."

"Yes?" she rasped.

"What is that stuff and where did you get it?"

"It is an energy drink," EBN said.

"Come on," Shale said. "Tell me what it really is."

"It is liquid nutrition," EBN wheezed. She sipped her drink and wiped her mouth with the back of her bandaged hand.

"Let me have a sip," Shale asked, reaching for the can.

EBN's brows rose. "No," her tone was grave. She coughed and cleared her throat. "It contains medicine," she rasped.

"For your digestive disorder," Shale said.

"That is correct," EBN coughed.

"What kind of digestive disorder turns your skin blue-green," Shale asked.

The canister slipped from EBN's grasp and hit the table with a *thunk*. "Shale, I apologize, but I do not have the energy for so many questions," EBN said. She turned her head and coughed.

"EBN, let me help you," Shale pleaded.

EBN shook her head and sighed. She pushed herself out of the chair then sat back down.

"What?"

"Nothing."

"Tell me."

After a pause EBN said, "Sometimes, you remind me of someone."

"Who?"

"My younger brother." Her breath sounded strangled.

"You have a brother? How old is he? What's his name?"

"Aix," EBN gasped, coughing harder.

"Ace," Shale repeated. "That's an awesome name. Your parents must be beyond cool."

EBN removed the boonie hat. "They are, in their own way," she said in a faraway tone.

"Where's your family?"

She hesitated. "At home, where they belong." Her face was thoughtful and sad. "Please help me inside and allow me rest. Repeat last night's assignment and come back tomorrow."

Shale's amused expression fell. He pushed his chair back, making a scraping sound against the concrete. He helped EBN move indoors and locked the door on his way out. As he walked home he wished there were more ways he could help her, but he didn't know what to do.

Chapter Seventeen:
Answers

"Another day slips from my grasp," I uttered as I awoke from heavy, dreamless decompression on Tuesday afternoon. The television remained on from the night before and announced the news. Anger smoldered from the Sent reporter as she spoke.

"Today marks day fifty of the oil spill. According to the latest government estimates, more than fifty million gallons of crude oil and one million gallons of chemical dispersants contaminate the Gulf of Mexico."

I moaned and turned the machine off. Aix had been right all along. Sents were only a threat to themselves. If they failed to stop the oil leakage, they would all perish slowly. I knew about dying slow and would never wish it upon anyone.

Overwrought with pain, I washed and dressed with care. The smallest movement caused excruciating suffering. Even the simple act of bandaging my leg and hands exhausted me. After resting, I attended the sick Sents waiting outside. Once they left, I rested awhile longer then exited the barracks to return to the *Surety*.

The day was warm and overcast. The gray sky brightened the landscape, aided by a white mist that rolled over the land like smoke.

My mind wandered as I moved through the desert. I found it ironic that it took a Sent's help to locate the Seemae activity Eesh had mentioned in his transmission. I wished my computer worked so I could report my findings. But Eesh was dead and there was no other Being to report the findings to. I wondered what the Seemae and Doug-M activity meant. I also questioned whether or not I would survive long enough to find out.

I felt terrible retreating to the ship, but it was the best possible outcome. I planned to die there, far from where Shale and Harmony could find me. It was the only way to spare them from suffering another loss.

When I reached the canyon, I heard helicopters approaching. At first I thought nothing of it because helicopters had been dropping loads of fire retardant and water on the fiery mountains all week. Then dark silhouettes circled overhead, curtained by the mist. The air churned and swirled around me, pelting my exposed skin with bits of dust and debris.

I scrambled under a rocky overhang for cover and peered up.

The shadowy outline appeared larger than any of the firefighting crafts I had seen. It sounded different too. A moment later one emerged through the fog and came into view. The black airships had two overhead rotors instead of one. They disappeared again but the constant *whomp, whomp, whomp* resonating through the canyon alerted me to their continued presence.

The noise grew louder, echoing in the canyon. I suspected the crafts landed nearby. Sent voices shouted over the din of the rotor blades. It reminded me of my first night on Erox and anxiety pulsed through my veins like blood. I pressed my body against the rocks and hid.

I remained in place until the shouting ceased and the noise from the rotor blades swelled. I crawled to the edge of the overhang and peeked up just in time to catch another glimpse.

A torpedo shaped object with an upright ring capsule and triangular rear engine configuration dangled from one of the Sent military helicopters. My jaw dropped. It was the *Surety*.

Once the canyon filled with animal and insect sounds again, I abandoned the hiding place.

It took all my strength and courage to continue moving toward the boulder outcropping. My bandaged hands trembled while my knees felt weak. I knew it was a horrible idea, but I had to verify what I had seen, whatever the risk.

Slowly and methodically I followed the ravine. No Sents lingered. If they left surveillance equipment behind to capture my image, I could not detect the vibration of any such devices.

When I reached the backside of the outcropping, no trace of my ship remained. Only piles of dried creosote, sagebrush branches and Sent trash lay scattered on the sandy ground.

I abandoned the site and hobbled back to the barracks as fast as I could manage, lest I be captured as well.

That evening, an eerie stillness held the desert in a firm grip. With Shale's lesson concluded, I sat in a plastic chair on the patio, bewildered by the quiet. The desert usually hummed with activity this time of night, but tonight no creatures stirred. No insects buzzed; no birds chirped. That milky white haze — neither smoke nor condensation — choked the air, obscuring everything beyond twenty letrs in all directions. Not even the sun was visible.

There was no denying my end was near. My lungs ached from coughing and fluid filled my ears. A scratchy sensation burned my throat. Pain blossomed behind my eyes and weighed my head, making it hard to hold upright. I felt weak, my muscles ached and the fever had returned. In an effort to minimize my symptoms, I had restricted my movements after returning from the outcropping.

Shale's fourth lesson went well. Within seven days he had undergone a remarkable transformation. Like the caterpillar who spins a chrysalis and emerges a butterfly, Shale had emerged from his self-imposed muteness a confident adolescent with formidable fighting skills. He no longer slouched and walked with his head held high. His facial tic was gone and he had grown to my height. I felt quite proud of him and loved who he had become.

As I searched the sky for the setting sun, I wondered who had stolen my ship, though I had an idea. It was only a matter of time before they came for me, too. Maybe they combed the desert right now, looking for evidence that would lead them here. This could be the reason why the desert sat in silence, because intruders lurked about. I half expected Sent agents to emerge from the haze and grab me.

I coughed and shook my head to end the speculation. The entropy fogged my mental acuity. With each passing hour my symptoms worsened. I expected the illness would incapacitate me soon. If there was another way out of this situation, I had overlooked it. The time to formulate a plan and gather intelligence had come and gone. I had never felt this alone in my life and would give anything to go home.

The last diffuse light of day faded quickly. As darkness draped the desert, I struggled to my feet.

While I brushed off the seat of my pants, a loud rumbling rushed across the land and the ground beneath my feet shook violently. Breaking, snapping, shattering sounds filled my ears, surging from every direction. The barrack's windows rattled in their panes. A cacophony of car alarms blared, including Harmony's car.

Panicking, I limped toward the desert. The ground rolled beneath my feet like waves in the ocean. Loud pops sounded over the car alarms. I turned and looked back.

Green clouds burst in the sky as transformers exploded and spewed showers of jade sparks. Darkness engulfed the mobile home park. Then, as quickly as it started, the shaking stopped and it was still once more.

I smelled natural gas and coughed into my bandaged hand. I was unaware I was shaking until I crossed my arms over my chest and felt the tremors. I did not know what to do; I had never experienced seismic activity on Pharralax.

Under the blasting car alarms, I heard a door open and the sound of voices. I limped toward the east side of the barracks. Harmony and Shale stumbled out of their mobile home. One of them held a flashlight. It was the only beam of light in the whole park.

"Shale, help me down the stairs before the first aftershock hits. Hurry, we've got to check on Mrs. Wiggins."

I cocked my head slightly and limped toward the light. I heard keys jingling on a ring. When they reached the bottom of the stairs, Harmony noticed me.

She directed the beam of light at my face and blinded me. "EBN, are you okay," she panted, sounding breathless.

"Yes," I said, raising a hand to shield my eyes.

"Sorry," Harmony said, lowering the light. "Shale and I are going to go door to door to check on everyone. Do you want to come with us?"

"I cannot walk far — my leg." The ground jolted and pitched beneath our feet.

Shale held out his hand. "It's okay; lean on me."

I gripped his hand through the bandages and looked at them with huge, frightened eyes. The aftershock lasted shorter in duration yet delivered a destructive force equal to the original quake.

Harmony led us down the unpaved street and shone the light on the ground before us.

I clenched my jaw against the discomfort in my leg as I struggled to keep pace.

"Your first earthquake I take it?"

"Yes," I replied, coughing into my shoulder.

"Don't be scared," she said, squeezing my shoulder. "We won't let anything happen to you, will we Shale?"

"No way," he said, shaking his head.

My terror subsided and my muscles relaxed. Although I still felt scared, for the first time since my arrival, I no longer felt alone.

The warm, humid night pressed against my aching skin. I looked up, seeking comfort from the moon and stars but the milky atmospheric haze blocked everything from sight.

We moved through utter darkness, stopping at Mrs. Perkins' home first. Mrs. Perkins was not what I expected with her round face, short, spiky blue hair and teal aura. She sat in her front doorway on a mechanized scooter holding Henry in one arm and her trusted baseball bat in the other.

The little dog turned ferocious as we approached. When she shouted over Henry's yapping that they were fine, we hurried down Stellar Way to the next group of homes.

Because of the power outage, most of the residents waited outside of their homes in small clusters. This eased our task.

As we circulated between the groups, I was amazed at Harmony's serene demeanor and friendly approach amid the crisis. She knew every resident's name and most of their pets' names as well, which impressed me.

Mrs. Wiggins lived two lots past the stop sign on the paved portion of Stellar Way. The petite, white-haired lady sat in a folding chair between her oxygen cart and her mailbox. She held a cat with long, white fur in her lap.

"Harmony and Shale, I'm so glad to see you," she said. "I checked on Mr. Townsend, but he didn't answer when I knocked on the door. I tried calling but the phone lines are down."

"We'll go right now," Harmony said reassuringly.

We crossed the street and banged on the door of Mr. Townsend's mobile home. There was no answer. Harmony put her ear to the door and shook her head. "I don't hear anything."

"I do," I said. I reached out and tried the door but it was locked. I heard a faint cry for help coming from inside. The hair on the back of my neck stood up.

"Stand back," I said, grasping the doorknob in my bandaged hands. I pulled hard, nearly yanking the door off its hinges, took Harmony's flashlight and limped up the three stairs leading into the recreation vehicle.

Inside the RV it looked like a bomb had gone off—a television lay face down on the floor. Newspapers, books, knick-knacks and broken dishes littered the floor. I heard another call for help from the back of the trailer and followed the sound.

I found Mr. Townsend trapped under a bookshelf on the floor of his decompression chamber. "Help is on the way," I reassured him as I hoisted the bookshelf off the elderly man.

Mr. Townsend moaned as the bookshelf's weight came off his body. The eighty-year-old man had watery brown eyes and a ruddy face covered in purple scar tissue welts. Blood poured from a cut on his right temple. "I think my leg is broken," he said in a shaky voice. He looked up at my bandaged hands with fear in his eyes.

"Who are you?"

I knelt beside him and stood the flashlight on end. Soft yellow light warmed the small chamber. I met Townsend's gaze and took his hand between my bandaged hands.

"My name is EBN. I am here to help."

As I spoke, the cut on Mr. Townsend's temple stopped bleeding and sealed itself. The man's breathing slowed. When he shuddered, I released his hand.

"Better now?"

"Much," Mr. Townsend replied. "How did you—?"

I heard shuffling sounds and knew Harmony was making her way through the dwelling. "EBN?"

"Back here," I called, waving the flashlight in the direction of the open door.

"I can't see a thing," she murmured. She appeared in the bedroom doorway. "Oh, Mr. Townsend," she gasped. "Are you okay?"

"I am now that our friend lifted that blasted bookshelf off of me. I was certain my leg was broken, but it feels right as rain now," he said.

We helped Mr. Townsend to his feet and through the earthquake mess to the ambulance waiting outside. While one paramedic examined him, another pulled me aside and asked me where the blood on Townsend's head, neck and clothes had come from. I shrugged in response.

After two examinations and an earful of fussing, the paramedics issued Mr. Townsend a clean bill of health, packed up their gear and left for another call.

While the ambulance pulled away, a middle-aged gentleman driving a golf cart arrived at the lot. Harmony introduced him to me as Néstor, the property caretaker. Small in stature, Néstor's salt and pepper hair was slicked back behind his ears. He wore silver-rimmed eyeglasses and had a belly that spilled over his tool belt.

Néstor asked about Mr. Townsend and Harmony told him what had happened. He then gave Harmony a full report in a deep, rolling voice I found quite soothing. Néstor said that he'd started at the front of the park and was working his way to the back, checking on the residents as well as the integrity of everyone's gas, electrical and water lines. He said some of the lines had ruptured, but that he'd closed them.

Harmony listened as Néstor checked Townsend's lines and thanked him for his hard work. When he finished, he returned to his golf cart and drove to the next lot on his route.

By the time we had visited every mobile home, it was 10:00 p.m. Whether from my illness, the seismic activity, or a combination of both, I felt vulnerable and emotional. The demonstration of caring displayed by my human neighbors overwhelmed me. Unbeknownst to them, they had acted in accordance with *The Way*. It reminded me of home.

As we crossed the property, I said to Harmony, "Are you always so calm during a crisis?"

Harmony held the light under her chin, unaware I could see her face with perfect clarity without it. "I never thought about it before; it's just what we've always done." She hesitated and smiled. "When we were little, our parents would—" she cut herself off and cleared her throat.

I saw tears well in the corners of her green eyes. "As you saw tonight, we have many elderly residents," her voice quavered. "I suppose I'd want someone checking on me, if I were elderly. You did great tonight. You were a real hero. Wasn't she Shale?"

"EBN's a saint," Shale said, nodding his agreement.

"I am nothing of the kind," I disagreed. "Helping others pleases me," I said, imagining Mr. Townsend's face. In many ways, Mr. Townsend reminded me of a younger version of my A-da.

We arrived back at our respective homes and stood in the drive behind Harmony's car. "Thanks for coming with us. Are you going to be all right tonight?"

I coughed and shook my head. "I suppose." I did not want to think about the aftershocks.

"Do you have any supplies, like candles, or a flashlight? I'm not comfortable—" An aftershock interrupted her.

I clutched Shale's arm until it stopped.

When the ground stilled, Harmony looked at me. "Why don't you stay at our house tonight?"

"I do not wish to trouble you," I said.

"We won't be able to sleep if we're worried about you," Harmony urged.

"But I am ill," I said, covering my mouth and coughing.

"All the more reason why you shouldn't be alone. Shale can bunk with me and you can have his room. You don't mind, do you Shale?"

"Stay with us," Shale said.

I looked between their faces. The truth was, I really did not want to be alone. The ground rolled and rocked beneath our feet as yet another tremor hit.

Harmony held out her flashlight. "Take this. Go get what you need and come stay at our house. I insist."

My lips curved in a shy smile. Her generous spirit touched my heart. "I will return."

When I limped around the front of the barracks and unlocked the front door, I noticed a countless cracks shattered the concrete foundation. But what alarmed me most was the scrawling fissure snaking under the patio that was as wide as my hand.

Inside the outpost, both recliners and the table had toppled over, dumping my computer, weapon, the televisions, offerings jar and bound bundles of money onto the floor. I would deal with straightening up the mess in the morning—if I were still alive.

I limped into the nourishment chamber. As I drank what remained in the last can of Re-breather formula, I remembered Eesh's orders. Involvement with Sents was forbidden.

I exited the nourishment chamber and limped down the hall to the bath chamber. While changing the dressing on my leg, I considered Eesh's melodramatic warnings, scoffed and shook my head. Compared to what I had observed, only half of what I had been told about humans was true. When blessed with good fortune, Sent behavior ranged between questionable and reprehensible. Yet, crises united Sents and brought out the best in them.

Adelians' misunderstanding of Sents surpassed comprehension, as did their abandonment of me. Since I was doomed to die here, I intended to experience joy where I could find it.

Another aftershock struck. I froze, terrified. My eyes arced over the chamber as the windows clattered in their panes and the ground lurched beneath my feet. The tremors were spooky, especially without electricity. I was glad I would not be alone tonight.

I secured the barracks and limped next door. Shale waited for me outside. He chomped on a red Popsicle, muttered a welcome and opened the door. I stepped inside their mobile home and looked around.

Dozens of lit candles cast a dim glow about the front chamber. The smell of cigarette smoke assaulted my nostrils and tickled my nasal passages. I sneezed and coughed.

Harmony shuffled into the chamber wearing baggy blue pajamas. "Hi EBN. Are you hungry? The fridge is full of food that will spoil unless we eat it," she said before disappearing down the opposite end of the hall.

"Thank you, but I am fine," I said. I crossed the chamber to look at the crooked rows of black and white photos hanging in identical frames above the television set, straightening each as I looked at it. A younger, slimmer Harmony was the subject of every portrait but I could not tell where any of the photos were taken. A strange black blot dangled into some of the pictures from outside the frame.

Shale stood next to me, munching on his Popsicle. I glanced at him, pointed to the photos. "What are these?"

He muttered with his mouth full of Popsicle slush, "Still shots taken on set, when Harmony was on the show *Wonder Kids*."

Stunned, I did a double take. That explained it! Now I understood why Harmony had seemed so familiar to me. She was the star of Aix's favorite broadcasted program.

Homesickness brought tears to my eyes. I looked at Shale. "Shale, would you mind taking your glasses off?" My voice cracked mid-sentence.

Shale removed his glasses, looked at me and blinked several times. I noticed his eyes no longer wiggled. "Can I put them back on now?"

I nodded, speechless. Without his glasses, Shale's resemblance to Aix was uncanny. Perhaps my attraction to him disabled me from seeing it before now. They shared the same archetype along with a similarity in their voiceprints that was downright weird.

"You're missing your brother, Ace?" It was more of a statement than question.

My head jerked back. "How did you know?"

Shale cocked his head slightly. "We talked about him yesterday. You don't remember?"

I coughed into my shoulder. I did not remember mentioning Aix to Shale. The illness was progressing.

"Where is your home?"

I sighed. "A long, long way from here."

290

"Did you come here for work?"

I nodded and pointed to the bottom row of photographs. "What show are those from?"

"Not *Wonder Kids*. She did a play; I can't remember the name of it."

"I see," I said. I felt tired; my eyelids were growing heavy. I turned away from the photos, limped over to the couch and sat down.

"Who do you work for," Shale asked.

"A foreign entity. No one you have heard of."

"What did you do?"

"I cannot discuss my former work."

Excitement sparkled in Shale's widening eyes. "Really? That only makes me more curious."

I shook my head. Even his mannerisms were like Aix's. Prejudice had blinded me from noticing their similarities until now. I found it sickening and unsettling.

Harmony shuffled into the chamber carrying a fabric bundle in her arms. "Okay EBN, Shale's room is this way. I put fresh sheets on the bed for you."

I limped after Harmony, thinking *I cannot believe I am sleeping in Harmony Bice's house tonight. Aix, Xtarr and Nyl are not going to believe me when I* ... Then I remembered I would never see my brother or our friends again and it was all I could do to maintain my calm composure.

Shale's chamber was located at the east end of the hallway. Harmony switched on a flashlight and stood it on end to light the room. Astrophotography crowded the walls. My eyes scanned pictures of binary star systems, red dwarves, white dwarves, supernovae and nebulae. Color posters of the Ultra Deep Field and the Pillars of Creation in the Eagle Nebula were tacked to the ceiling over Shale's narrow decompression platform.

A glow-in-the-dark poster entitled *Constellations of the Milky Way* hung on the wall opposite his decompression platform. A three-dimensional model of the solar system hung suspended from the ceiling by the closet.

A telescope sat in the corner, underneath the model. Glow-in-the-dark stickers of stars and planets plastered the walls and ceiling. Tables sat on both sides of Shale's decompression platform. Polished geode halves anchored the stacks of books and magazines cluttering the tabletops while more books and magazines lay scattered about the floor.

I sighed longingly and half-smiled at Harmony. "Thank you," I said in a half-whisper on account of my hoarse voice. "I feel right at home."

Harmony leaned against the doorway. "I'm going to bed," she announced. "Please blow out all of the candles before you turn in, and don't stay up too late. Shale still has school tomorrow."

Shale groaned behind her in protest. He carried two lit candles in his hands and edged around her, entering the chamber while I eased myself onto his decompression platform. Just then another aftershock shifted the trailer and jarred the windows. I inhaled sharply and coughed into my bandaged hand. The quaking stopped with a violent shudder.

"I won't have school if the power's still off," Shale corrected.

"We'll listen to the radio in the morning and hear what they say. Goodnight you two," Harmony said. She turned and shuffled into the darkness. When her door clicked shut, the sound resonated down the hallway.

Shale set the candles atop the stacks on his bedside table and sat at the foot of his decompression platform. "You wanna play cards?"

"I do not know how," I said. I leaned against the wall and closed my eyes. The events of the day had worn me out. It hurt to breathe and cough from the fluid collecting in my lungs. I feared the window on my life was closing.

"I could teach you," Shale offered.

I did not respond. I sat quietly with my eyes closed and listened to the sound of my breath. Each time I exhaled, phlegm rumbled my diseased lungs.

"I can tell something's bothering you, E," Shale said. "I thought playing cards might take your mind off it."

293

"I'm scared, Shale," I said, barely above a whisper.

"Because of the earthquake?"

I opened my eyes to slits. "No. Not the earthquake." I took a deep breath and slowly exhaled. My gaze drifted to the floor.

"Then what?"

After a long silence, I said, "It is time we had that conversation." I glanced at him. Shale's expression changed. His brows drew together and his forehead furrowed.

"I am very sick, Shale."

He stared at me. "But you won't go to a doctor."

"I would if they could help me." I hesitated. "I have lied to you and am very sorry. I withheld information out of necessity, because I have many secrets," I said. The words caught in my throat and I coughed for a while. It took some time to catch my breath.

"Maybe I should let you rest," Shale said. He went to get up but I reached for his hand.

"Do not go," I said hoarsely. Shale sank down again and watched me with concerned eyes.

"I hoped for more time. This is more difficult than—" my words trailed off.

"What can I do?"

"I need your help, but I dread asking," I whispered.

"Don't," Shale protested, taking my bandaged hand in his. "I'd do anything to help you. That's what friends do, right?"

I nodded. "And we are friends, are we not?"

Shale nodded. "Of course. You're my best friend."

A sad smile curled my lips. I glanced at the candles on the bedside table and watched the flames flicker. The chamber suddenly scorched. "And you are mine," I said, holding out my arm. "Please help me remove my jacket?"

Shale pulled the jacket sleeve. I shrugged out of the bulky camouflage jacket and let it fall to the floor. "You are more light Being than you are human, Shale. The question is, can you keep a secret?"

"I told you my biggest secret."

"You must promise to never repeat what I am about to tell you."

"Okay."

"Please say it," I urged.

"I promise to never repeat what you're about to tell me."

"Very well," I said. I let out a sigh that ended with several hacking coughs. "I have evaded your questions because I am not human, Shale. Earth, or Erox as my people call it, is not my home.

"I am an Adelian-Nadreen hybrid and the very first of my kind to set foot on this planet. My home world is located in the constellation your people call Ophiuchus. The star known as Barnard's Star, my people call Scyros. It is our sun. I hail from the planet Pharralax."

Shale stared at me.

295

"My ship crashed in the desert. I was supposed to be rescued."

Shale's expression hardened and he blinked several times. "Are you making fun of me?"

"I would never do that, Shale. I would show you, but this morning a Chinook helicopter flew away with my ship. Now I fear being hunted, like an animal. Whoever stole it will come looking for me.

"Whether alive or dead, I must not be captured. I fear this more than I fear dying. They must not discover or experiment on me. This is why I need your help."

"Wait," Shale said. "So, two weeks ago, that light in the sky the papers claimed was a meteorite … that was you?"

"Yes."

"You don't look like someone from another planet," Shale said.

"This is not my true appearance," I explained. I lifted a hand to my mouth, pulled the bandage with my teeth and began unwrapping my hand. Shale scrutinized my movements. When I finished, the unwound fabric formed a pile between us. I lifted my teal, four-fingered hand and held it next to the candlelight so Shale could see.

"I did not fall into a cactus, like I said. I apologize for lying about that too. Perhaps you understand the reasons behind my dishonesty."

Shale cleared his throat and stared at my hand. "Did you have anything to do with my dad's disappearance?"

"No. I know not what happened to him. I am very sorry."

Shale lifted his hand and pointed at mine. "You only have four— Can I touch your hand?"

I grabbed one of the candles and gave it to him. He took it, held it close to my teal flesh and laid his hand over mine.

"Your skin feels hot."

"It burns with fever."

"Why?"

I told Shale about my leg injury, the subsequent infection and my inability to heal due to environmental pollutants. I confessed that I caused the wildflowers to grow and explained why people flocked to see me. Shale listened with rapt attention and hung on my every word.

"I collected an enormous sum of money from the people who visited me. Currency bundles sit on the floor next door. I want you to take them, keep them safe and when the time comes, spend it on your education."

Shale swallowed loudly and looked down. "How long before you—"

"One day, maybe two. Hard to say."

He sat silent for some time. Finally he said, "What do you need me to do?"

I let out several barking coughs. "Dispose of my remains," I said weakly.

"But how?"

"Bury me deep in the desert, where no one can find me. Will you?"

"I don't know. I don't know if I can. How would I get you there, once you're...?" Shale's voice broke off. Tears glistened in his eyes. His lower lip trembled and he looked away.

"There is a wheelchair on the patio next door. You can use it."

"No," Shale shook his head. "This isn't fair. You can't go, EBN. You just came into my life. I can't lose you."

"I wish circumstances were different Shale. I hate asking such a task of you," I whispered.

A rolling aftershock hit. I closed my eyes and waited for it to pass. The trailer's walls shifted and creaked. The tremor subsided and faded into silent stillness.

"Help me rewrap my hand, please?"

Shale did so. When he finished, he said he would think about my request and tell me his decision tomorrow. As I drifted into decompression, Shale blew out the candles, lay on the floor and stared at the ceiling.

Chapter Eighteen: Risk

It is the first day of the lunar cycle *Nej* and the last feast of Rings. The day slips by without the date registering and I forget about Preece's party until after school. When I pass under the front door, I notice the house bustles with Loredi.

In honor of the holiday, they shave their bushy black hair and wear coarse burlap garments in a demonstration of humility for the Source. They speak in whispers and move silently about the house, carrying decorative food-laden baskets to altars set up in each chamber.

Incense burns everywhere—the air is thick with floral and spicy smells. Shrill Adelian music rings through the house. I cringe and clap my hands over my ears because I long to hear aesthetically pleasing music—Sent music.

I cross the foyer and move from chamber to chamber but A-ma isn't downstairs. I climb the spiral walkway and peek into the nourishment chamber. Several Loredi mill about but A-ma isn't among them.

The smoky smells of grilled natches, orange peaz and other seasonal dishes mingle with the heat and incense and overpower my senses. Feeling lightheaded, I retreat to my decompression chamber but the incense and food odors permeate the walls. I usually love flaky white fish and spiced vegetables but not today. Something about it turns my stomach.

In need of fresh air, I exit the chamber. I almost collide with two Loredis in the hallway because they stop abruptly and cast their eyes to the ground until I pass. It is difficult to navigate the short distance to the terrace because every Loredi does this. These holiday demonstrations of humility make me glad I'm not bound to follow the same customs.

I step outside, cross the terrace and lean against the marble balustrade. The balmy spring air suffocates. The sound of pounding surf drifts up to where I stand, punctuated by the shrieks and caws of shela birds hunting their evening feed.

The holidays aren't the same without EBN. Only now do I realize how much I rely on her. I know I'm wrong, but it seems like I'm the only one who remembers her and cares about her whereabouts. A-ma no longer shows her concern and weeks have passed since I last saw A-da.

I hear the terrace door open and turn. A stunning Loredi with shimmering copper skin steps onto the terrace. Her bare feet pad silently across the white marble. She lowers her gaze and speaks in a hushed voice.

"There is someone here to see you."

300

"Thank you."

"My service to you pleases the Source." She hurries to the door and opens it for me. I walk inside and make my way to the first floor, expecting to see either Xtarr or Nyl but as I descend the elliptical walkway, my heart drops to my stomach. Five Protectorate Guards in black uniforms stand in the foyer below. Have they come to deliver bad news about EBN? Feeling dizzy again, I grip the walkway half-wall.

"Can I serve you?" I step unsteadily onto the stone entryway floor in anticipation of bad news.

The Adelian leader has periwinkle skin and humorless compound eyes. "I am Commander Ammes of the Enforcers. We are here to arrest Guardian of the Sky EBN-Reyoz-X," he barks. He doesn't look at my eyes as he addresses me, but over my head.

It takes a moment to compute his words. "Arrest her? For what?"

"Failure to report for duty."

I shake my head. "I don't understand. She deployed on her assigned date. Our Gran-Ada, Protectorate High Chancellor Eesh-Slic escorted her."

The Commander checks his palm-sized computer and says, "That's not the information I have." The other four Enforcers fan out from behind Commander Ammes. One of them darts toward the hallway while the others run up the elliptical walkway.

"Wait—what are they doing?"

"Searching the premises," the Commander says.

"But—I told you," I say. I turn to follow the soldiers but Commander Ammes grabs my arm and holds me in place.

"What are you doing," I demand. "Get your hands off me."

"Wait here."

"EBN is not here," I insist, raising my voice.

The guard who searched the first floor chambers returns first. "All clear."

The others appear one by one. They lean over the second floor half-wall and shout down, "All clear, Commander."

"Clear."

"She's not here, Commander."

Commander Ammes releases me. "Thank you for your cooperation," he says. He turns on his heel and leads his men out the front door.

I stand in the foyer, stunned. A moment passes before I dare to move or breathe. I'm uncertain what just happened.

I go straight to my decompression chamber and don't come out. In need of time to think, I lie down and drift into decompression. It is the best decompression I've had all Scyros cycle, since before EBN's deployment. When I awake, the feast is underway but I don't want to face anyone. I can't tell A-ma about the guards with a house full of guests.

The time for evening nourishment passes, but I'm not hungry. I sit at my computer desk and try to focus my bleary eyes on my assignments, but it is useless. I replay the guards' visit over and over in my mind. I cannot accept that EBN is missing.

I open multiple windows on my tabletop computer and access the broadcasted news clips required for current events class. The first item, a story broadcast on Xionin's Protectorate Network, features Gran-Ada Eesh.

The Protectorate High Chancellor wears a slate gray suit the same color as his deep-set eyes. I can't discern where Eesh is speaking from, only that he stands at an opaque podium with his hands clasped in front of him. Eesh leans forward and addresses his audience.

"Regarding the ban on items from Erox, I am extending it to include Sent literature, music, film and video broadcasts. Any citizen possessing or accessing banned materials will be arrested.

"Over the course of recent Scyros cycles, Sents have expanded their space exploration efforts, launching more probes, telescopes and satellites to further colonization efforts. Their rovers invade Odos as I speak. It is only a matter of time before they capture proof of our existence.

"The time has come for us to ask, what are we going to do about the Sent problem? The best among them are animals with intelligence—urban primates. Sents are creatures of appetite and passion, not reason.

"Some would argue that between climate disruption and resource depletion, Erox's inhabitants might as well be extinct. Unless their numbers are drastically reduced, Sents will exhaust Erox's resources before the end of one hundred Scyros cycles. Why prolong the inevitable? We must take preemptive measures to ensure our safety and the safety of the multi-verse.

"Sents must be contained on their home world. Upon approval of the Zuma Neway, Guardians must be deployed to occupy Erox."

Applause and cheers sound from off camera. I scoff in disgust and close the computer window. I've seen enough and don't understand why Beings are not outraged.

The assignment includes a supplemental article to the video clip entitled, *Sents: Future Terrorists of the Multi-verse,* but I'm in no mood to read it. I open a new window on my computer and select a news segment off the same network that highlights the day's Protectorate proceedings.

The clip opens with the Zuma Neway taking their seats on the High Council platform. The council members listen as the Speaker — my A-da, Ulem — calls the meeting to order and introduces the first citizen speaker slated to address them. I smile at the sound of Ulem's deep, soothing voice, but when I notice the Chancellor's seat is empty, my smile fades, my mouth hardens and eyes narrow.

The enlarged image of the guest speaker, a slender Adelian female, appears on large projection screens above and below the High Council's dais. She wears a black hooded mourning cloak and steps up to the tier's speaking podium. A lock of silver-white hair falls forward and rests on the curve of her light blue cheek. She tucks it behind her ear.

"Thank you esteemed High Council Beings and Protectorate Delegates," she says. "I am Semaj-Divad, Adelian citizen of Pharralax. I stand before you to protest the deployment of Guardian Forces to Erox."

"Finally," I mutter over the broadcast. "A Being with sense."

"Recent reports state the Protectorate intends to deploy Guardian Force troops to Erox to ensure the safety of the multi-verse. While I acknowledge the importance of protecting the multi-verse from Sents, I strongly discourage deploying Guardians to Erox. Many citizens feel that a Protectorate presence on Erox is wasteful and unnecessary because Sent threat is minimal at this time.

"It cannot be disputed that Erox missions, however valuable, are dangerous. Simply entering Erox's atmosphere is treacherous due to the abundance of satellites and space trash orbiting the planet.

"One study showed that seventy-one percent of Guardians returning from Erox suffered a myriad of contamination-related illnesses, many of which permanently altered brain chemistry. In addition, the exposure to pollutants often resulted in the onset of entropy.

"In the past, there was much to gain by deploying Guardians to Erox as there was much to learn about the Sents. The Protectorate's tireless work has elevated Sent Studies to a prestigious field, but recent reports suggest we have learned all there is to know and have exhausted our reasons for being there. If this is the case, and there is little more to be learned, how can we justify the potential loss of life resulting from such deployments?

"My offspring, Ranx, attended the Adelian Conservatory on Pharralax. He was an exceptional student, earned top honors and joined the Forces. He underwent the rigorous training with enthusiasm. Nothing excited him more than the opportunity to serve the Protectorate. He completed training, was recruited by the Guardians and eventually deployed to Erox," she says. She takes a deep breath, scratches behind her ear and clears her throat.

"During his mission," her voice trembles, "he failed to metabolize environmental pollutants and slipped into entropy. He died on Erox," she wipes the tears streaming down her cheeks. "He died while serving the Protectorate. This is why I address you. It is my responsibility to speak on Ranx's behalf, since he's no longer here to speak for himself.

"For these reasons delegates, I strongly urge you to vote against all Erox deployment programs. Thank you," she says and steps away from the podium. She sits and sobs quietly.

I wave my hand over the desktop, close the screen, settle back in my seat and stare across the chamber. I hoped my assignments would distract me from my concerns about EBN, but now I feel worse. My intuitive sense says EBN is on Erox.

I need a break. In spite of the bans and risk involved, I open a new window on my computer and try the Sent channel. To my surprise, it remains accessible. I glance through the program titles and select the most recent news broadcast available entitled, *Teen Angel*.

A brunette reporter dressed in a magenta suit walks through a field carpeted with gold and orange flowers. "Something mysterious, some say miraculous, is happening in our community," she says. "Church officials from all over the city contacted our station with reports of miraculous recoveries experienced by their parishioners. What do these people have in common? They all visited the same teen—a girl some say holds the power of healing. No one knows who or what she is—healer, angel, prophet or saint, but one local resident, Sally Broderick, has seen the strange goings-on."

The broadcast cuts away from the Sent reporter and switches to footage of Sally Broderick, a Sent with wrinkled, sepia skin and a mass of black hair piled on top of her head. I think the name of her hairstyle is 'beehive.'

"Right after the flowers bloomed I noticed people gathering outside my neighbor's house." Sally says.

The reporter speaks off-camera. "According to doctors, fifty-eight-year-old Rich Jeffries had terminal lung cancer. Eight months ago, he lost his ability to walk when the cancer metastasized and spread to his spine."

"I've known Rich for years," Sally says. "He came to my house after seeing this girl and he could walk. He said this girl healed him."

"Word spread fast and soon people were coming from all over to see the teenage girl some are calling an angel." Behind the reporter, many Sents stand in a queue outside a rectangular, white dwelling.

"Mr. Jeffries' dramatic recovery has baffled his doctors. Doctor Lawrence Grass, a Los Angeles oncologist and Rich Jeffries' treating physician, confirmed the spontaneous regression of Mr. Jeffries' cancer. Dr. Grass, an expert in his field, can't explain it," the reporter says.

The broadcast cuts to footage of a moon-faced man with thinning brown hair and dark, bulging eyes dressed in a long white coat. "Rich Jeffries came to my office after seeing the girl he calls 'The Healer.' After examining him, we ran some tests and there was no sign of cancer in his system," Dr. Grass says.

"Dr. Grass didn't know what to make of Rich's test results. There was no scientific answer Dr. Grass could come up with explaining his patient's recovery," the reporter says.

"Scientifically, it's inexplicable. That kind of recovery is almost unheard of considering the severity of Rich's cancer," Dr. Grass says.

"I prayed constantly, asking God for an answer. I believe he sent this girl to heal me," Rich Jeffries says.

"All of a sudden, Rich just got up and walked. To me, it's a miracle," Sally Broderick says.

"Every time I think about it, I get chills. I'm living proof that miracles happen. I've been given a second chance at life," Rich Jeffries says.

"Channel 37 contacted the girl whom believers are calling the Teen Angel. No one knows her name or where she's from and she declined our request for an interview."

The reporter pursues a girl three heads taller than her. Her white-blond hair is the same color as mine. "Excuse me, miss. We'd like to ask you a few questions."

"No thank you," she says. She raises her hands and backs away.

The reporter shoves her microphone into the girl's face. "Is it true you can heal people?"

"No. You should not be here. Please go away." The girl limps inside the white building and closes the door.

I replay the video clip. There is something oddly familiar about the blonde Sent. She looks nothing like EBN, though.

My brow wrinkles as I watch it again. I know that voiceprint. When it finishes, I replay it again. After several viewings I'm convinced it's EBN.

I play the broadcast one last time and listen closely, determined to learn her location.

At the end of the segment, the reporter says, "Coming up later, more residents in the area speak out. This is Dana Cain reporting live from—"

The computer screen goes black.

"No," I say. I inspect my computer, but it works fine. I open a new screen and return to the Sent Channel site. A prompt appears in the screen's center that says, "Unavailable." I try accessing the channel over and over but nothing restores the video clip.

Moments later, Preece's voice sounds in my head and startles me.

Aix, are you awake? Come ingest some nourishment.

As I get up and walk down the hall to the nourishment chamber I don't feel my feet.

The house is a mess. Half-filled nectar glasses and dirty dishes rest on every available surface. A few guests linger in the hallway while others make their way to the tube. Everyone except me is dressed in Rings colors, white, green, silver and gold. Loredis circulate through the house, cleaning and collecting dishes.

It is one of those rare occasions when Ulem is home from Nilotic. He and Preece sit at the annex hover table while several Loredi clear away evidence of the feast in the nourishment and formal dining chambers. Preece's strapless emerald gown matches Ulem's silk suit. Her long, elegant neck and earlobes drip with sparkling Blu-rays, the most precious gemstone on Pharralax.

Ruby-red flashes of light also refract from the small blue gemstones on Ulem's misshapen earlobes. Our parents exchange glances and smiles and engage in quiet conversation. When I slide into my seat, Ulem serves from the dishes on the table.

I watch A-da's brisk movements and wonder how I should deliver the news about the Enforcers' visit. Perhaps I should speak with A-da later, in private.

"Not too much for me, A-da. I doubt I can eat after what I've seen," I grumble.

What's that, Preece vibes. She nibbles on a vegetable stalk and chews.

I can tell from the sound of her voice that she consumed too much nectar as usual. "Your A-da intends to deploy Guardians to occupy Erox," I repeat, my tone sharp with anger.

I did not know, she clarifies. *I have been seeing to others' spiritual concerns.*

I can't stand it anymore. "Perhaps you ought to see why Gran-Ada isn't doing more to locate EBN. Last lunar cycle Gran-Ada told me EBN was due back at the PLEXUS station, but he lied. EBN isn't on PLEXUS. No Being knows where she's at," I growl.

"That—is—enough, Aix," Ulem commands. "What has gotten into you?" His basso voice fills the annex.

Preece passes my plate. I almost blurt out what happened earlier but stop myself.

312

I glance at A-da, who stares at me then look down at the fish and vegetables on my plate. I'm too angry to eat. "Has he mentioned EBN's whereabouts to either one of you? Have you even asked about her?"

"No," Preece says, lifting her nectar glass and daintily sipping from it.

I rearrange my food with my eating utensil. "Is he still trying to get you to send me away? Gran-Ada wants EBN and I out of the picture. I haven't figured out why though."

Ulem raises his eyebrows. "What makes you say that?"

"Something I overheard. Ask A-ma," I say, dropping my utensil on my plate. I feel eyes boring holes into my back and glance over my shoulder. Eesh stands behind me, leaning in the doorway.

I jump in my seat, startled. "Gran-Ada."

Ulem and Preece tear their eyes from me and look up. "A-da, you made it after all," Preece chimes, pushing out her chair and standing. Swaying on her feet, she touches foreheads with him and lets out a loud hiccup.

Ulem also stands and touches foreheads with Eesh. "Sit. Dine with us," he says, walking into the nourishment chamber for another plate.

Eesh's pink lips curl into a wicked smile. His yellow suit reminds me of bile. "Don't mind if I do," he says, casting a glance at me. He takes Ulem's seat next to Preece and sits opposite me. "Please, don't let me interrupt your conversation."

An uneasy feeling comes over me. I return Eesh's look and glare at him.

"Ulem was just telling us about his day," Preece quips, quickly changing the subject. A loud hiccup escapes her lips. She giggles and covers her mouth with her hand.

"Really," Eesh says, accepting a full plate from Ulem. Ulem slides into EBN's empty seat next to me.

"Gran-Ada," I say, "Why were you absent from today's special session?"

Eesh's cold laughter fills the chamber. "Who are you, and what have you done with my offspring's offspring," he says, seasoning his food. "I had more important business elsewhere."

"More important than hearing your constituents protest the occupation of Erox?" I glower at him.

"Well of course," he says, shoveling orange peaz into his mouth. He points his utensil at me. "Care to brief me on what I missed?" He cocks his head slightly, challenging me.

"I shouldn't have to — you should've been there," I answer in a matter-of-fact tone.

"Aix," Ulem warns. He turns to Eesh. "Forgive his impertinence, High Chancellor."

Eesh stares at me while slowly chewing his food.

Pressure builds behind my eyes. Gnashing my teeth, I force down two bites of cold fish. "Can I be excused?"

Back in my decompression chamber, I check my computer for messages—I have two, one from Nyl and one from Xtarr. My thoughts race as I reply to both.

I hear the chamber's door open and close with a *whoosh* sound and sweep the transmission windows closed. I look up. Eesh saunters toward me. My empty stomach tightens.

Eesh strolls to the chamber's center area and drums his fingers on the tabletop. "I know you're worried, but EBN is fine," Eesh says in his gritty, raspy tone.

"Then why did the Guardian Police come here looking for her today?"

Eesh leans on the horizontal computer screen. Faint hints of leaf litter and wet soil drift into my nasal passages. I know that smell, but can't place it.

"They did? There must be some mistake. I'll look into it. Her reports have been timely and just yesterday I spoke with her myself."

I don't believe him but play along. "You did? What did she say?"

Eesh smiles. "We discussed her mission of course."

"And?"

Eesh musses my hair. "Protectorate business, but she's fine." He places his hands on my shoulders and holds my gaze. "She's being taken care of and shall return soon."

I almost gag from that smell. "Thank you Gran-Ada," I give Eesh a wan smile while my eyes dart between his. I want to believe him, but something feels wrong. It's only a feeling, but it's strong and clear.

All of a sudden, an image of conservator Faux flashes through my mind. That's it—Eesh smells like ... a Seemae? I stare at him, concentrating. *Gran-Ada, did EBN ask about me?*

Eesh looks at me and lowers his arms. He gives no indication he received my vibe. "How did Preece handle the Enforcers visit," he asks in a nonchalant tone.

I shake my head. "She wasn't home." *Gran-Ada, I asked you a question,* I repeat.

"Did you tell your A-da, or any other Being?"

"Not yet." *Gran-Ada, please tell me if EBN asked about me.*

Eesh still doesn't respond.

You can't you hear me, can you?

Eesh narrows his compound gray eyes. "If I tell you something in confidence, can you keep what happened today our little secret?"

"That depends." The hair on the back of my neck prickles.

Eesh stares into my eyes. "EBN is on a special assignment. She's on Erox."

So it is true. "Really," I ask, feigning surprise. "When did you send her there?"

"Yesterday," Eesh says. He taps his fingers against my desktop then waves dismissively.

316

"Was she excited? She's always wanted to go to Erox to see the Sents."

"EBN was so excited she could barely contain herself," Eesh chortles.

"That sounds like her," I lie, returning Eesh's smile. "If you'll excuse me, Gran-Ada. I have assignments to complete." I glance down.

"Of course," he says. He withdraws a few steps and stops. "Before I go, Aix."

"Yes?"

"Now that you know where EBN is, no more hacking into the Protectorate's computer systems. A young, inquisitive Being *like you* would be wise not to trouble with other Beings' business … like, Protectorate issues, or my whereabouts," Eesh says in a cold, definite tone. His compound gray eyes narrow to slits.

Pressure expands behind my eyes again. My hands fly to my temples.

"Do you understand?"

"Yes Gran-Ada," I whimper, rubbing my aching head.

Eesh nods, silent. Then he turns and exits the chamber.

I spend a restless night tossing and turning.

The next morning I wake before Scyros, watch the double sunrise and leave for the Conservatory earlier than usual. Few students congregate in the halls. On the twenty-third floor the crystalline hallways project images from Pharralax's tropical southern region. Massive jungle plants like charcoal horned leaf trees and obsidian palms sway in a gentle breeze.

Tiny primates swing from branch to branch, carrying young on their backs. Pink porpoises jump from a clear river mouth and careen through the air. In deeper water, a family of five whales hunts in southern waters. As I walk down the hall, I stare at the whales and think of EBN. Seeing the image feels like a kick in the stomach.

Xtarr and Nyl wait outside their class chamber at the opposite end of the hall. I hurry to join them.

Dressed in white, Xtarr holds a Sent book, William Faulkner's *The Sound and the Fury,* open while she practices hovering inches above the floor. Her vibrating lavender wings shimmer like moonlit dewdrops. She looks up as I approach.

"Greetings, Aix," she coos. "Nyl and I were discussing the theme of madness in Faulkner's *The Sound and the Fury.* I argue both Quentin and Jason went mad; however, the madness manifested differently in each brother, and you clearly are not listening to me," Xtarr glances over the top of the book at Nyl.

"You better put that away before the Conservator arrives," Nyl says under his breath. "No sense of humor, that one." He stands watch and surveys the hall in both directions.

Xtarr lifts her chin, defiant. "As a member of the Nadreen Royal Family, the Sent literature ban doesn't apply to me and you know it. Now as I was saying," she says, lifting herself to his eye level. She bats her eyes at him.

Nyl stands transfixed by her — frozen.

Satisfied, she continues. "Sents are fragile; they have delicate constitutions. Since you and Aix are Adelians and thus, share Sent DNA, I figure that puts you at greater risk for madness than, say, your Nadreen counterparts, who share no Sent DNA."

Nyl mumbles something about Xtarr being elitist, but if she hears him, she ignores it.

Xtarr closes the book and presses it to her chest. "Quentin reminds me of you, Aix. You're both so conflicted," she sighs, easing down to the floor.

"Fitting discussion, Xtarr," I reply. My expression is dead serious.

"What's wrong, Aix?" Nyl says.

I look behind me then glance over Nyl's shoulder. We're the only ones in the hall. "I can't stand it anymore. I'm through waiting."

"Still no transmissions, I take it," Xtarr asks.

I shake my head and lean closer to them. I tell them about the Enforcers showing up to arrest EBN for desertion, my subsequent conversation with Eesh and my suspicions about him.

"Remember the SRF attack on Nilotic? What if Eesh didn't really survive? What if—"

"Slow down, Aix," Nyl says.

"What does that mean," Xtarr asks.

I shrug. "All I know for certain is my family's gone supernova," I say. "A-da hides behind work, A-ma hides behind religion, Gran-Ada—I'm not sure it's really him. Meanwhile, EBN is still missing."

"That's not fair," Xtarr says. "Nadreen royals inherit station. None of us asked for the duties we were born into—not your A-ma and certainly not I."

Nyl rolls his eyes. "This isn't about you, Xtarr. This is about Aix and EBN."

"I've got to do something or I will go mad," I whisper.

"And you want our help," Xtarr says. Worry flashes in her mahogany eyes.

Nyl looks at us and glances down the hall. Students are starting to arrive. "What are you going to do?"

A mischievous grin spreads across my face. *I stole A-da's access codes to the PLEXUS way station. It's the only place I can find out where EBN is.* My eyes alternate between their faces.

Have you lost your mind? Nyl stares at me. Xtarr's mouth falls open. "You're not serious," she says. "The risk is too great."

Nyl stares at her.
You — need — to — shut — up — and — vibe.

Only if we get caught, which we won't. We'll be back before they realize we were gone. I look at them. *Well?*

Nyl's compound eyes sparkle. *Sounds interesting.*

Xtarr fidgets and her forehead creases. "I don't want to get caught," she says.

Quiet, Nyl looks at her.

Xtarr rolls her eyes at him and shakes her head. *I'll think about it.*

If you decide to join me, meet me at half past fifteenth hour tonight, at the community Matter Transference Station in Upper Sheltdonic, I vibe.

Under cover of darkness and long past when other Beings are decompressing, I dress in jeans, my "Save the Humans" t-shirt and blue backpack then steal into the night to meet Xtarr and Nyl at the Upper Sheltdonic community Matter Transference Station.

"Are you sure you want to do this," Xtarr says. She looks around the empty station and wrinkles her nose. "It's so risky."

I take a deep breath. "Not anymore. I've given my plan some thought and decided it was selfish, immature and wrong," I say, looking at my computer's chronometer.

"That's a relief," Xtarr replies with a smile.

Nyl turns to her. "We were worried, but we'd go anywhere you needed us to."

"Worry no more," I answer. "It was wrong of me to ask you to get involved, let alone expect you to go along with my plan. I'm sorry."

"Apology accepted," Xtarr yawns. "Can we go home now?"

"Yes." I put one hand on Nyl's shoulder and look him in the eye. "If anything happens to me, take care of Xtarr."

Xtarr lets out a small cry. "No."

I stand in front of Xtarr and put my hands on her slender shoulders.

"What are you going to do?"

I gaze into her eyes. "I won't implicate you in my mess."

"What about your doubts about the High Chancellor?"

"Never speak of it again. I'm probably wrong. I'll not have you harmed."

"I want to go with you," Xtarr cries.

"As do I," Nyl says. He steps forward with his chest pushed out.

I smile at them. "You are my best friends. If we were caught and you were punished, I wouldn't forgive myself."

"If anything happened because we weren't there to protect you, I wouldn't forgive myself either," Xtarr says.

Nyl nods.

I stand before a Matter Transference Chamber and wave my palm across the metal door. When it lifts open, I step inside.

"I won't allow you to come. You're staying here," I say. I pull my computer from my pocket and enter a series of coordinates into the Transference Sequencer.

Nyl and Xtarr jump into the Chamber before I enter the last coordinate. "We're going. Change the number of travelers to three," he says.

"No," I protest. "Go home."

"No," Xtarr sniffs and turns her nose up.

Nyl refuses with a curt shake of his head.

I give them an uneasy glance. "Remember I warned you," I say.

"Let's go already," Xtarr fusses.

"Ready?" I fidget, unable to contain my excitement.

"Ready," Xtarr says in an uncertain tone.

Nyl nods.

The Chamber door lowers. We're thrust into darkness.

Within seconds we Matter Transfer to the PLEXUS station. Invisible to Sents' eyes, the way station circles Erox in a geosynchronous orbit so that it sits suspended over Erox's northern hemisphere, approximately 25,000 k-mets above Erox's surface.

The Chamber door slides up. We step onto the station platform.

"Celestial heavens," Xtarr says. Her eyes widen as she turns in slow circles.

"Unbelievable." Nyl looks around, awestruck.

Starlight floods the circular platform. Transparent plasma walls provide a 360-degree view of space and the spinning planet below. The station's interior glows with diffuse blue light, creating a shadowy stillness.

The smells of burned plastic and molten metal hang in the air. On the planet below, the North American continent is covered in darkness, but sunlight shines over the Hawaiian Islands. A shooting star streaks past. Distant stars glow and wink at us.

The soft blues and grays of the station's interior lull us, as does the view. I stand before the wall, staring at Erox. I've never seen anything so beautiful. Brilliant shades of blue, brown, green and violet glow under layers of white clouds. Erox sits so close, yet so far away.

"It's just like A-da described," I say. "They've completed installing the basic components of this platform for Erox missions. The dock's down a few levels."

I cross the area and move to a wide console spanning half the platform. "Above us, they're finishing the second dock." I swipe my palm above the console. Three rows of five laser light screens materialize in the air over the console, suspended at eye level. I access the surveillance system to show Nyl and Xtarr different areas of the way station.

"You can see the construction on these screens."

Nyl and Xtarr cross the platform and stand next to me. The top row of laser screens shows exterior areas where construction is in progress. Mechanical cranes and arms secure beams to exterior walls. The middle screens monitor critical areas, like entrances and exits while the bottom screens display corridor areas and the docks.

Nyl moves to a window. His eyes widen as he points at Erox. "Look at the contrasting light and shadow over here," he says. An orbiting satellite floats some distance from the station.

Xtarr grabs my arm in a startled flash of comprehension. She points at the screens, "Aix, are you sure it's safe?"

My expression turns serious. "Nothing about being here is safe," I warn. "If a Cruiser flies by, duck behind the console. Don't let anyone see you and don't touch anything," I say, pointing to the security screens. "If you see any Beings approaching the platform, quietly let me know." My fingers dance with dizzying speed over one of the station's computers.

Her eyes widen and she looks at Nyl. "This is a bad idea."

"You weren't forced to come along," Nyl says. He moves to a different computer and goes to work. "Come on Aix. It's now or never."

Nyl and I search for information on EBN while Xtarr monitors the surveillance screens. It isn't long before her attention wanders. "If we're so evolved, why hasn't anyone streamlined this process and built Matter Transference stations on Erox?"

325

I don't look up from what I'm doing. "I think Beings have, but A-da denies it. He says Erox's atmosphere's not conducive, that it's too corrosive. But if we did open the doorway to Erox, what would stop the Sents from accessing it eventually?"

Xtarr frowns. "I'm getting a bad feeling," she says and shudders. She moves away from the screens and gazes out a window.

"I should have found something by now," Nyl says, his enthusiasm dipping.

"See any Cruisers out there, Xtarr," I ask.

"I don't see anything," Xtarr replies. "But I sense something."

"*I sense something*," Nyl warbles in his best falsetto voice.

Xtarr shoots Nyl a dirty look. "Stop acting childish and hurry up. We need to go," she urges.

"Find anything yet, Nyl," I ask.

"Nothing so far."

Xtarr's wings twitch nervously. "We have to leave, now." She moves away from the window and returns to the screens.

"Not yet," Nyl and I say in unison.

"This is weird, Aix. There's no files or service records of any kind for EBN," Nyl says.

"Keep looking," I say, my voice shaking a little.

Nyl nods and runs a hand over his bald scalp.

I glance up from the computer screen and look at Erox. As I stare, an idea strikes me. With another palm swipe in the air and a series of clear, commanding thoughts, I access the mainframe where Sent broadcasts are recorded and stored. If I can just find that broadcast I watched. I search the directory but there are billions of files listed. I slap my palms against the console. I'll never find it.

"Aix," Xtarr warns in a low voice, "we have company."

Nyl and I shut operations down, rush to Xtarr's side and look at the security screens. An imposing Being in a black uniform approaches the platform door.

"Quick. Follow me," I whisper, swiping the screens to make them disappear. I open a large panel beneath the console; Xtarr and Nyl crawl inside. I back into the dark, confined area, push and jostle my friends with my backside and pull the panel shut. It won't close all the way, nor does it latch.

"Move back," I whisper.

"I can't," Xtarr replies. "There's no room."

"Be quiet," Nyl urges.

The platform door slides open. I suck in my breath and pull the panel door but it still sits ajar. Craning my neck, I peer through the narrow crack.

The guard steps onto the platform. Time slows to a crawl as his black shiny boots move toward our hiding place. He steps too close and kicks the panel with his boot, startling us. I hold the door closed and listen to my friends' breathing. Everything seems unnaturally loud. My thumping heart echoes in my ears; it's so loud I worry the guard will hear it.

We hear a series of clicking sounds and a loud beep. The guard mumbles something unintelligible and the beep sounds again. He steps away from the panel and out of sight. I hear his footsteps, feel a slight vibration as he moves about the platform.

Another loud beep sounds. "Area One clear," the guard utters. He moves into sight again and walks toward the door. "False signal, equipment failure. Don't know," he says. The door raises open. He steps through it and it lowers after him.

I open the panel to get some air inside the tiny hiding space. The others push and bump against me. "Wait," I whisper over my shoulder. "He might return."

Xtarr whines in protest. She crawled into the space first and is pressed all the way back.

When enough time passes, I whisper, "Come out slowly; don't make a sound." We crawl out from beneath the console, stand and look at each other. Xtarr's face is pale; her hands and wings tremble. Nyl watches me with wide, frightened eyes.

"I want to go home," Xtarr says, her voice quivering.

"But we haven't found the information we came for," Nyl says.

I shake my head. "I've got a bad feeling too. Let's go."

We Matter Transfer back to the community station in Upper Sheltdonic. Nyl tries to hide his anxiety but his darting eyes and quick movements betray his calm pretense. We all feel shaken by our experience at the PLEXUS station.

We exchange goodbyes but no one moves. Xtarr and Nyl stare at me expectantly.

"You two go. I'll wait," I offer.

Xtarr narrows her eyes. "Go home, Aix,"

I look away. "I can't. I'm going back."

"You can't. You'll get caught," Nyl says.

"Remember what I said. If anything happens to me, take care of Xtarr."

"I will," Nyl says. "What are you going to do?"

"What I should have done long before now."

I touch foreheads with my friends and wait for them to enter the Chambers. Xtarr hangs back and urges Nyl into the Chamber before her. As the Chamber door lowers with Nyl inside, she pulls something from her pocket and unclasps her necklace.

I watch her and work up my courage. "What's the story with you and Nyl? It seems you've … grown apart."

Xtarr shrugs one shoulder, shakes her head and looks away.

I fight the urge to smile. Without saying a word, I know she's lost interest in him.

She takes my wrist, places two items into my hand and closes her tiny hand around mine. The cold objects vibrate and make my palm tingle.

"What's this," I ask, growing dizzy from her touch. She stands dangerously close and locks eyes with me. I want to kiss her. Instead, I open my closed fist and look down. A delicate Blu-ray encrusted key hangs from a thin platinum chain and a dazzling Blu-ray encrusted ring sit in the middle of my palm. The objects feel heavy.

"This jewelry belongs to my A-ma. It comes from Doridaen," she says. "Both pieces hold special properties. The necklace will shield your thoughts except from those you engage. Wear the ring for stealth and protection."

My eyebrows arch. I've heard myths about items crafted on Doridaen but have never seen any with my own eyes. "I'll guard these with my life." I embrace her and hold her close. I must return if only to see her again.

"Be sure you do." She gives me a gentle squeeze before stepping into the Chamber.

"Please consider what I've said about your Declaration ceremony," I say.

"I expect to see you there," she says, as the Chamber door slides closed.

I lower the necklace over my head and tuck it inside my shirt. I hold the ring for a moment then slip it onto the middle finger of my left hand. Immediately a sense of calm steadies me. The anxiety I felt earlier at the PLEXUS station now seems like a distant memory. Feeling strong and confident, I step into the Matter Transference Chamber.

When I return to the PLEXUS way station, I creep down to the dock level, raise the door and peek out. The door opens onto a catwalk located high above the loading dock floor. The semi-circular catwalk spans the mid-level's circumference but stops short of the huge metal launch door opposite where I stand. Many smaller doors lead off the catwalk. Below me, scores of identical, cylindrical, silver Protectorate Cruisers line the expansive loading bay. My eyes scan the rows of sleek ships. I wonder which to choose.

As I stand there, I realize I might not survive the journey. I might never see my family, friends or home again. The Protectorate is unforgiving to law breakers and I can hardly plead ignorance of the law. Odds are slim I'll survive. The smallest oversight or mistake means sudden death. I consider this and my lack of hesitation. I am neither conflicted nor doubtful about what has to be done, which makes this departure so easy — exciting even.

Criss-crossing walkways sit just beyond the door. I stick my head out and look around. I see no guards or workers in the loading dock. I stalk down the walkway and hide in the shadows beneath them. There are more doors positioned underneath the catwalk and I duck inside one. The lights switch on automatically.

I stand in a dressing chamber of sorts. Long cabinets line the windowless walls. A small nameplate hangs over each cabinet. My eyes scan the nameplates. When I see the cabinet labeled 'EBN-Reyoz-X,' my heart stops beating.

I rush to it and fling the door up. A black flight suit with iridescent undertones lays folded on a shelf. Holographic images of our family hang inside the cabinet door. I grab the flight suit and pull it on over my jeans and t-shirt. As I zip it up, I notice the holographic emblem over my left pectoral. The image shows the nine planets of the Xionin star system in their respective orbits. I press my lips together. I'm wearing EBN's flight suit.

Unable to bring myself to search the other pilots' cabinets, I exit that chamber and look for a supply chamber. I find it two doors down, duck inside and ransack it.

I shove whole food supplement packets, bottles of Re-breather formula, entropy solution packets and two medical kits into my backpack. Then I exit the chamber and sprint for the ships.

EBN, please answer me. Can you hear me? I visualize my thought energy racing through the multi-verse along the intricate web of ethereal silver cords connecting all Beings. The white-hot ball of light reaches EBN's image, but she doesn't respond.

My heart slams against my rib cage. I've never felt such determination before in my life. I'm through waiting; I need answers. I have to find EBN, regardless of the consequences. I have to know if she's okay, or if she's even alive.

I select the Cruiser nearest the dock door. As I approach the airship, the hatch automatically opens. My brain teems. I'm really doing this. I climb inside and stow my gear in a compartment. The ship's hatch closes automatically and seals out all sounds.

The flight suit rustles as the pilot's seat swells to adjust to the contours of my body and webbing stretches across my chest, securing me for flight. The airship hums to life. The control panel glows with turquoise light.

I survey the control panel, locate the power supply and imagine it activating. Laser light screens form on thin air. My fingers fly over the console and screens as I familiarize myself with the ship's features and controls. EBN is a Cruiser expert and spent many, many mangnas boring me with her vast knowledge. I never guessed the information would be useful.

Sweat trickles down the center of my back. I lower my hand onto the command module recessed in the right armrest. The ship makes a faint *whrrrr* sound. I feel a slight vibration as the vessel lifts off the dock floor.

EBN, can you hear me? Please answer if you can hear me.

The cramped control deck warms quickly but the temperature will plummet in space. My breathing grows shallow. I mop the moisture beads from my brow with my hand. It's still inside the capsule; too quiet. A feeling of dread washes over me. There is no turning back now. I hope I don't die.

According to EBN, the navigation systems in Protectorate ships are linked regardless of distance. How many Protectorate ships could possibly be on Erox? I access the Cruiser's navigation system and enter the phrase 'Protectorate ships on Erox' into the computer.

A satellite image of Erox's continents pops up on an adjacent light screen. Five dots flash over different landmasses. My eyebrows arch. It seems Eesh has moved forward with his plans to deploy Forces to Erox without approval from the Zuma Neway. There is no time to speculate on what this means.

I tap the screen over each dot. The navigation system lists each geographic location at the bottom of the screen:

Monterrey, Mexico
Santiago, Chile

Nanking, China
Groom Lake, Nevada USA
Lancaster, California USA

I tap each destination twice to reveal the languages spoken. The Sent reporter in the broadcast spoke English, so that rules out Mexico, Chile and China. I know enough about the Groom Lake facility, also known as Area 51, to know that it's a military installation, not an actual city, and it lacks a Sent population. That leaves only one option.

I enter Lancaster, California, USA, into the Cruiser's navigation system. The coordinates appear on an adjacent screen along with a flashing black dot. I tap the black dot.

A satellite image of the continental United States flashes on the screen, followed by a topographical image of the state of California. A solid black dot marks the city of Los Angeles. Above it, a black dot blinks. I tap the screen again and a miniature map of the city of Lancaster expands. The dot blinks from the upper right hand portion of the screen, over a place called Edwards Air Force Base. If EBN's ship sits on a Sent military base, then she's been captured.

In a flash of inspiration, I snap my computer onto a console jack and a laser screen materializes above it. It lists the computer's model, manufacturer, memory capacity and bandwidth frequency. Since EBN and I use the exact same computer, if I can locate the computer's signal using the Cruiser's sensors, then I can locate her.

I access the ship's systems computer and program the search parameters for the Cruiser's sensors. After a moment, a blinking red dot appears outside a city called Lancaster, California. I tap it and the coordinates appear on the bottom of the screen.

I imagine the ship moving forward and the small vessel advances. The circular door at the end of the runway lifts open. The ship passes under it and enters the launch dock.

The computer's automated voice says, "Entering launch area ..."

Once the airship moves into the launch area, the loading dock door clangs shut behind me. The expansive launching bay sits empty save for the stolen Cruiser.

I enter the coordinates into the navigation system. The label 'Oasis Mobile Home and RV Park' glows above the pulsing red dot. I tap the screen over it, enable the autopilot mechanism and initiate the launch sequence.

The launch door slowly lifts onto blackness—the vacuum of space.

The computer's automated voice says, "Prepare to launch in ten, nine, eight ..."

Sweat trickles down the side of my face. I press back, squirming in my seat, but there is no give. I squeeze my eyes closed against the nausea gripping my belly.

"Five, four, three, two ..."

The stolen Cruiser catapults into space and streaks toward Erox.

Chapter Nineteen: Slipping Away

Aftershocks thrashed the trailer all night. I awoke in terrible pain and lay doubled over on Shale's narrow decompression platform, moaning and clutching my stomachs. When it seemed like the intestinal malaise would never end, the discomfort faded long enough for me to sit up.

I called out for Shale and Harmony but the mobile home sat silent and still. Not even the hum of electricity flowed through the dwelling. Gauging from the light pouring into the chamber, I guessed it was mid-day, maybe later.

I slowly pulled on my jacket and rose. My unsteady legs wobbled. My injured leg no longer hurt; both felt weak and unused though. I limped down the hall and peeked in Harmony's decompression chamber. Princess lay curled in a ball, snoring in the center of the rumpled, unmade decompression platform covers.

As I withdrew down the hall, more cramps struck my midsection. I bent forward and clutched my stomachs against the sharp, hot pains that felt like knife stabs. I staggered out the front door and across the deck, toward the wooden stairs.

Hot wind blasted my face, but it felt cool and welcome against my scorching flesh. Wispy cirrus clouds floating high in the atmosphere did nothing to cool the desert. I squinted against the blazing afternoon sunlight and fixed my eyes on the mass of Sents congregating around the barracks.

The street and field writhed with people. Their brilliant auras, like undulating rainbows, dazzled my eyes. Waves of nausea squeezed my stomachs, twisting my intestines.

I gripped the wooden hand railings to remain upright and descended the stairs one at a time. Silver stars sparkled before my face. A black curtain fell over my field of vision, blinding the church vans and tour buses lining the street.

When the curtain lifted, I watched Sents of all ages emerge from the vehicles. They wore white garments, carried white candles and streamed toward the barracks.

I blinked several times and opened my eyes wide. The barracks seemed very far away.

At the base of the stairs I lost all sensation in my legs. I fell across the hood of Harmony's car with a *thump* and remained there, feeling my internal temperature spike.

Desperate for warmth, I pressed my body against the hot metal as my skin broke out in tiny raised bumps and shivers ran down my spine. My teeth chattered, which reminded me of traveling by Matter Transference. How I wished I could Matter Transfer to my home world right now.

Before I could imagine my cherished home world Pharralax, turbulent spasms attacked my midsection. I grimaced, turned on my side and regretted having left the safety of Shale's home. More stars fired in my field of vision. I had to get inside. The barracks sat so close, yet I lacked the muscle control and strength to reach it.

Death was imminent and very, very close. While I pondered this fact, delirium stole me from reality. Vivid colors burst against my closed eyelids like fireworks. My brain swelled inside my skull; my head felt too heavy for my shoulders.

The agony swelled to a crescendo. Just when I thought I could take no more, the painful spasms ended and a floating sensation overcame me. My ethereal body floated over my physical body and I stared down at the empty shell in wonder. There was no pain, fear, guilt or sadness in this transcendent state. The sensation felt similar to flying, my greatest passion.

I thought of my Gran-Ada, Eesh, and felt a subtle flutter of movement. Carried on the wind, I floated up and away, surrounded by pale yellow light and swirling white mist.

Soon Eesh appeared before me dressed in a plain white suit. I flew toward him, touched my forehead to his and embraced him. I clung to him as long as I could and basked in the serenity radiating from my Gran-Ada.

Eesh loosened his hold and regarded me with his smiling compound eyes. *You are a welcome sight, offspring! But what brings you to Other World? I did not expect to see you here so soon.*

I lowered my head. *I am sorry, Gran-Ada.*

Eesh placed a finger under my chin and lifted my face. *What are you sorry for?*

I failed you. I failed the Protectorate. I disobeyed orders, befriended Sents and fell in love with one. I forgot who I am and lost honor. My light has dimmed. I am no longer worthy of the rank of Guardian.

Eesh's expression grew serious. *Tell me what happened.*

I told him the whole story starting with Princess. I explained what happened with Melody, Betty, Shale and Harmony and all the Sents I had helped through my healing touch. When I finished, Eesh lowered his gaze.

I stared at him and braced myself for his reaction. *It is I who owes you an apology,* Eesh vibed with a sad shake of his head.

I do not understand, Gran-Ada.

My one regret is that you were not rescued before my death.

Please tell me what happened.

After attending Aix's Ascension, I traveled to Nilotic for Protectorate business. Shortly after our arrival, a Seemae rebel faction ambushed us. Every one of us died. I never saw our family again.

But why did no other Beings attempt to rescue me?

Only I knew your whereabouts, another colossal mistake.

So it was never your intention to leave me marooned on Erox?

Divine Source, no!

Relief filled my entire Being. Eesh had not abandoned me after all.

As for the rest of it, Eesh continued, *I do not see how you could have avoided disobeying orders. However, I think you remembered exactly who you are. In my estimation, there is no light Being more worthy of the title Guardian than you, EBN-Reyoz-X.*

A surge of gratitude filled my spirit and energized me. I embraced Eesh again and held him close. Now that we were reunited, I intended to remain at Gran-Ada's side for eternity.

But, it is not your time yet, EBN, Eesh vibed. *You must endure this tribulation, resist and fight. You must return to Pharralax and see these events through. You must avenge my murder.*

Although I held him tight, an unseen force yanked me from Eesh's arms. Carried on another gust of cosmic wind, my ethereal body raced toward Earth and plunged back into my physical body.

I awoke with a violent jerk, shivering atop Harmony's car. As my eyelids popped open, there was no confusion or disorientation. I occupied the physical plane and had evaded death ... for now.

Every muscle ached worse than before and my head felt like someone was hammering a spike into my skull. It hurt to hold my eyes open.

The hot, dry conditions sucked moisture from my body to feed the clouds swelling in the sky.

I vaguely remembered leaving Shale and Harmony's house. It seemed less real than my experience with Eesh. I closed my eyes for a long moment and attempted to return to the Eesh's side, where it was warm and comfortable. To my dismay, I remained anchored in my useless, diseased shell.

With my eyes fixed on the silhouette of a solitary bird soaring across the crowded field, I wondered what use was my service to the Guardians? It had taken me from my family and would soon take my life.

I had to see Shale one last time. Of all the Sents on this planet, I had found and befriended two unique human Beings. I missed them and longed to be with them. I did not want to die alone.

Other than seeing Shale and Harmony, the only urge I felt was to get inside the barracks. I stared down at my legs but could not feel them or my feet. When I tried to wiggle my toes, my efforts failed and the stomach cramps returned. I whimpered against the torture wracking my weakened body and wondered how much longer it would be before Shale returned from school and noticed my absence.

Fresh pain exploded behind my eyes. I squeezed them shut, hoping for relief. After a few minutes, I gave up, exhausted.

My energy dwindled and I drifted in and out of consciousness. This time there were no bright explosions against my eyelids, only darkness. I felt the floating sensation lifting me out of my body once more and welcomed it, until I remembered Eesh's words and forced my eyelids open.

Cold sweat trickled off my face and dripped onto the hood of Harmony's car. I pushed my torso off the vehicle, but could not remain upright and fell against the hood again with a *bang*. A number of heads turned and gawked.

Although I fought to hold them open, my eyelids lowered against my will. I heard footsteps crunching in the dirt and gravel and thought I sensed another's presence. Hands slid under my body and gathered me close. I felt too sick and weak to protest. It took all my energy to open my eyes to slits.

A trio of muscular male Sents surrounded me. With their thick necks and massive, rippled arms, they reminded me of young Silverback gorillas I had read about at the library. That mission day seemed so long ago.

Golden energy enveloped me as a Sent named Grant lifted me off the hot vehicle and carried me toward the barracks. Grant's friends walked ahead of him and parted the growing sea of bodies.

"Excuse me, Ma'am, Sir," one friend said. His name was David and his aura resembled Erox's daytime sky.

"Make room, make room," another named Tony commanded in a deep, terse tone. His scarlet energy reminded me of blood.

"Coming through, people," Grant said. "Kindly excuse us."

When they reached the barracks, Grant eased me into the patio chair nearest the front door and squatted next to the chair. "You okay sweetheart?"

I nodded and gulped air. "Thank you," I whispered.

"Anytime." Grant patted my shoulder. He rose to standing and addressed the waiting queue of Sents. "I hope you folks don't mind me cutting in line, but this girl collapsed over yonder and needs to sit in the shade. Do any of you have a problem with that?"

Eyes widened and heads shook no.

The edges of my lips curved up. Based on their expressions, none intended to disagree with the hulking figure before them.

A hollow-cheeked Sent with tubes running from his nose to a tank strapped behind his wheelchair stared at me. The young female standing next to him told Grant, "We don't want any trouble. We're here to see a girl who heals people."

"Grant," I croaked.

Grant turned around and regarded me with a bewildered expression. "How did you know my name?"

I lifted my bandaged hand and beckoned him to move closer. As he leaned down, I rasped, "I am the girl who heals people."

Although I did not ask them to, Grant and his friends cleared the patio to give me space. While they attempted to control the mass of people, the media arrived in brightly painted news vans and set up their cameras at the mob's edge.

Reporters approached the patio and asked to interview me but I declined with a shake of my head. Others in the crowd took pictures of me with their cell phones. I felt too weak to shield my face.

At the same time, a black pick-up truck rolled past the wooden barricade and parked in the desert. Inspirational music thumped from the vehicle's open windows at earsplitting volume. A group of male Sents piled out and unloaded dark cases and equipment from the bed.

The suffering was too much to bear. I settled back into myself and accepted my fate. I longer felt any sense of urgency and I no longer feared my end. I felt my body shutting down and welcomed the inevitable. Soon I would be permanently reunited with my ancestors. I looked forward to joining them, especially my Gran-Ada.

Grant, David and Tony stood at the patio's edge and used their bodies to form a barrier against the growing crowd. Someone produced a bullhorn and passed it to Grant, who used it to organize the throng of followers.

345

By the time the hollow-cheeked man's daughter pushed his wheelchair forward to receive my touch, a funky drumbeat resonated in the dusty air. I glanced up. A makeshift stage surrounded by speakers had been erected next to the truck.

Four male Sents holding musical instruments stood on the stage, while a female sat behind a drum kit with many gold cymbals. I watched and listened to the drummer bang her sticks together.

She yelled, "One, two, three, four!" and the band launched into song.

An overwhelming sense of peaceful humility overcame me while the faithful approached. For the first time since my ordeal began, I felt grateful for coming to Erox. I knew I was helping my people by healing Sents. If anything, I wished I had more time to make a greater difference in the multi-verse.

Whether sick or healthy, young or old, as I looked into each human's eyes, I wondered if my family would ever know what my final days were.

Chapter Twenty: The Faithful

Shale laid awake most of the night, tossing and turning on the hard floor. In the morning, he awoke in a glum mood and got ready for school.

Nothing worked because of the earthquake. There was no water to shower or flush the toilet with, plus there was no milk to pour into his cereal. He dressed in clean clothes and left the house hungry.

He just knew it was going to be the worst Monday ever.

But when he arrived at school and heard the morning announcements, his mood brightened. He'd forgotten about the half-day scheduled for the senior class. Between the earthquake, the power outage at home and EBN's request, early dismissal had slipped his mind. Go figure. The morning still dragged along at a snail's pace, though.

At the sound of the lunch bell, Shale rushed to the auditorium and was among the first to be fitted for his graduation cap and gown. While his classmates lined up inside the auditorium, Shale dashed from the building and hurried to the bike racks. He'd felt anxious all morning and needed to get home to see EBN.

It was a hot, blustery day. Patches of blue peeked out between the puffy white clouds streaming across the sky. Once beyond the school's chain link fence, he raced down Enchanted Drive.

Because of his preoccupation with EBN, Shale didn't notice Tommy Nutter or Chaz sitting astride their bikes, smoking and talking to two girls. When Shale sailed past them, Tommy and Chaz exchanged a glance then gave chase.

They caught up to Shale at the three-way stop sign near the soccer field. Tommy arced around the front of Shale's bike and stopped, his tires screeching to a halt. He jumped off his bike and gripped Shale's handlebars so he couldn't ride away.

The smell of hot rubber burned Shale's nostrils. A second later Chaz stopped on Shale's left and blocked him. Shale's heart thudded against his breastbone. He cast a nervous glance around. There were no cars or people in either direction.

Without uttering a word, Tommy swung at him, connecting with Shale's jaw. The punch sent Shale's glasses flying and shook his senses. Pain exploded in his head as he and his bike fell onto the sidewalk.

"Get up, pussy," Tommy chided.

"Yeah, get up," Chaz said.

Stars winked amid the blurred shapes in Shale's field of vision. He untangled his legs from his bike and felt where Tommy had hit him. A knot was forming under his stinging skin.

Anger boiled and rushed through him. He groped the sidewalk and located his glasses a few feet away. A shadow passed above him as he slid them onto the bridge of his nose. Both boys had ditched their bikes and stood over him.

The taste of blood filled Shale's mouth. He scrambled backwards and slowly got to his feet. His heartbeat echoed in his ears. Shrugging out of his backpack, he set it on top of his toppled bicycle and took the defensive stance EBN had taught him. Remembering her words, Shale squared his shoulders and stood up straight.

"Holy Shit, dude," Tommy said, staring up at him with huge eyes. "When did you turn into Andre the albino Giant?" Tommy retreated a few steps. "Go on, Chaz," he said, eyes narrowing. "Show him what you got."

Chaz's head snapped toward Tommy. His fearful expression spoke volumes, yet he moved closer, stepping over the curb and onto the sidewalk.

"Don't do it," Shale warned and raised his arms on guard. "This has nothing to do with you."

Tommy's mouth fell open. He looked at Chaz and said, "The geek speaks." When they finished laughing, Tommy held his arm across Chaz's chest to hold him back. "He's right, Chaz. Leave the pussy alone."

Chaz grunted and turned away as if to heed Shale's warning, then quickly spun around with his arm pulled back. The swing came at Shale in slow motion. In an effortless move, Shale blocked the hit with his left arm, formed a 'V' with his right hand and jabbed Chaz's eyes.

Chaz's hands flew to his face. "My eyes," he cried and stumbled toward the curb.

Without hesitating, Shale delivered a crushing blow to Chaz's head. Chaz pitched sideways, toppled his bike and fell against it in the street. He let out a yowl as the bike pedal's metal teeth bit into his side.

"That was payback for torturing my cat. Now get out of here," Shale roared.

Chaz rose to his feet, his pinched expression revealing his discomfort. A red lump swelled near his temple and his yellow t-shirt was torn and grease stained. He picked up his bike, withdrew several feet — all the while opening and closing his eyes in exaggerated movements — then sat down to watch the spectacle from a safer distance.

Shale turned and faced Tommy, who stared up at him with a slackened jaw. Tommy snapped his mouth closed, but Shale noticed the color had drained from under the kid's freckles. Shale considered stopping the fight until Tommy charged forward with his right arm pulled back, aiming for Shale's face. Shale ducked the hit and extended his foot.

Tommy tripped and landed face-first on the pavement. He jumped to his feet and examined his scraped, bloody palms. "That was a pussy move," he chided.

"So is having someone else fight your battles," Shale replied.

Tommy yelled and lunged at him. Shale blocked the hit, launched his fist and delivered a fierce blow to Tommy's cheekbone. His knuckles cracked against Tommy's skull and Tommy's head flew to the side.

Tommy staggered sideways and propelled himself forward again, bent at the waist. He lowered his head to ram Shale's stomach, but Shale jumped him like a hurdle. When Shale landed, he spun on his heel to face Tommy again. Tommy curled his lips and bared his gnashing teeth.

"Chaz," Tommy yelled and glanced over his shoulder. Still seated on his bike, Chaz shrank away. His face was red; water poured down his cheeks. Blood spots surfaced near the edges of his torn shirt.

"This is between you and me, Tommy," Shale growled, tasting more blood in his mouth. He spit it out, aiming for the gutter but missed his mark and hit Tommy's shoes. The bloody saliva stood out against the dusty white leather of Tommy's sneakers. Tommy looked up at him with a flushed face, enraged.

Adrenaline and fury raged in Shale. His hands trembled. "What's the matter Tommy," Shale taunted in a falsetto voice. "Too scared to fight me yourself? Now who's the pussy?"

Tommy let out a yell and ran at Shale with his right fist cocked. Shale ducked too late and caught an undercut to his chin. Shale heard a knock as his teeth slammed together. His glasses flew off his nose again and clattered against the pavement. More stars appeared in his blurred field of vision. He shook his head, hoping to dispel the painful ringing in his ears.

"Want your glasses, kid," Tommy said in a cold, sardonic tone.

"Yeah," Shale said, keeping Tommy's blurred shape in front of him.

"Then come and get them," Tommy said. He stamped them underfoot and ground them into the pavement.

Shale heard his glasses crunch along with Tommy's cruel laughter.

"Come on, Chaz. Let's go," Tommy said, turning away.

Although he could only see Tommy's blurred form, Shale knew what to do because EBN helped prepare him for this moment. Shale jumped to his feet, let out a fierce battle cry, sprang forward and knocked Tommy down. They rolled on the asphalt, beating each other. Shale squirmed away, jumped to his feet and continued throwing punches while Tommy rose on Shale's heels.

They pummeled one another, using fists, feet, knuckles, palms and elbows. Focusing his awareness like EBN had taught him, Shale threw his entire being into every hit and made each one count. He knew this wouldn't end until Tommy learned. He refused to live the rest of his life looking over his shoulder, in fear for his family's safety.

It wasn't long before fatigue wore on him. Shale used all his strength, aiming several punches at Tommy's face, but none connected. Tommy, on the other hand, showed no signs of fatigue and punched Shale in the face. Shale heard a *crack* and felt warm liquid flow down his face, lips and mouth. He wiped at it and his hand came away bloody.

"That's payback for busting my tooth," Tommy yelled. He hesitated, which was the worst thing he could have done.

Shale's adrenaline spiked. He delivered jabbing blows to Tommy's face, ribs, jaw and stomach. Shale heard Tommy's breath rush out of him with an *umph* before Tommy doubled over and staggered backwards, but Shale did not relent. He stalked forward, delivering more blows to each side of Tommy's head until Tommy fell to the ground with a *thud*.

Shale stood over him. "Don't you *ever* come near me, my sister or pets ever again, Tommy," he yelled, seething. He pointed at Chaz's blurred form. "Same goes for you. Understood?"

"Yeah," Chaz muttered under his breath.

Shale looked down. Tommy's blurred figure lay on the asphalt, clutching his stomach and gasping for air. "Have I made myself clear, Tommy?"

Tommy grunted.

Shale bent down, seized the front of Tommy's shirt, twisted it in his fist and yanked Tommy's face close to his. "Say it so I know you understand."

"What?" Tommy cried in a shrill, high voice.

"Tell me you've learned your lesson. Say you'll never bother me or my sister again."

"I won't bother you or your fat, ugly sister ever again."

Shale clenched his jaw and spoke through his teeth. "Not good enough." Releasing his grip on Tommy's shirt, he pushed him down, brought his leg back and kicked Tommy hard in the side. Shale heard a cracking noise as Tommy's breath rushed out of him for the second time. It was a satisfying sound. Shale stood on top of Tommy's feet to avoid a kick in the groin and waited.

When Tommy could finally speak, Shale demanded, "Apologize. Say it."

Tommy grumbled an apology and assured Shale he wouldn't bother them again.

"Then it's over," Shale said and stepped away.

Tommy groaned and coughed several times. "I hate you," he hissed.

"And I pity you," Shale said. He picked up his bike and backpack and raced toward home.

Instead of taking his usual route, Shale cut over to Columbia Way. Westbound traffic congested the main thoroughfare. Without his glasses, Shale could only make out the automotives' shapes, but it was clear the vehicles weren't moving. Shale wondered where everyone was going.

A few blocks down, Shale noticed several tour buses and vans lining the street, while several more sat parked in the empty lots near the Oasis. He heard live music playing in the distance and an uneasy feeling crept over him. He wished he had his glasses so he could see what was going on.

By the time he arrived at the mobile home entrance, the weather had changed. The wind blew harder, clouds blotted out the sun and humidity thickened the air. A yellow school bus blocked the Oasis' driveway. Shale rode behind it and stopped on the sidewalk. A long line of people dressed in white exited the vehicle and walked onto the mobile home park's grounds.

Shale stopped the nearest person. It felt weird speaking to someone he couldn't see. "Excuse me. What's all the commotion about?"

The person placed a flyer in his hand but he couldn't read it and said so.

"We're on a church outing to see the Teen Angel," said the featureless face.

Without uttering his thanks, Shale turned his bike and sped the opposite direction down the sidewalk. When he reached the pink stucco wall surrounding the Oasis, he turned and shot through the desert, kicking up dust clouds behind him.

The wind roared in his ears. The closer he got toward home, the louder the music swelled.

Shale was still shaking when arrived home. After pushing his way through the mass of people gathered in the driveway, he put his bike inside, located his spare set of glasses and glanced in the bathroom mirror. His face was a puffy, bloody mess; his red knuckles were swollen and covered in cuts.

Harmony would freak out when she came home. His shirt was ruined; he took it off and slung it over his neck. Discolored splotches covered his stomach and ribcage — they would be bruises within a matter of hours. Once he washed his face with bottled water and changed into a clean shirt, he ran outside and stood on the elevated deck.

People swarmed the area. Photographers stood near the road, snapping pictures. Camera crews and reporters stood near the photographers, shooting video and interviewing people. A live band played Christian rock music on a stage one hundred feet beyond the wooden barricade.

With his limited view, Shale estimated two hundred people crowded around EBN's mobile home, blocking his access. He walked down the steps and nudged through the mass using his shoulders and elbows.

When he rounded the west corner of EBN's house, he couldn't believe his eyes. A growing wall of empty wheelchairs, crutches, canes and walkers cluttered the patio and spilled over into the desert. Shale glimpsed EBN on the other side of the mound, sitting at the patio table near the door.

A wide line of people ran parallel to the mobile home then turned and coiled into the desert. A woman and little girl stood at the front of the line. Metal braces gripped the girl's legs and she leaned forward on metal crutches. When it was their turn, they lumbered toward EBN, laid flowers at her feet and placed a woven crown of miniature white roses on her head.

EBN touched the little girl's hand and the child's body jolted into a rigid line. A few seconds passed before she relaxed. The woman made the sign of the cross, uttered, "God bless you," and stepped aside. The little girl smiled wide then removed her leg braces and threw them along with her metal crutches onto the pile of abandoned medical equipment in front of Shale. The smiling child grasped her mother's hand and skipped alongside her singing the tune of *Old McDonald*.

As Shale marveled at the scene, commotion broke out. He heard yelling over the music and scanned the crowd. A number of heads turned toward the road, where a dozen people dressed in matching red t-shirts hurtled insults into the crowd. Several of them held crudely fashioned signs that read "Death to False Prophets," "Charlatan," and "Blasphemer."

A tall lady who wore her gray hair twisted in a tight bun at the nape of her neck shouted back, "She's not claiming to be anything. You're making that up!"

Shale knew he had to get EBN away from the crowd and considered calling the police until he remembered the phone lines would still be down. Just as he wondered where Harmony was, the wind shifted, carrying the smell of rain with it.

To Shale's relief, a black and white patrol car rolled down their street and parked. Two uniformed officers got out and approached the group of protesters. While Shale watched them, anxious for the disturbance to end, he noticed a group of five guys shuffle forward in line.

The men sported identical crew cuts and similar stylish sunglasses. Their regular clothes, suit jackets worn over polo-style shirts and khaki pants, stood out against the ocean of white garments worn by the rest of the church crowd. But unlike the other people in line, there wasn't an ill or injured person among them.

Something else also set them apart. The men's serious expressions seemed out of place. Shale disliked them at once, especially the short guy who stood in front of the others like he was their leader. The short man stared at EBN with an intensity that made Shale uncomfortable. There was something about the man's pale skin, receding black hairline and dramatic widow's peak that creeped him out.

Feeling an urge to protect EBN, Shale edged between the house and mountain of medical equipment and stood behind her chair. As the line inched forward, Shale laid his hand on EBN's shoulder and leaned over. "You sure know how to throw a party."

EBN turned her head and smiled weakly. She looked withered, just awful. A chalky substance coated her bluish skin. Her lips were blistered and scabbed. Dark circles ringed her sunken eyes. Sweat-drenched clothes clung to her bony frame and the stench of sulfur and rotten eggs wafted from her body.

EBN lifted her bandaged hand and hacked into it. Shale could tell the effort wracked her body. Across the field, the band paused between songs then launched into Leonard Cohen's *Hallelujah.*

"That favor you asked me about last night," Shale continued. "I'll do it."

When the line moved forward again, EBN turned toward him and nodded her understanding. The corners of her eyes crinkled in appreciation. EBN opened her mouth to speak but was interrupted by a hand clamping down on her arm.

It was the short man with the creepy widow's peak.

EBN tensed and her bottom lip quivered. "Sir," she whispered.

"Nice cult, Eden. You're coming with me," Sir said. The men with him fanned out and surrounded them. A sinister grin spread across Sir's face.

Shale stepped forward and wedged his arm between them. "Let go of her, Napoleon," he demanded.

Sir's eyebrows drew together as he looked up at Shale's face. "Nap—" his forehead smoothed in understanding. "That's funny. Get out of here, kid," he said with a jerk of his head.

Out of nowhere, a woman shrieked as a shot rang through the air and the music crashed to a halt. However, Sir neither averted his gaze nor loosened his grip on EBN's arm. Behind Sir, a gunman in a red t-shirt pushed through the crowd.

At first glance, the box-like, padded fit of the man's red t-shirt and trousers made Shale think he was an escaped figurine from Lego-land or a reporter dressed in a fat suit. Then Shale realized the man wore body armor under his clothes, North Hollywood shoot-out style. He held a screaming woman in a headlock and used her as a shield. That woman was Harmony.

The ground rumbled beneath Shale's feet. Scattering people shook the ground like an aftershock.

"Watch out!" Shale yelled, flipping over the patio table.

While Sir spun around, the gunman shot two of Sir's guys then aimed his gun at EBN. The downed agents drew their weapons and pointed them at the gunman, but held their fire.

Behind them, the police moved in with their weapons drawn.

The gunman yelled something about glorifying a false prophet then popped off another round that blew a hole in the wall next to Shale's head. More blasts cut through the air.

Shale dropped to the ground and tipped EBN's chair sideways. Another shot exploded as Shale dove forward and shielded EBN with his body. Someone heavy fell on top of Shale, knocking the breath from his lungs. He looked up and saw the gunman turn around, dragging Harmony with him.

Shale shrugged out from under the body pile and grabbed EBN by the shoulders. As he pulled her behind the mountain of discarded medical equipment, EBN reached out and touched the wounded person's hand. Shale recognized the guy's jacket—Sir had been shot.

Shadow engulfed them as the sky darkened.

"Are you okay," Shale whispered to EBN. "Were you hit?"

EBN shook her head.

Shale peered through the medical equipment. The gunman, somehow, still stood. He turned in slow circles, yanking Harmony with him.

Lightning bolts flashed behind the dark clouds rolling and banking across the sky while thunder rumbled overhead.

"Shale?"

"Yeah?"

"Take me into the desert," EBN said.

"Now?"

"Yes."

Shale glanced around. An empty black wheelchair sat at the edge of the equipment mound. Shale grabbed it, lifted EBN into the seat and sprinted full speed toward the riverbed. Shots pierced the air. A bullet streaked by Shale's shoulder; others pitted the ground near his feet. Shale pumped his legs harder. Their lives depended on it.

More lightning flashed. Thunder exploded and diagonal sheets of rain poured down on them. Shale threw his head back and cackled at the absurdity. He was wheeling his extraterrestrial girlfriend into the desert to die, provided she wasn't assassinated or captured first. Another shot sounded over the roaring din. The bullet whizzed by Shale's ear.

"Aix!" EBN called and pointed.

At first, Shale wasn't sure what he was seeing. Midway through the field, an oval doorway appeared a few feet above the ground. A boy about Shale's age stood in it, beckoning to them. Shale slowed his pace in shock and disbelief.

"Go! Go!" EBN urged. A bullet skimmed Shale's arm, burning.

Shale sprinted toward the doorway with everything he had. When they neared it he yelled, "Hold on," planted his heels in the mud and brought the wheelchair to a stop.

Shale moved to the chair's side. As he leaned over to collect EBN in his arms, EBN said in a soft voice, "I must ask two more things of you."

"Anything," Shale said.

"Harmony and Princess need you. Take care of yourself, and them."

Shale couldn't stand how final EBN's words sounded. He nodded sadly, hoping to loosen his tightening throat. "What else?"

"You must never return to the door in the desert. Will you avoid that place?"

Shale choked back his tears. "I can't," he said.

363

"You must," she insisted.

"No. And I won't lie about it either," he said.

Thunder rumbled overhead. Shale brushed his wet hair out of his eyes.

"I am sorry for missing your graduation ceremony." Moisture welled in EBN's dull, lifeless eyes. "Know that I will miss you, my friend."

Shale blinked back his own tears. "What will I do without you?"

"You are ready to take it from here." A single tear slid down EBN's bluish cheek. "There is much to admire here ... and so much to learn."

Rainfall stung Shale's eyes and washed away the tears trailing his face. He removed his glasses and brushed the moisture with the ball of his palm. "Thank you for being my friend," he said, his voice cracking with emotion.

Shale embraced EBN then lifted her out of the chair. He carried her forward and lifted her emaciated frame into the doorway. As he lowered EBN into Aix's outstretched arms, EBN reached out her bandaged hand. Shale grasped it.

EBN said, "If I make it back to my home world, I will look for your father."

Shale hadn't expected that. He gulped loudly, dropped EBN's bandaged hand and staggered backwards.

With his sister securely in his arms, Aix regarded Shale for a long moment and nodded once. Shale stared at the extraterrestrial siblings to seal their image into his mind.

364

A lightning bolt scrawled to the ground, searing the atmosphere. An ear-splitting thunderclap followed. The electric current passed through Shale, shocking him.

His knees buckled and he fell sideways but caught the doorway's edges, narrowly avoiding landing in the mud. Dazed and a little confused, time slowed to a crawl. While he stood and righted himself, he watched Aix retreat inside the ship with EBN.

This was it. She was really leaving. When Shale raised his hand to wave goodbye, a final shot sliced the air behind him. Aix lifted his gaze as the doorway closed and his expression changed in slow motion. Aix's brow creased and his mouth opened. "NOOOO!" he yelled.

Shale pitched forward. Scalding pain tore through his body. Then everything went black.

When the blackness cleared, Shale stood, stepped through the round doorway and entered Aix's ship. EBN sat in the pilot's seat wearing a pristine white uniform and she appeared perfectly healthy. She turned, waved to Shale and instructed him to sit down because it was going to be a bumpy ride.

A steady *beep … beep … beep … beep…* issued from the ship's console. If EBN heard it, she ignored it.

The noise grew steadily louder. When Shale opened his mouth to ask EBN about it, Shale heard voices coming from the back of the ship.

"You mean you didn't see anything?" Harmony said.

"I was unconscious. I got shot in the chest," an unfamiliar male voice said.

Shale turned, searching for Harmony but he stood alone at the back of the control deck. He felt a subtle vibration humming under his feet as the ship lifted off the ground. He opened his mouth to tell EBN to wait because he wasn't strapped into his seat yet when a rush of cool air blew across his face.

His eyelids fluttered open. He lay in a strange bed in a dim room. The smell of antiseptic and bandages lingered in the air. He craned his neck back. Behind him, a machine beeped.

A uniformed sheriff guarded the door. Harmony sat in the corner, talking with a man in a hospital gown. Without his street clothes or sunglasses, Shale almost didn't recognize the man EBN had called Sir.

"I was shot once before, while serving in Iraq. I know what it feels like."

Harmony glanced at the bed. "Shale," she said, leaping from her chair and rushing to his bedside. Sir followed and stood beside her.

"What did I miss," Shale asked.

"Funny, I've been wanting to ask you the same thing." Sir reached under the hospital bed, lifted a plastic bag and dumped the contents onto the stark white sheets. Shale's bloodstained clothes lay in a stiff pile on his stomach. He stared at them.

"What happened?"

Sir grabbed a pen and held up Shale's t-shirt with it. "Judging by the blood, the entrance and exit holes in your shirt, I'd say you were shot," Sir said. "But you're not wounded and neither am I. That fundamentalist whack-job blew a softball-sized hole in my chest. My guys saw it go down. I've got the ruined clothes to prove it, yet I stand before you a whole and healthy man. You want to explain how that could happen?"

Shale pressed his lips together to avoid smiling and shook his head no.

TO BE CONTINUED …

END OF BOOK ONE

Acknowledgments

A huge thank you to:

My late parents, who met and fell in love while working at NASA;

My beloved husband, Jim, for his endless support, encouragement, inspiration and fearlessness;

My brother, Steve, and sister-in-law, Tori, for having my back and being the first to buy this book;

My sister, Sharri, for being a force for change in many lives;

My in-laws, Jim and Della Mousner for making me the daughter they never had;

My awesome step-mom, Mary, for many things, including sharing her library;

My niece, Alexis, for believing in me, my nephew, Nathan, for his enthusiasm and patience and my nephew, Jason, for inspiring me with his courage;

My Los Angeles surrogate family, the late Al Lapin, Jr., and his amazing wife, Yona Lapin. There's not enough room to list the many things they did for me;

My friend, beta-reader and literary buddy David Fee, for his dedication and help in making *Being* so much better than it started out;

My soul sisters Jennifer Page and Kathryn Yeatman Pasio for their unconditional love;

My friend Angel Page, who inspired EBN;

My friends Amanda Howe and Katrina Mahler, who read early versions of this tale, provided feedback, encouragement and talked me off the ledge countless times;

My friend, author and Jedi Knight David Sheppard, for sending me <u>Novelsmithing</u>, which proved indispensable while writing <u>Being</u>;

My friend and David Sheppard's daughter, Bear Sheppard, for starting me down the writing road in our teens;

My friend Joshua David Gray, for reading various drafts, providing feedback and his support;

My friend Alice Fulks, for reading early drafts, making suggestions and sharing her light;

My friend and idea juggernaut Robert Smedley, for making me LMAO, his invaluable suggestions that took Being to a whole new level and for keeping it real;
My friends Melissa Rodriguez-Wyer and Sierra Thompson, for being the little sisters I never had and putting up with me;
My friend and neighbor Alexjandro Herdocia, for his support, feedback, sharing his pets and wanting to beta-read the sequel — I'm really looking forward to working together;
My friend, the incomparable James Warren Gaile III, for his artistic brilliance, finesse and divine Virgo vibe;
My friends Lilya Issacson, Kelly Grimm, Claire Mahler, Susan Mansion and Sumish Shankar for their continued support;
My friends Ronada Davis and Polly Weimar for their generosity, enthusiastic support and outstanding care;
My friends and fellow writers in various workshops and writers' groups for their guidance;
My new friends in the blogging world who took a chance on an unknown writer: LunaMoth a.k.a. Jessica Maxson at Far From Reality, Kristen at Seeing Night Reviews, Talina Perkins at Bookin' It Reviews and Night Owl Reviews; Megan McDade at Reading Away the Days; Tracy Riva at Midwest Book Review; Babs Hightower at Bab's Book Bistro; AOBibliophile at AO Bibliosphere; Zareen at Reach for the Books; Jennifer at Fictitious Musings; Holy Polk at Full Moon Bites Reviews, Andrea Thompson at The Bookish Babes; Amanda Pizzolanti at Paranormal Romance Novel; Deborah Previte, The Bookish Dame at A Bookish Libraria; Christin at Portrait of a Book; Yara Santos at Once Upon a Twilight; Savannah Valdez at Books With Bite; Albert Robbins III at Free Book Reviews, Lisa Faber, aka Bookworm Lisa; Mishel Zabala at Creativity Gone; Jen Stewart at Jenisreading; David King at killie-booktalk; Jenny Needham at Moonlight Gleams; Shannon at Wicked Kitty;
My friends and fellow authors Tiffany King, Christine M. Butler, David Sheppard, Richard Sheppard, Richard Goodship, Nathaniel Wyckoff, Karen Morgan, and Thomas Amo for their generous support; and
Every reader who purchases this book — infinite thanks for supporting my dreams.

www.ingramcontent.com/pod-product-compliance
Lightning Source LLC
Chambersburg PA
CBHW071304200626
46813CB00015B/33